MW01123887

Razor Sharp

A Western Novel by

BERT LINDSEY

Copyright © 2019 Bert Lindsey
Second Edition © 2023 Bert Lindsey

RC LAKE PUBLISHING
Streetman, TX

Originally published by Page Publishing, Inc. 2019
Second edition published by RC Lake Publishing, 2023

ISBN 978-1-7364791-6-2 (Paperback)
ISBN 978-1-7364791-7-9 (Digital

Printed in the United States of America

Dedicated to Amelia Grace Julian,

our three-pound miracle granddaughter.

Contents

Chapter 1

The Sharp Massacre

No one knew why Clayton Sharp and his wife, Wynona, were there alone, with their wagon stuck and their team of horses and scalps missing. The wagon of Razor Sharp's parents had been stuck in the great white gypsum sands of New Mexico. The wagon had been on a trail hugging the foothills of the Capitan and the Sacramento Mountain range heading south to Mesilla. The drifting gypsum sands pile up, making shifting dunes rumored to stretch out covering thirty-five miles long, six to eighteen miles wide, and as high as fifty feet.

Well-protected freight wagons used this trail to haul freight from Santa Fe and Las Vegas to Mesilla and El Paso. They then hauled freight from Mexico and Texas, back to Santa Fe and Las Vegas. Most freight haulers would not attempt this without an escort of at least fifty guards. To do otherwise, the Mescalero Apache living around the Capitan Mountain and the Ruidoso River would be tempted to attack any lesser protected enemy.

The only information they had was from their eight-year-old son, Razor. According to Razor, his father saw the Indians coming down the mountain in the distance. His father raced the team forward. While looking back for the Indians, he guided the wagon into the gypsum sand and became stuck.

With the Indians nearing, he had grabbed Razor and run into the towering dunes. His father gave him two canteens of water and instructed him to stay in the dunes until the Indians left. He pointed out the closest landmark on the nearest mountain and told him that he must not sit down or go to sleep in the dunes. Razor was told that when the Indians left, he should walk toward the landmark, and it would take him out of the dunes. His father told him he was going back to the wagon and that he and his mother would try to hold off the Indians until the wind had time to push the sand over his tracks.

He didn't mention that his father had given him a small leather pouch, extremely heavy for its size. He had told Razor not to show it to anyone or let anyone know about it.

He was to hide it as soon as possible.

Ten minutes after the freight convoy found his parents, Razor Sharp appeared on top of a dune. His tall and slender frame held his head high as he looked down on the twenty freight wagons, teamsters, and guards.

Some of the guards were busy digging a single grave for Clayton and Wynona, while others were on guard for an attack. The teamsters were checking the conditions of their teams and wagons.

Anxiety was building to move out. The time spent burying the Sharps would have to be made up. It could also cost them their lives and cargo. With the wagons moving, everyone was in place to defend life and cargo. Not so in a situation like this.

The clothes and food stuff had been taken by the Indians. The only things left on the wagon were three pieces of well-made furniture. It was being removed and placed on the freight wagon hauling the least weight. The wheels of the stuck wagon were being salvaged, and they too were placed on the freight wagons.

Jacob Walters, the guard supervisor, spotted Razor and walked into the dunes and led him down. Remounting his horse, Jacob reached down and lifted Razor to the back of his saddle and took Razor to the wagon master.

The wagon master, Ray Calhoun, asked Razor if his father had any money or jewelry hidden in the wagon. Calhoun had searched the wagon for any trapdoors but had found none. When Razor responded that he knew of none, Calhoun assumed the Indians had taken it if there had been any.

The grave was finished, and the bodies were placed in. The wagon master said a few last words, and the guards started filling the grave. Razor had kneeled at the foot and corner of the grave. His knees were on top of the sand and gravel that had been taken from the grave. Tears rolled down Razor's cheeks, but no sound left his mouth. Razor rocked forward, leaning over the grave. In one motion, he dropped the leather pouch from under his shirt and followed it with sand and gravel pushed in by his knees. The gravel filled the grave, and a cedar marker was placed. While this was happening, Razor sought out unique rock formation markers in the surrounding mountain range.

The wagon master pulled out in a rush to make up the twenty minutes they had lost burying the Sharps. Razor was sitting by his side.

Raiman Callaway was standing outside the freight office, looking at his gold watch, when the first wagon entered the yard. He was not happy. The wagons were eight minutes late. Standing beside him was his six-year-old daughter, Bonnie Lou, with her arms wrapped around his legs and peeking up at Razor. Razor was aware that she was peeking at him but didn't let on that he knew. Calhoun got down from the wagon, leaving Razor in his seat. After Calhoun explained the reason why he was late, he told Callaway about the wagon wheels and furniture.

Callaway was impressed with the design and construction of the various pieces of furniture. The three pieces consisted of a chest lined with cedar, a chest of drawers, and a large armoire, or a chifforobe, as it was called in the South.

Callaway gave instructions to have the furniture delivered to his home, a large mansion overlooking the Rio Grande. In a loud voice, Callaway said, "The furniture will help pay for some of the expenses for burying the Sharps."

"What do you want me to do with the kid, boss?" Calhoun asked.

"Take him to the stable and tell Stew I want him put to work. I'll talk to the marshal and see if he can find some kin or some place to take him. Until he does, the kid must earn his keep. If he's not willing to work, tell Stew to run him off. I'm not going to take him in to raise."

When Callaway arrived home with Bonnie Lou, his wife, Priscilla, excitedly asked about the furniture that had been delivered. After telling Priscilla how he came to have the furniture, Bonnie Lou spoke up.

"What's going to happen with the boy, Daddy?"

Chapter 2

Hello, Everyone, I'm Razor Sharp

Stew told Calhoun he was not happy about having to look after the boy and expressed those feelings in front of Razor. "That's your problem, not mine," said Calhoun as he turned and walked away.

"What's your name, boy?" Stew asked.

"Razor Sharp, sir," he replied.

"How the hell did you get that name, Razor?"

"My father started calling me Razor when I was around two years old because he thought I was sharp as a razor."

"Well, I hope that sharpness helps you around here. I'm going to show you around, and I hope your daddy taught you how to work because I damn sure don't have time to teach you. The only thing I can tell you is, if you see anything that needs done and you can do it, then do it."

"You heard Calhoun tell me that the boss said if you didn't work for your keep, I was to run you off. So, it's up to you. I ring the chow bell at five in the morning, noon, and seven in the evening. If you aren't present, you don't eat. The chow hall is over there," he said, pointing at a long adobe building.

He walked in the bunkhouse and pointed out a bunk for Razor. "You can put your things under the bunk."

"Mr. Stew, I don't have any things. The Indians took all my clothes."

A sad expression came over Stew's face.

"Mr. Stew, I can get by with what I have on for a long time. By then, I'll have figured out what I'm going to do. I know how to work. I know there will always be things that needs doing that I can do. I think you will be happy with my work." "We'll see," Stew softly replied.

"Will you let me sleep in the barn, Mr. Stew? I love the smell of hay and horses. I would also be out of the way of the teamsters and guards."

"Okay, Razor, find you a place to sleep in the barn. Stay busy, and don't get hurt."

Razor was relieved that he could sleep in the barn. The bunkhouse reeked of body odor, cigarette smoke, and tobacco spit. Razor found two old worn-out saddle blankets. He put the best one down over a patch of hay in the loft and would use the other for cover.

The bell rang, and Razor hurried out to the chow hall. He thought he would be one of the first in. He was last. When Razor walked in, it was obvious the wagon master, Ray Calhoun, had been telling everyone about the Sharps. The conversation ceased. Everyone turned and looked at Razor.

"Hello, everyone, I'm Razor Sharp." He ate silently, as most of the others. It was his first meal of the day. When he was full and felt he could not eat another bite, he slipped a biscuit in his pocket and went to the barn. After settling down on the blanket in the hay, Razor pulled the cover blanket up over his head and cried. He didn't try to stop or continue, but after an hour, he stopped. He pulled the biscuit out of his pocket, ate it, and went to sleep.

The next morning, he was first in the chow hall. Razor had gotten up around three o'clock and washed his clothes in one of the horse troughs. He wrung the water out, hung them out on the corral fence, and then bathed. The desert stole the remaining moisture from the clothes by the time he finished bathing.

Razor was the first to eat, first to leave, and first to go to work. He washed the two saddle blankets he used as bedding and hung them out to dry. Razor had already spotted several other things that needed his attention. He decided to start with cleaning and saddle soaping the extra reins to restore the limpness of the leather. If this is not done regularly, the leather gets stiff and cracks. At the end of the day, the teamsters were rushing to get the saddle-soaped reins. They left the ones they had been using for Razor to saddle soap.

Chapter 3

The Rebellion

The next morning, Raiman Callaway went to the US Marshal's office and found Marshal Lester Block. After greetings, Callaway spoke up.

"Guess you heard about the Sharp killings by the Mescalero!" "Raiman, I'm not so sure that the Mescalero did those killings."

"Why not?" asked Callaway.

"I've heard that some of the Comanche have been driven out of west Texas. You know the Mescalero Apache and the Comanches are longtime blood enemies. The Mescalero have been staying in the Capitan and the Ruidoso River area, minding their own business unless Geronimo shows up. The thing that makes me think it might have been the Comanches was that they didn't burn the wagon. I feel that they didn't want to bring themselves to the attention of the Mescaleros," said the marshal.

"I think if Geronimo stays away, we could have a lasting peace with the Mescalero Apache. The hatred the Apache have for the Comanches and the size of the other Apache tribes in the area, would indicate that any insurgence by the Comanches should be short-lived."

"You could be right, Lester, but what I came to talk about is the Sharps' son, Razor."

"What has the boy told you about himself and his parents?" asked the marshal.

"That's none of my business, so I didn't ask. Just because my crew buried his parents and picked him up in the white sands, doesn't make me responsible for raising him. I want you to pick him up, find some kin, or put him in the orphanage in Santa Fe. I'm already out twenty-five hundred dollars in lost time burying his parents and am now having to feed and house him. I want him gone by the end of the day."

"I wish you would give me a little time, Raiman. Where is he now?"

"He's at the freight yard," said Callaway.

"Raiman, I've got to talk to him and see if he knows of any kin. If he knows where any might be, I'll try to find them. If he has none or I can't find them, I'll have to do some checking about how to get him in the orphanage. You've got to give me an extra day."

"Okay, Lester, you've got your extra day. If you haven't figured out what to do with him by then, just put him in jail until you get it figured out."

When the chow bell rang that evening, Razor entered the chow hall. Several teamsters greeted Razor, asking that he sit next to them. Jacob Walters made room for himself next to Razor. He complimented Razor for the job he had done with the reins and asked how long he thought it would take to do the rest.

"I'll have them finished in two days," replied Razor.

"If you need help with anything, Razor, come to me," said Jacob Walters.

The next day Razor was busy saddle soaping reins when Callaway drove his carriage into the freight yard with Bonnie

Lou sitting at his side. Callaway got down and lifted the young girl to the ground. He held her hand while they walked forward to greet Stew. When he let go of her hand, Bonnie Lou wrapped her arm around his leg, and peeked around at Razor. When she caught Razor's eye, she moved her hand close in front of her body and gave a slight wave to him. Razor acknowledged with a movement of his hand and a nod of his head then looked away.

Early the next day, Marshal Lester Block set out for the freight office. He had contacted the orphanage in Santa Fe but had not heard back from them. He felt under pressure from Callaway to get the kid out of the freight yard, especially after getting the extra day.

The marshal needed to find a place for Razor today. He didn't like the idea of having to put him in jail for the lack of another place. Upon arriving, Marshal Block sought out Stew and asked if he had found out anything about Razor.

"Razor is a good kid and seems to have been reared right. Everything is 'Yes, sir' or 'No, sir' with him. He is always polite and courteous. He's a good worker. The teamsters and guards seem to have taken a shine to him," Stew said.

"Stew, let's go and talk to him and see if we can get some information. Callaway has insisted I get him out of here by tonight. I'm checking on the orphanage in Santa Fe. If we can't find some kin, I'll probably have to put him in jail until I find someplace for him."

"Marshal, Callaway isn't being fair with Razor. He told me he had to earn his keep, and he damn well has been doing that. Only if he would not work was I to run him off."

Razor looked up from his work. When he saw the badge on the marshal's shirt, he knew what was coming. He was mentally prepared for it. He was not to tell anyone about where they came from and to trust no one. He was to never mention gold or act as if he knew anything about gold. There were a lot of things he didn't know, but he did know his mother had gone to college somewhere back east. He had no relatives that he knew of. Razor lowered his head and continued his work.

"Razor, hold up there and meet Marshal Lester Block," Stew said.

"Nice to meet you, Marshal Block."

"Razor, Stew has told me what a fine young man you are and what a good job you have done here these past few days. I need to ask you a few questions. I hope you don't mind answering them. I'm not trying to pry into your business, but we need to find your kin, if you have any."

"Marshal Block, I don't mind. If I have any kin, I don't know of them. The only people I ever knew was my mother and father. It wasn't that my mother and father weren't friendly, it was that there were no towns around. My father was cautious and very protective of my mother and me."

"How did you learn to speak so well and be so polite?"

"Our house was full of books. Mother read to us every night and would often call on me or my father to read. She would correct us on any mispronunciations. She also corrected us on any grammar mistakes either of us made. My mother had gone to college back east and insisted that my father and I know everything she knew. Politeness was stressed by my mother and my father. Many of the books we read dealt with politeness. It was great fun for all of us, and we looked forward to the reading each night."

"Where is your home, Razor?" the marshal asked.

"I don't know. It was a long way from here. It was not in the desert or mountains, but both were close by."

Stew turned to the marshal, saying, "That could be thousands of places, even close by."

"Yeah, that's no help. It's as long as it is short," replied the marshal.

"Marshal, I don't know anything else I can tell you. May I go back to work? I promised the teamsters I would be through saddle soaping the reins by today."

"Okay, Razor, if you think of anything else, tell Stew to get in touch with me."

The marshal told Stew that he would be back to get Razor that afternoon. "I do not know where I could put him other than in jail." Stew expressed his displeasure of that thought.

Stew told everyone that came in the situation that faced Razor. Everyone he told passed it on to the others as they arrived in the freight yard. By the time the marshal arrived, everyone except Razor knew what the marshal had in mind. Razor was still working to finish the reins.

Stew was surrounded by the teamsters and the guards. When the marshal announced to Stew that he had come to take Razor, a loud protest of defiance erupted. Jacob Walters was the most outspoken. He had found Razor in the great white sand dunes and had led him out. He told the teamsters and guards that he wasn't going to let the marshal take Razor. Both groups backed him. The marshal didn't want to take him in the first place. "Stew, get Raiman Callaway down here!"

Callaway had seen the cloud of dust racing in his direction and waited for it to arrive. "Boss, you need to come back with me to the yard."

"What's the problem?" Callaway demanded.

"The teamsters and guards are rebelling and are not going to let the marshal take Razor."

Razor knew something was going on but had no clue as to what. He was still working on the reins when Mr. Stew and Callaway arrived back at the freight office.

Stew tried to push his way into the freight office with everyone else. He wisely turned to the chow hall, and everyone followed, including the marshal. When everyone was in, Stew got everyone quieted down.

Marshal Block came forward with his hand raised, reinforcing a demand for quietness and took the lead. "The only way we can get this worked out is for everyone here to get their say."

Callaway lunged forward and was stopped in his tracks by a glare and a stiff outstretched arm toward him by the marshal. "It's going to be one at a time, and I'll give each permission to have their say. I'll start first.

"Mr. Callaway came to me and told me he wanted the young Sharp off his property." The marshal's hands went up instantly to silence the moans. "This is his property, and he has that right. He told me he didn't want the expense of feeding the kid and that he had already been out twenty-five hundred dollars of time burying his mother and father." Again, the marshal's hands went up to silence moans and words about wheels and furniture. "Stew told me that Razor was to work for his meals and housing. He told me he was pleased with Razor's performance so far." Claps and cheers were quieted by the raised hands of the marshal. "I think I may have a solution to this problem.

"I want to ask a couple of questions of Callaway, then to you as a group. Mr. Callaway, is it just the cost that makes you want Razor Sharp off your property?"

"Yes," he replied.

"Does it cost you anything for Razor Sharp to sleep in your barn?"

"Well, no," Callaway slowly replied.

"How much a day does it cost to feed just one of your men?" the marshal asked.

After some thought, he replied, "Thirty cents a day."

"You just told us that you had no objection for Razor Sharp staying on your property, sleeping in your barn, and taking his meals in the chow hall if you were paid, let's say, ten dollars a month. Now I'm going to pass my hat, and I'm putting in the first dollar. I'm sure we will come up with much more than ten dollars."

There was a rush of teamsters and guards digging for loose change. The final count amounted to thirty-five dollars and thirty-five cents. The money was handed to Raiman Callaway, and he left.

Marshal Block told Stew and his crew the importance of passing the hat each payday. "We never want to give Callaway a reason to back out on this agreement." The marshal told them he had talked to the schoolteacher and told her Razor would be in school the next morning. "I'll pick him up and take him the first day."

Callaway felt he had been tricked by the marshal and was boxed in with no way out. It did solve a problem and made him some money. Razor could not eat as much as a man, and the real cost was only fifteen cents a day anyway. It still made him mad.

Chapter 4

Golly! Doesn't He Have Anything?

Mr. Stew told Razor that evening that he no longer worked for Raiman Callaway. "The crew is paying for your meals, and you can continue to sleep in the barn or move into the bunkhouse. We all agreed that you should go to school. The marshal will pick you up early in the morning and take you."

"I'll repay them for their kindness," promised Razor.

Razor was excited about going to school. He had never been before. He had never played with other kids. For that matter, he had never met or talked to another kid.

Razor did know how to read, write, spell, and do arithmetic, thanks to his mother. He also knew how to read maps, a lot about geography and history.

Razor had bathed and washed his clothes. He was finished eating when Stew handed him his lunch wrapped in a piece of rough paper.

"Thanks," Razor said. Marshal Block pulled Razor up behind him and told him to pay attention so he would know the way back from school. The teacher was standing out front, greeting her students, when the marshal arrived with Razor.

The soon-to-be new student slid down from the horse before the marshal could dismount and went straight to the teacher.

"Hello, ma'am, I'm Razor Sharp."

She had expected Razor but expected someone who would reflect the sorrow and fears he would have to face without his parents. "I'm Miss Mary Ann Scott, Razor. Marshal Block told me a lot about you. Let's go in and I'll introduce you to the rest of the class. Why don't you give me your lunch and I'll put it in my desk drawer to keep the ants away."

"Thanks, Miss Scott. I haven't had time to build me a lunchbox, but I'll have one in the morning."

"Class, this is Razor Sharp. Each of you call out your names as I point to you."

Razor paid close attention to every name and took mental notes. Buster Marlow was big and threatening. Nell Simmons was the prettiest. He recognized Bonnie Lou Callaway but had not known her first name. She was the sweetest. After the introductions, Miss Scott assigned Razor his seat and asked everyone to take out a pencil and a piece of paper. She realized Razor didn't have a piece of paper or a pencil.

"Would someone loan Razor a pencil and piece of paper?" she asked.

Nell Simmons spoke. "Golly! Doesn't he have anything?"

"No, Nell, I don't, but I'll someday," Razor said.

By the end of the morning class, Razor had not said another word. At lunch, Miss Scott asked, "Razor, have you been able to keep up with the lesson? I haven't seen you take any notes."

"Miss Scott, I take mental notes on everything. Everything you went through I already knew."

"How did you know, Razor? I thought you had never gone to school."

"My mother taught me. I can read, write, do arithmetic, and I know a lot of other things."

"Razor, please go to the black board for me and do this problem: add nine plus five and tell me the answer."

"Fourteen," Razor said without writing the numbers.

"Add thirty-three and twenty-two and subtract nine." "Forty-six," Razor instantly replied.

"I'm impressed, Razor."

Razor ducked his head and smiled.

After lunch, Miss Scott had each student read a chapter out loud, and she corrected any mispronunciations. Then they were asked to give a review on what they had read. There had been several mispronounced words, and many of the students had hesitated, changed, and wallowed around in their reviews. Razor was last. He was assigned the longest and most difficult chapter of the book. He read it without error then reviewed it for ten minutes without hesitation.

When he finished, the room was in total silence. Miss Scott thought, *What have I uncovered here*? Nervous and excited, she broke the silence by clapping her hands. Several others joined in. Nell Simmons threw her nose in the air and looked away with a "humph" coming from her closed mouth. It had not gone unnoticed by Razor.

When the school day was over, Buster Marlow bumped into Razor. "If you plan to have something someday, you had better stop bumping into me," Buster snarled.

Razor walked away, delaying the inevitable fight. He would have a plan when it happened.

Bonnie Lou Callaway rushed up and said, "Razor, I don't know if you recognized me, but I'm the one who waved at you in the freight yard."

"Of course, I recognized you, Bonnie Lou." Bonnie Lou was surprised and proud that Razor remembered her name.

"I want you to be my friend."

"We will definitely be friends, Bonnie Lou," Razor said. "I have to rush now, but let's talk again tomorrow."

After he found his way back to the freight yard, Razor went straight to the barn. He remembered seeing the hand saw, hand drill, nails, a pig tie, and hammer. He rounded them up along with loose scraps of wood and, in a few minutes, had a lunch box. He had watched his father make fine furniture since he was born. He thought his father would have been proud of him.

He had a couple of hours before the evening chow bell was rung. He felt a little guilty about the crew having to pay for his food and wanted to help them any way he could. He decided he would clean and wash the spittoons in the bunkhouse then wash the floor around them. He washed all the wash pans, filled them with fresh water from the well, and filled the water pitchers.

Razor washed all the loose towels, rung them out, and hung them back on nails to dry. He took the two roller towels from above the wash basins and took them to the horse trough, unrolled them, washed, and strung them out to dry before rerolling them. It was probably the first time they had ever been washed. They looked like they had been at the end of the roll for months.

When the teamsters and guards came into the bunkhouse, they noticed that things smelled a lot better. Then they noticed the spittoons, clean towels, and wash pans. Everyone was pleased that the two roller towels had been washed. They talked among themselves about everyone taking a better aim at the spittoons. They knew that it was Razor who had cleaned the floors and washed the towels. Later, they wanted to talk to him about his first day in school and thank him for cleaning the bunkhouse. They all liked Razor.

Razor asked Mr. Stew if he could have a pencil and paper for school. He readily gave them and apologized for not thinking to give him paper and pencil the previous day. Razor told him no apology was needed and promised him he would pay him for the pencil and paper someday. “Forget about it, Razor,” Mr. Stew replied.

Chapter 5

Bonnie Lou's Sadness

Ms. Scott had stayed awake half the night thinking about Razor Sharp. His intelligence astounded her. Was she the only one who realized the depth of his knowledge? Did she even know the understanding that he had? What was she going to do with him? What *could* she do with him in this small school where all the other students would be well behind him academically?

The next morning, she arrived early with a plan. "Class, I want you all to get your reading books and go sit under the shade tree. Read the next six chapters starting at chapter ten. If you finish before the others, read it again. I am going to stay inside with Razor and bring him up to date with what we've covered this year. I'll be watching you through the window, so you all had better behave!"

When they had settled under the tree, she turned to Razor. "The real reason I want to talk to you, Razor, is to find out how advanced you are in your studies. After yesterday, I know your intellect is far superior to the rest of the students."

"Miss Scott, I didn't mean to act superior. I want everyone to like me. I just got carried away with the critical analysis of the chapter."

"Oh! Razor, I didn't mean you acted superior. I just want to know the upper range of your knowledge so I could possibly challenge that range."

"I read the books you gave me yesterday. They were all very elementary. I would like to be challenged," said Razor.

"Razor, what books did your family read?"

"Shakespeare, Plato, Aristotle, Socrates, and books by the American novelist James Fenimore Cooper. Mother thought Mr. Cooper could become the first internationally recognized American novelist. We always started the day with a scripture from the Bible and a prayer to God. At the end of the day, we ended with the same. There were many other books we had. The Bible, the Cooper novels, and the philosophers were our favorites. We always had lengthy discussions about their meanings and thoughts. We embraced the Bible and some of Socrates's sayings in our way of life along with our favorite from Aristotle that happiness is a goal of life."

"Where are those books now, Razor?"

"I'm not sure where they are now, Miss Scott."

"Tell me, Razor, what is the one thing that you want to do next in your educational endeavors?"

"I want to learn Latin. I know it's the dead language of the great Roman Empire, but as you know, Latin is the root of many words in many languages."

"I'm wondering, do you speak Spanish?"

"I speak Castilian Spanish. I've heard of the Mexican Spanish spoken in northern Mexico and along the border. It's my understanding that it's a mixture of Castilian Spanish, English, and Indian. Many expressions are used and referred to as Tex-Mex by the gringos. I've never heard it being spoken, but I understand that if you speak Spanish in any country, or any of the dialects, you will understand what is being said. I'm looking forward to someday hearing it."

"Razor, I'll talk to the Catholic priest and see if he can help us with information on Latin."

"Miss Scott, many philosophers and other smart people have been shunned and killed because of what they thought or said. Socrates drank hemlock given to him by his political opponents, which killed him. They thought he was corrupting the minds of youth. I don't want to be shunned or killed because I know about more things than the others do. My goal in life is the same as Aristotle's, and that is to obtain happiness.

Please don't tell the priest or anyone else about this, and from now on, I'll act more reserved. I want to be the same as any other eight-year-old boy."

As tears came to her eyes, she turned away and assured Razor she would tell no one. She asked Razor to join the class outside and told him she would join them shortly.

She didn't know if her tears were for sadness, happiness, or fear for Razor. She knew she would never forget this moment of enlightenment concerning the unusual boy named Razor Sharp. She also knew he would never be the same as any other eight-year-old boy.

Razor and Bonnie Lou Callaway did become best friends. Razor often helped her with her schoolwork. When teams were chosen for games or schoolwork, they always seemed to be on the same side. Confrontations with Buster Marlow, the banker's son, seemed to be increasing throughout the year. Although Razor had always won with words alone, he didn't know how long this would continue.

Miss Scott had been able to secure a book on Latin from the Catholic priest. It was worn from much use by the priest in preparing for church services. The priest gave it to Miss Scott as a gift, and she gave it to Razor. It was now his prized possession.

Razor had continued his work in the bunkhouse. He was now washing blankets for the teamsters and guards. He cleaned and polished their shoes, boots and did many other odd jobs. He often received tips, which he reluctantly accepted at their insistence. After a while, the tips enabled Razor to buy a horse and saddle and to replace his worn-out and too small clothes. He enlisted Miss Scott's help. She complained about him insisting on buying his clothes two sizes bigger than those that fit. He assured her they would be a perfect fit in less than a year.

Razor loved riding his horse bareback or saddled. He had read of Indians riding bareback and practiced their techniques. Jacob had taken him to see several bronc-busting contests in Mesilla. He marveled at how the successful rider's bodies stayed in rhythm with the horse. *I could do that,* he thought.

Bonnie Lou told her mother that Razor was her best friend. Her mother told her that her best friend should be a girl and that she didn't want her best friend to be Razor Sharp. Her father had caught the tail end of the conversation and insisted Bonnie Lou not associate with Razor Sharp. He ended the demand with "He will never amount to anything."

Bonnie Lou began to cry and told them how smart Razor was and how he helped her with her schoolwork. "I don't like any of the other three girls in school," she said.

"I don't care how smart Razor Sharp is and how he helps you with your schoolwork. Razor Sharp as your best friend would be an embarrassment to our family. Now go to bed," her father demanded.

That evening, Raiman Callaway contacted Miss Scott. He told her he didn't want Razor Sharp to have any contact with his daughter. If he did, he would whip the hide off him. She tried to persuade him to change his mind, to no avail.

Bonnie Lou told Razor what had taken place at her home.

"I figured that your father didn't like me, and I know why. It doesn't bother me, Bonnie Lou. You will always be my friend, and there is nothing that I wouldn't do for you if it's in my power."

"But why doesn't my father like you?"

"It's a social thing, Bonnie Lou, it's not me personally. I have no family; therefore, I don't fit in socially, and it's difficult to amount to anything without family support. There are a few who will amount to something without family support, and I plan to be one of them. He just doesn't know that. Bonnie Lou, you must honor your father's wishes to not associate with me, but I hope you will always be my friend."

"I promise. This is going to be so hard for me."

Later, Miss Scott told Razor of her conversation with Mr. Callaway and Razor shared the conversation that he had with Bonnie Lou that morning and that they would remain silent friends.

Razor missed his daily conversations with Bonnie Lou that they had been having throughout the year. He did appreciate the slight smile, eye contact, and the small hidden waves he received. Razor realized the only benefit he was receiving from attending this school was the rapport with Miss Scott. He discussed this with her, and both decided it would be best for him to use his time discovering new avenues to enhance his education.

There was one last thing Razor wanted to do before leaving, and he was ready. As the class was being dismissed, Miss Scott announced that Razor would be leaving the class. Razor caught Bonnie Lou's eye and offered a small wave. Bonnie Lou returned a look of shock and soon had tears streaming down her face.

Buster Marlow was coming forward for his daily bump and taunt. This time Razor was not feeling inclined to talk his way out of the situation. When Buster bumped him with his right shoulder, Razor walked by him and placed his right leg behind Buster's right leg. With his left hand, he grabbed Buster's shirt at his right shoulder and kept walking forward with his left foot. Buster went sprawling on his back, knocking all the air from his lungs.

Razor stopped, reached down as to pick Buster up, and fell on him with his right forearm going in on top of his nose. He was sure it was broken. Razor asked for help to get Buster on his feet and apologized for falling on him. Miss Scott couldn't help from grinning.

Buster was helped to his feet by Razor and a fellow classmate. He caught his breath but was having a hard time stopping the nosebleed. Both of Buster's eyes were black and swollen shut before his nosebleed stopped. Not wanting anyone to know the younger and much smaller Razor Sharp had thrown him to the floor, broke his nose, and blackened his eyes, he feigned that he had tripped. Miss Scott went along, readily accepting his explanation.

Bonnie Lou was heartbroken that Razor was leaving school even though she had not talked to him in several weeks. Now she would not see him unless she ran into him at the freight yard, and then she would have to be very careful. She would not want to get Razor or herself in trouble.

Chapter 6

Buster's Attack

Razor prayed each morning and before going to sleep. He thought of the past and future. He continued his odd jobs and kept the bunkhouse spotless. The tips kept coming in. One day he would change the coins into paper money, roll the bills tight, and slip them into his waistband and pant cuffs. He thought of the leather pouch often but had no desire to retrieve it. Its contents might attract attention he could not now give.

He was loving his Latin book and studied it daily. Even more fun was learning to do tricks on his horse. His favorite was the ability to mount the horse while the horse was running and riding while standing on the horse's back. He could also mount the horse from the rear or either side.

Razor always let Mr. Stew and Mr. Waters know where he was going and when he would be back. He visited Miss Scott at least once a week after all the students had left the classroom. She was always glad to see him.

He had become friends with the Mexican stable boy and his family. He had been invited to the boy's home on several occasions. His father spoke only the Spanish language spoken along the border and northern Mexico. It was very easy for Razor to learn. His father wanted to learn to speak and understand English. Before long, Razor was teaching as many as twenty kids and several adults from the neighborhood. Others came from across the Mexican border to sit in on the English lessons. They were informal classes. Come if you could. Feel free to ask questions.

Seven years later, he was still teaching English, and doing his odd jobs. Razor was known and well-liked by every Mexican in Mesilla and ever teamster and guard in the area. Favorable knowledge of Razor Sharp had also spread across Northern Mexico.

Razor found and stole a large horse blanket from a family of packrats. They had chewed and made fodder for their nest from the rear end of the blanket. He trimmed and hand sewed the chewed area of the blanket. After a good washing, he used it as part of his bedding. He had drastically outgrown the two saddle blankets.

Razor had heard about Apache raids over these years. It brought back sad memories each time, even though he was convinced Comanches killed his parents and not the Apache. The increased firepower of the repeater rifles was taking a toll on the Indian Nation, and they were becoming more and more hostile. It was said that Geronimo maintained a following of fifteen to twenty Apache braves recruited from the different Apache tribes as needed to raid and pillage for the Apache cause. Geronimo was constantly raiding and constantly having to replace his dead with recruits. Razor noticed that raids in the immediate area declined when Geronimo left the area.

Razor had seen Bonnie Lou at a distance several times and once close enough to slip her a smile and a discreet hand wave. He was shocked and surprised when he saw Bonnie

Lou and Buster Marlow ride into the freight yard in a carriage. Buster was now seventeen years old, six feet tall, and weighed two hundred pounds. He also had a very crooked nose. Razor was now sixteen years old, five feet, nine inches tall and weighed one hundred and eighty pounds.

Stew came out to meet Bonnie Lou and Buster. He knew all about the incident between Razor and Buster that had happened when Buster was only nine years old. Stew hadn't heard a word of it from Razor.

Before the sun had set the day Buster's nose was broken, nearly everyone in Mesilla was snickering when they heard Razor Sharp was the one who broke it.

Stew spoke up. "Buster, Mr. Callaway wants me to put you to work. I don't want any trouble out of you concerning Razor Sharp."

"Mr. Stew, you couldn't melt Razor Sharp and pour him on me.

He would just run off," Buster said with a smirk and looked at Razor. "Buster, don't talk about Razor that way," snapped Bonnie Lou.

"Shut your mouth and stay out of this!" he said as he jerked Bonnie Lou from in front of him and roughly threw her to the ground while clearing his way to Razor Sharp.

Razor stood his ground as Buster rushed toward him with his head lowered. Just before reaching him, Razor stepped aside and stuck out his foot, tripping Buster. Before Buster could get up, Razor placed his right foot on Buster's upper ankle, balanced his body directly over it, and stood on the one ankle with all his weight. The one hundred and eighty pounds shattered the ankle when Razor jumped up and down on the ankle one time. Buster's scream could be heard all over Mesilla.

Razor rushed to Bonnie Lou and picked her up off the ground. "Are you okay?"

"I'm all right, Razor, just a few skinned places. I'm sorry, Razor, Dad made me bring Buster down here. Dad is pushing him off on me all the time. Buster's dad is Father's banker. I would not do anything that that might damage our friendship. This was out of my control."

"I know that, Bonnie Lou. Give me a few seconds to make sure Buster is being taken care of."

As Razor started toward Buster, Stew started toward him. "Razor, we're taking care of Buster. His ankle is busted, and he's in a lot of pain. That might be good for him. It might just save his life someday. I'm sure he will think twice before jumping on someone he doesn't know well."

"I really hope he uses the same excuse he used last time, that being he just tripped," Razor said.

"Well, one thing for sure, he'll have plenty of time to think about it," Mr. Stew said.

Razor went back to Bonnie Lou. "Let's go to the kitchen and clean up those scratches."

Chapter 7

Left for Dead

Ralph Marlow, Buster's father, pulled up in his buggy and rushed to Raiman Callaway's door. His two bank guards waited with the horses out front. When Callaway opened the door, Marlow crashed in. "Raiman, you're going to have to do something with Sharp! He jumped Buster at your freight yard and knocked him down before he had a chance to defend himself. Bonnie Lou tried to break it up, but Razor threw her out of the way and then crushed Buster's ankle. This is the second time he's attacked Buster."

"Where is Bonnie Lou?"

"She's been fixed up and is at the doctor's office with Buster. She had several scratches and some bruises," Marlow said.

"Marlow, I had gotten word to Sharp that I would skin him alive if he didn't leave Bonnie Lou alone. I plan to do that tonight and drive him out of the territory. Then if he ever comes back, I'll kill him. You want to help?"

"Absolutely, Raiman!"

"The kid doesn't work for me. He works for my teamsters and guards. They like the kid and are protective of him. I've already had a run-in with them over the kid and don't really want another. Sharp sleeps in the barn. If you will let your guards slip in and grab him and then bring him to me, I'll take care of him."

"I'll go with them myself. I want Sharp to know he can't mess with Ralph Marlow or my family and get away with it. I want to help you skin him. I'll beat him within an inch of his life for what he has done to Buster and Bonnie Lou."

At midnight, Razor was struggling to breathe. The rag they had stuffed in his mouth was not the only reason. His hands were tied in front of him. The rope around his neck pulled tighter as he stumbled and tried to keep up as he was being pulled out of the freight yard. He had to keep up or be hung by the rope as they dragged him away. His captors were hugging the shadows of the buildings on their way out. After they got through the gate, he had to run half a mile until they came to a side street.

A buggy was waiting, and Razor was dragged into the back. The rope was jerked occasionally to maintain the tightness around his neck. He flexed his neck muscles and slipped his tied hands around the rope and pulled it to get enough air into his lungs. The rope was cutting deeper into his neck and blood covered most of his body. The buggy raced off toward the west for at least ten miles, then stopped.

Razor's feet were tied, and then he was pulled out of the buggy onto the ground. He landed on his side as the rope dug deeper into his neck. Again, he flexed his neck muscles and pulled on the rope.

"Sharp, I'm Ralph Marlow, Buster Marlow's father. I think you know Mr. Callaway. You've messed with my son and Mr. Callaway's daughter one too many times. You were warned. We don't want people like you in Mesilla or even the

Territory. We're going to beat you within an inch of your life for what you did to my son today and for knocking Bonnie Lou down when she tried to talk you out of continuing your assault on Buster. If you survive this whipping and come back to Mesilla or don't get out of the Territory, we'll kill you."

The small slit in the parted eyelid let in a glimmer of light. The rocking of his body was foreign to him. He couldn't see anything out of his right eye. Razor trying to keep the tiny slit open in his left eye hurt, so he let it close. He remembered nothing. His next thought was that he was blind. It was pitch-dark, and the tormenting rocking had ceased.

Razor heard a voice. He tried to hide, but his body wouldn't move.

"See if he's still alive, Walks."

Razor felt a rough hand grasp and close his nose, and another hand was placed over his mouth. He was struggling, trying to breathe. When the hands were removed, he gasped for air.

"Alive," reported Walks with Pride.

"You are safe! My name is Water Finder. I need for you to sit up and drink a little water."

Three days had passed before Razor's head cleared enough for him to remember the beating. He raised his hand to his throat and removed it as fast as he could. He reached for his waist and his trouser cuffs to make sure he still had his money. He was relieved that he did.

He remembered that his hands were tied, and he wouldn't be able to defend himself. He knew that Bonnie Lou had not contributed to the lie and knew that a verbal defense would have been a waste of time. Marlow and Callaway had taken turns beating him, concentrating on his upper body. He had tried to cover his head and had curled into a fetal position.

Did I deserve this beating? He thought. *All I did was protect myself from a beating Buster Marlow intended to give me. Doesn't a person have a right to defend himself?*

Razor was convinced their intention was to kill him without being present when he died. Why else would they leave him tied hand and foot in the desert without water, food, or horse? They would have to believe that he would not survive. *I guess they didn't want my death on their conscience. If they had one.*

Now that he had survived, he prayed for guidance. He thought of an attack against them. He would beat the two and drive them away. If that failed, he would be forced to kill them both. *I know they could hire people to fulfill their promise to kill me. If the beating I am going to give them does not convince them to leave me alone, I'll have no other choice.* He was sure they could hire such people. He would be ready when they came for him and would make sure they weren't successful.

He remembered that they had gotten tired lifting their large clubs. They threw them down and started kicking him.

That was the last thing he remembered. He didn't know how long the beating continued. For that reason, he was glad that he had lost consciousness.

Until that day, Razor had never feared anything or anyone. That day changed everything in his future. How could he have been so naive about what had happened. In packs, dogs do things that they would never do if they were alone. In the wild, most animals protect their young with their lives. In the animal world, the weakest one is the first to be attacked.

Razor was now determined to never be attacked because he showed weakness or fear. He was attacked because he was young and didn't outwardly show any strength. He would show them soon that they had made a mistake in not having killed him. They could not see his intelligence and determination. He vowed that he would become physically strong and knowledgeable about preventing such attacks.

Water Finder had been increasing Razor's food intake daily, and the injured young man was regaining his strength steadily. The rocking of the wagon didn't seem to hurt as much as previously. Razor was ready to find out more about his rescue and his rescuers.

Water Finder and Walks with Pride were Lipan Apache Indians. They were converted to Christianity by Catholic missionaries who had a strong presence around San Saba, Texas, their native home area. A lot of the tribe members were serving as scouts for the military.

Water Finder and Walks with Pride were hired by the missionaries to lead and scout for them to enable their endeavors in New Mexico Territory. The missionaries had run short of money in Mesilla and could not afford to feed Water Finder and Walks with Pride. The missionaries helped the Indians hire out to a mining company to deliver a wagon loaded with mining equipment to Animas, New Mexico Territory. Water Finder and Walks with Pride wore western clothes, and their ability to speak English helped them land the job.

The two Lipan Apache Indians had found Razor the day after he was beaten. They would not have seen him if the buzzards hadn't been gliding over him. The buzzards had picked up the scent of blood, but Razor was not putting off the odor of death. The buzzards were biding their time, continually gliding high over their potential meal. They didn't leave even when the Indians approached their intended feast. They untied his hands and feet and removed the bloody rope from around his neck, moistened his lips, and washed his bloody face.

Ants covered his body, seeking moisture from his blood. Water Finder brushed them away as gently as he could. Only a few stung Razor in the process. The sting of the pissant is always minor in pain, and the pain from his beating masked any pain that they caused.

Finder and Walks were concerned with the deep rope burns on his neck. They had sought out and found several large purple *Opuntia* cactus, cut off the spines, and cut open the pads to allow the slick sap to escape. They cleaned his neck and applied the sap from the plant to the rope burns. The sap would keep scabs from forming and let the wound heal with minimum scarring.

Water Finder had wrapped a clean cloth, loosely tied, around Razor's neck. Walks dug up the plants and transplanted them in a bucket. He placed the plants in the wagon to be sure they had a ready supply of the cactus sap. Water Finder would apply the sap at least three times a day. The disappointed buzzards were still circling when the two braves left the area with the buzzards' intended feast.

Water Finder, who was twenty years old, spoke English as if it were his native tongue. Walks with Pride didn't know how old he was but knew he was something over twenty-five. He had settled on that number. His English was broken. Water Finder insisted that Razor call them Finder and Walks. He also insisted that Razor stay with them at least until he could take care of himself. Razor had no better choice.

Finder drove the wagon each day and had his horse tied to the back. Walks would walk or run far ahead. His horse always followed behind with no bridle or lead rope attached. The horse was regal in looks and had no brand. Razor finally asked, "Why does Walks' horse always follow behind without a bridle or lead rope?"

"The horse is smart. Walks is carrying the horse's oats," Finder said. They both had a good laugh.

Walks would be ahead of the wagon as far as a mile at times. Often, he would go out of sight. He carried a long bow with a quiver of arrows and a hunting knife. Finder wore a Colt .45 on his right hip and a ten-inch blade Bowie knife on his left. He had a .45-caliber Winchester repeating rifle and a short bow and a quiver full of arrows in the seat beside him.

Finder told Razor that they had heard that several Comanche hunting parties had been seen in southern New Mexico. He heard the Comanches were being driven out of Texas, and Walks was looking for them instead of the Comanches finding him first.

The Mescalero Apache preferred the timbered mountains, streams, and rivers over the extreme south and southwestern parts of New Mexico, which were dry and arid. It was known that some Comanches occupied parts of

Northern Mexico south of New Mexico Territory. The Comanches were a nomadic tribe, and hunting parties sometimes went north to hunt but would try to stay clear of the larger Mescalero Apache tribe.

Finder explained to Razor that they would be in little danger of the Mescalero Indians. The dialect of the Lipan Apache and Mescalero Apache were different but similar. The Mescalero Apache spoke the western dialect of the Athabaskan language, and the Lipan spoke the eastern dialect. Finder knew both. Finder and Walks had talked many times with Mescalero Apache, and they had no problems communicating. Most Indians signed when talking, and hand signs were used often to clarify meanings. All the Apache tribes were friendly with each other except the White Mountain Apache tribe located in the southwestern part of New Mexico Territory. It was rumored that they could not get along with themselves, much less get along with another tribe. Finder felt the Comanches and banditos were their main concerns.

Razor kept his thoughts to himself. He knew he was lucky to be alive. He was also lucky to have been rescued by Finder and Walks. He didn't want to depend on luck for his survival.

He had to have a plan. He was determined he would return to Mesilla without being killed. All this ruckus made him think about the battles of the Roman Empire and of the British in the Revolutionary War and their War in 1812 with the United States and France in North America. He marveled at the brute force results of the Roman Empire in Europe and the defeat of the great British Empire by the small Army of the United States. The guerrilla war tactics used by the States helped in the defeat of the mighty British Empire in both the Revolutionary War and the War of 1812. Both times the armies of the States were outnumbered and outgunned.

Razor realized that his return to Mesilla would not be the same as those two countries, but he too would be outnumbered and outgunned. He made up his mind he would prepare for a guerrilla war with Raiman Callaway and Ralph Marlow. His first objective was to finance his return. Then he would select the weapons he would need and learn how to use them.

He had never wanted his life to turn in this direction. In the short term, it wouldn't lead him to his main goal in life—happiness. His retaliation and defeat of Raiman Callaway and Ralph Marlow would lead him in that direction. He prayed he would be successful, and for the first time in his life, he realized how wars were started regardless of pain or cost.

Chapter 8

Plan for Return

Several years before, Razor had started rolling one-hundred-dollar bills and placing them in the waistband and cuffs of his pants. Around the bunkhouse, it was usually quite a long time from one washing to the next. Some days Razor would just hold the waistband and cuffs of his pants just out of the water and wash the rest of the pants instead of trading out the money into another pair. He decided he would count his money tonight.

Razor went to sleep in his usual place under the wagon. As usual, Finder and Walks bedded away from the wagon and the campfire. One of them was awake and on guard throughout the night.

Around midnight, Razor slipped off his pants and pulled out the rolled-up money. The glow from the campfire gave him enough light to count. In seven years, he had saved a little over eleven hundred dollars in tips from the many teamsters and guards who worked for Raiman Callaway.

Razor thought that it would take him at least five years before he would be prepared to return to Mesilla and that eleven hundred dollars would not be enough money to cover everything he'd need. He made a mental list: horse, saddle, bridle, lariat, Winchester .45-caliber rifle, two Colt .45-

caliber pistols, ammunition, and a ten-inch Bowie knife. To cover all this, he needed a way to make money immediately.

He knew the United States Army needed horses. He had heard and read of the wild mustangs in Arizona, Mexico, and New Mexico. The origins of these horses were developed from the mixture of the pure bloodlines of the Barb, Arabian, and Andalusian horses. The very best of them were brought to this country from herds in Spain, Portugal, and Egypt by the conquistadores of Spain. They came from herds that belonged to the royal families of those countries.

Razor was convinced he could sell the horses at Fort Fillmore, named for President of the United States Millard Fillmore, which was six miles southeast of Mesilla and close to the Mexico border. He had enough money to buy all the supplies needed and pay wages for the first roundup and sale. Then from the next roundup and sale, he would save for his return to Mesilla.

Razor had been observant of Finder's and Walks' work ethics. They were careful along the trail. Finder was always checking his back trail for dust in the daytime. In the late evening, Walks would make a five-mile figure eight to see if anyone was on their back trail.

Finder continued putting the cactus sap on Razor's rope burns three times a day and would give Razor a report on the healing process.

Neither of the Indians asked anything about the beating Razor had received. He was confident of their character and wanted to talk his plans over with them. He told them what had caused the beating and the threat that he would be killed if he ever returned to Mesilla and didn't leave the territory. He assured his rescuers he would return. He learned from them that when the wagon and supplies were delivered, they would be out of work.

"I am grateful for the help both of you have given me, and I'll reward you greatly. I am young, and I desperately need your help, for which I can pay. I know a lot about the world, but there is so much I don't know that you both can teach me. I need to be as strong physically as you are. Walks, I need to walk and run as fast as you. I know little about firearms. I want to know everything you know about them. I want to know about the bow and arrow, tracking, hunting, and how to fight with a knife. And, I want you to teach me the Athabaskan language that the Apache use."

Razor told of his plan to trap the wild mustangs and sell them to the military. He assured them he had enough money to pay and feed them and buy supplies to last through the first roundup. "I don't want either of you to be involved in the combat that will take place between Ralph Marlow, Raiman Callaway, and me. It is my battle, and I plan to fight it alone."

Finder and Walks liked the plan but knew they would fight for the one who paid them, or better said, fight for the brand. Finder and Walks readily accepted Razor's offer.

By the time they reached Deming, Razor was walking, gaining strength, and carrying on conversations with Finder in the western dialect of the Apache Athabaskan language, with corrections as needed.

Deming was an oasis in the desert with a large trading post and blacksmith shop. Razor gave Finder instructions to pick out the weapons and ammunition. "I'll choose the bridle, saddle blanket, and saddle that I want. I'll be back for Walks to pick out a horse for me, and then I'll pay for everything."

At the local blacksmith shop he gave the proprietor a piece of paper with a drawing of an open shaving razor. "How long would it take for you to make a pair of branding irons shaped like this?"

"It's pretty simple. It will take me longer to fire up my forge than to make them. I can have them ready for you in about three hours."

"Do it," said Razor.

Razor went back to the trading post. He had spotted a brass telescope he felt he must have. He had previously checked the price and decided he could not afford it. Now he had decided that he could not afford not to have it.

He had wrapped a clean white cloth around his neck to cover the ugly, unhealed rope burns. At the trading post, he picked out six colorful bandannas, a change of clothes, and a hat. Razor had never worn a hat before. Walks had told him he needed one to shield the sun out of his eyes when scouting or tracking.

Razor, Finder, and Walks went to the corral to pick out a horse. There were two lookalike bay horses that caught Walks' eye. "We need a packhorse also," Walks said.

Walks looked at their hoofs, mouth, and legs. "Best horses here, and they are young. They have no brand or shoes, and they are mustangs," Walks said.

They walked back to the trading post, and Finder asked about the price of the two bays. They dickered over the price until there was an agreement.

"Is there a good farrier in town?"

"The blacksmith is an excellent farrier. People come from miles around to use him."

The blacksmith had just finished the last branding iron and was burning it into a board. "How's it look to you?" he asked Razor.

"Looks great! Let's heat it up and slap it on those two bays and put shoes on both," said Razor.

"Show me the bill of sale and I'll do it."

Razor looked with pride when he looked at his first razor-branded stock.

"It'll cost twenty-five cents to register the brand in the New Mexico Territory Brand Logbook, and I'll be glad to send it in for you," said the smithy.

Thoughts ran through Razor's mind. *Do I want to let Ralph Marlow and Raiman Callaway know I am alive?* He quickly determined this would be a good thing for him to do. He had planned to do things that would taunt them. This would be his first taunt of many others to come.

"Let's do that," said Razor.

After adding a rifle scabbard and a packsaddle to their supplies, they went to the corral and picked up the two horses. They loaded all the supplies securely on the packsaddle. Razor paid close attention as the packhorse was being saddled and cargo was loaded. Special attention was paid to the many different knots that were used. "Can someone teach me to tie all these different knots?" Razor asked the clerk.

Chapter 9

The Vaqueros

Razor saddled the other bay for his riding horse. Walks and Finder were surprised at how well Razor handled the horse. They were even more surprised when Razor showed them his trick mounting and riding.

With the wagon loaded with mining equipment, it was necessary to skirt Pyramid Mountain, throwing their trail north toward Lordsburg. It too had a large trading post. They would stop there and replenish their supplies then swing south at Lordsburg and drop down to Animas, where they would leave the mining equipment and wagon.

If traveling by horseback, some forty miles could have been cut off the trip. Razor was splitting his time on the way to Lordsburg evenly between Finder and Walks. Razor was now riding his bay bareback and without a bridle. Razor's bay horse kept pace with Walks' horse, and, on signal, the horse would rush forth for Razor to mount him from any direction.

The heat was up to 110 degrees Fahrenheit during the daytime hours and down to 60 at night. To help build his strength, Razor would seek a boulder each day and lift it over his head numerous times. Each day he tried to find a boulder that weighed more than the one he lifted the day before.

The wounds on Razor's neck stung and the scars looked ugly. His hand went to it involuntarily several times a day, which fueled his urgency and determination to return to Mesilla. The running, lifting the boulder, and other physical work brought on long lean muscles, height, and weight to Razor's body.

Finder and Walks didn't know Razor's age but thought he had to be at least twenty. They were astonished at how fast he picked up their language and how much he mimicked them in the use of the bow and arrow, scouting, tracking, throwing his knife at targets and tying knots.

Razor's previous riding experience helped him adjust well to the trail. He was always observant of his surroundings, especially the back trail. While walking out front with Walks, he was the one who picked up the first sign of the dust cloud five or six miles behind the wagon. He pointed it out to Walks.

Razor mounted his horse and stood on its back. He scoped back toward the cloud. Heat waves were shimmering off the desert floor, making it hard to locate movement. Only after moving the scope above the heat waves and picking up the top of the dust cloud and lowering it back toward the ground did he pick up the sight of the two riders racing toward them.

Walks disappeared, and Razor rode back to alert Finder.

There were rock outcroppings in the area. "We want to be the only one with cover. We will race ahead where there are no rocks, and we will have the cover of the wagon, and Walks will have the cover of the desert," said Finder.

Razor had shot his rifle numerous times but was a long way from being a good rifleman. Finder had turned the wagon sideways from the trail. Razor took a position up front in the wagon behind some of the equipment. Finder took his position at the back. Walks was nowhere to be seen.

Razor watched the riders' approach. One held up a hand in peace. The other held his hands high away from his guns. They stopped about fifty yards from the wagon and asked for permission to come closer. Only Razor understood them because they asked in Spanish. They looked the same as the many vaqueros he had seen around Mesilla.

Razor asked if they spoke English, and they answered that they didn't. He asked if they were vaqueros, and they answered that they were. Razor asked them to hold up for a moment.

"Finder, they want to come closer to the wagon. They said they are vaqueros."

"Tell them to ride in with their hands held high and that they will be shot if their hands drift lower," said Finder.

Razor relayed the message to the two vaqueros, and they rode in closer while complying. The vaqueros showed no signs of hostility and seemed pleased that Razor was talking to them in unbroken Spanish.

"Finder, I'm going out to meet them halfway. Cover me!"

The vaqueros told Razor that they had driven a small heard of Longhorn cattle out of the Rio Casas Grandes area of Mexico to the mines in Silver City. Silver City lay northeast of Lordsburg. Rio Casas Grandes in Mexico lay thirty miles due east of Antelope Wells, New Mexico. "We pitched camp near our trail going back to the Rio Casas Grandes area. We both live in the Villa de Jonas, thirty-five miles southwest of our destination. We were attacked by seven Comanche. We had unsaddled and hobbled our horses. We had eaten and moved away from our campfire for the night. We were alerted to the Indians' presence by one of their horses. We cautiously made it back to our horses and resaddled just before they chased us from the area. The Comanche acted as if they were starved and that they were more interested in our food stuff than chasing us for our scalps and horses," one of them said.

The vaqueros had lost their food supplies and bedrolls. They were hungry and offered to pay for any food and coffee that we could spare.

Razor escorted the vaqueros back to the wagon. After Finder heard of their plight, he decided to set up camp and feed them. Walks appeared from nowhere. "Razor, find out where the vaqueros were when the Comanches showed up," said Walks.

It was determined that they were between the Tres Hermanas Mountains and the Cedar Mountain range. The vaqueros were very familiar with this area, which was about thirty miles southwest of Deming and just a few miles from Mexico.

Walks had wanted to make sure the Comanches had not crossed their trail. The vaqueros assured them that they covered their retreat from the area and pushed them away from Mexico. When they found the wagon tracks, they followed, with thoughts of food and being farther away from the Comanches.

The names of the vaqueros were Enrique and Roberto Mendoza. They were cousins. They were born near the Rio Casas Grandes in the Villa de Jonas. They both were twenty-five years of age. They had worked on seasonal roundups in and around the lower Chihuahua State. Razor casually asked them what they knew about the wild mustangs in the Rio Casas Grandes area. He was told there were hundreds of them. "Does anyone try to catch them?" Razor asked.

"There is no market for them that I know of. We have wild longhorns. They are harder to catch than the mustangs, but there is a market for them in the mining camps along the border," Enrique said.

"You have caught wild mustangs?"

"Roberto and I get a request for a specific horse, such as Walks', once or twice a year. We catch it and break it to saddle. It takes more time to find the specific horse, but when we find it, we usually can break it to saddle in an hour or so. We charge four pesos," Enrique said.

"Does anyone else round up the Longhorns?"

"Some are killed to eat, but no one that we know of rounds them up. Rounding them up is just part of the problem. They are mighty ornery to drive. We drag twenty of them out of the brush and corral them. When we get them started, we stampede them and keep them running until they want to sit down. Only then is it easy to keep them bunched and headed in the right direction," said Roberto.

"How many vaqueros would it take to drive a herd of a hundred mustangs a hundred miles?" Razor asked.

"Horses like company. They stick together. Six vaqueros should make it in two and a half days," was Enrique's immediate answer.

"Would you and Roberto be interested in a steady job capturing, saddle breaking, and herding mustangs?" Without hesitation, an affirmative answer was given. "Roberto and I know of a perfect place to trap mustangs in the Rio Casas Grandes area," said Enrique.

"I'll work out the wages with you to your satisfaction later. I need for you to start now. I want a list, in the morning, of the supplies we will be needing. You will go with us to

Lordsburg. There, we will buy supplies and another packhorse."

Finder and Walks had remained sitting and silent. They were amazed that Razor had listened so intensely to the vaqueros and spoke without hesitation. They knew there was mutual respect and agreement among them.

In the Athabaskan dialect, Razor told them everything that was discussed. He added, "The Mexican vaqueros were renowned throughout the world for their ability to rope and herd animals."

Razor then introduced the vaqueros to Finder and Walks, using a mix of the Athabaskan dialect, Spanish, and English. It would be Finder and Walks' first of many Spanish lessons, and Enrique and Roberto's first of many English and Athabaskan lessons.

Throughout every day, Razor would repeat everything he said in English, Athabaskan, or Spanish depending on who he was talking with. Razor increased his runs with Walks and his tracking lessons. He was practicing his quick draw with his Colts and was dry firing throughout the day. In the evening around the campfire, he threw his knife at targets for an hour each night.

He was not even close to being ready. He was not going to be patient. He would have to work harder. Several times he realized his hand was moving toward his throat and he would stop it. He would never do that again. If his hand started for his throat, he would let it go. It would remind him how badly he needed to return to Mesilla. His pursuit of happiness had a large roadblock, that being Marlow and Callaway.

Before they reached Lordsburg, Razor expressed his thoughts on ammunition. He felt that one could never have too much, but it would be limited to how much they could carry without displacing other necessities. They would buy more ammunition and cut back on food stuff, except coffee, bacon, flour, and salt. There were plenty of game animals that could be harvested as well as maverick longhorns. Traps, knives, and bow and arrows could be used to kill game instead of ammunition.

Razor knew that the rope burn would always be with him and decided to buy more bandannas, mostly plain. He did want to hide the scar, but it was a strong motivation for him to always be strong, alert, and ready for anything. He also bought a suit of clothes and a string tie.

After buying supplies, another packhorse and packsaddle were acquired. Razor planned that they move out early the next morning and reach Animas by nightfall.

Animas was thirty miles from Lordsburg but had an excellent straight road and was deemed safe by the mining company and the trading post.

It had been a leisurely ride for Razor and the vaqueros. Before Walks and Finder turned the freight wagon west toward the mine, Razor removed the purple *Opuntia* cactus from the wagon and tied them on top of one of the packsaddles. Nothing but a dim trail led forward. Razor and the vaqueros continued on and set up camp to wait on Finder and Walks' return.

Enrique and Roberto heated up Razor's branding iron and branded the packhorse bought in Lordsburg. When Finder and Walks returned, hardtack, coffee, and cooked bacon were waiting.

Chapter 10

Antelope Wells and Rio Casas Grandes

It was a hard two-day ride from Lordsburg to Antelope Wells. The trail weaved its way around peaks as high as eight thousand feet. The wind was guided by the mountains and peaks which flooded the trail with whimsical gusts, making it much cooler than the desert.

Walks ran and walked, usually staying out front of the others. His horse was always close, but he seldom rode it. If Walks did ride, he rode bareback and without a bridle.

Everyone continued trying to speak the language of the other with Razor or Finder correcting them as they went. It was natural for the Apache to sign as they talked regardless of the language they were trying to speak. Before long, the Mexicans were signing also. Walks' broken English was disappearing into full sentences. If he did speak with the broken English, he corrected himself before Razor or Finder did it for him.

When Razor's hand was raised to his neck, the pace of his horse picked up.

That night after eating, Enrique and Roberto started teaching Razor how to throw a Mexican riata. The riata was tightly plaited strips of cured leather. Most were thirty feet long, but some were fifty feet long or longer. A large loop for the Longhorns required the longer riata. This was the preferred lasso of the vaquero. The riata didn't stretch and seldom broke, as the hemp ropes often did.

His first lesson was roping while standing still, then roping from a run while still on the ground. Then they resaddled and threw the lariat while sitting in the saddle. They threw from the horse while it was trotting and running at full speed. Razor threw until dark thirty, a cowboy's way of saying thirty minutes after dark. Throwing the lariat correctly was his top priority. It was a vital tool in his plan concerning Ralph Marlow and Raiman Callaway. To fail in what he was going to do with the lariat could get him killed.

Razor's hatred for Ralph Marlow and Raiman Callaway was eating at him constantly. He wouldn't wait two or three years to get back but would start thinking in terms of months. He promised himself that he work harder and longer on the skills he needed.

Late in the evening the next day, they saw a herd of about 40 mustangs. When they first saw them, they were standing still with their heads held high, looking back at them from maybe a hundred yards away. There was one horse standing off about twenty yards looking at the mustangs. The horse stood proud with his tail and head held taller than any of the other mustangs. They realized that it was Walks' horse.

There came a bleating sound from one of the horses and then Razor witnessed one of the most beautiful sights he had ever seen. The mustangs turned with their heads and tails held high and raced off and held them high until they were out of sight.

They were the proudest-looking animals he had ever seen. It didn't seem that they were panicked, but more like it was simply the proper way to get somewhere fast. This sight would stay in his memory for the rest of his life.

Razor wanted to ride a wild mustang. He didn't want to break the mustang's spirit but would let it go and do whatever it wanted to. He just wanted to stay on.

The sight of the mustangs lingered in his mind and would not leave his memory but a few of the horses looked different from the mustangs. These few horses were regal in structure and performance. He knew now why Roberto and Enrique had often been hired to seek out and capture these special horses. They were bred with a dominant bloodline of the Barb, Arabian, or Andalusian.

Antelope Wells was in the boot heel of the New Mexico Territory and on the border of Mexico. There were several cottonwood trees and many sightings of Pronghorn Antelope and other animals. Tracks, including the wild mustangs, and game trails were abundant.

Water came from flowing artesian wells. They provided water to the area year-round. The water pooled up in low areas around the wells. After flowing away from the pools, the water would be reclaimed by the thirsty earth. Various vegetation was abundant but was eaten as soon as it poked its new growth forth.

The next morning, Enrique and Roberto led the group into Mexico. Along the way, Razor practiced his draw on every movement and sound. It was a thirty-mile trip to the Rio Casas Grandes. They continuously spotted herds of mustangs along the way.

When they arrived, Razor was surprised to see the abandoned large stone structures. He had read about the conquistadors building such structures in the sixteenth century in Mexico. All the roofs were missing as well as many of the walls. The river ran behind the structures.

"Enrique doesn't anyone live here?" asked Razor.

"No! The conquistadors were brutal conquerors of Mexico and Peru and occupied the better parts of both countries. They were far outnumbered by the Incas in Peru and the Aztec in Northern Mexico but much better equipped. The conquistadors defeated the Indians with their horses, rifles, and swords they brought with them from Spain. They robbed anyone who had anything of value, and those who resisted their authority were killed. Hernando Cortez defeated the Aztec and claimed Mexico for Spain in the year 1521.

"Most of the Aztec who once lived here were killed, and only a few escaped. None of them or their relatives wanted to come back to this area because the conquistadors' ruins brought back bad memories. The stories had been handed down for generations by their relatives. Some included rumors of ghost occupying the area to persuade others from coming back," Enrique concluded.

Enrique suggested one of the structures be used as their headquarters. They decided to add a covered fire pit out front where they could cook their meals. Roberto suggested that they do a quick rattlesnake hunt in and around the structure before settling in. After finding several dens, it was decided they would pick another. The second building had good walls and an abundance of gun portholes. The roof had been burned off, as had most of them. The flagstone floor was intact, eliminating possible snake dens, and would be easy to clean.

Only three rattlesnakes were found around the house, but that would be plenty for their evening meal.

Most of the huge wooden doors in the structures had survived at least partially. In all the abandoned structures, the dry air preserved many of the doors and window frames. Fire had destroyed a few. The next day, a roundup of enough doors and hardware was completed. The doors were hung, and supplies were moved in. Many of the doors had religious crosses carved in them, and some of the stones had crosses chiseled into their faces.

Enrique and Roberto led the way to the narrow valley that would serve as an entrance to the canyon where they could trap horses. The valley floor covered eight hundred acres or more. In the far reaches of the valley were several stone pools that held water from the mountain's runoff.

On the north side of the river, the mountains maintained their three hundred or so yards distance from the river all the way northeast to the New Mexico Territory.

Enrique suggested they build a six-foot-tall brush fence starting five feet out in the river to the center of the valley's entrance. They could block off either side of the entrance with a brush gate, and the mustangs could be driven into the enclosure from either side of the center fence. A smaller drift fence would be built on both sides of the center fence.

Razor reached up and rubbed the rope burns on his neck. "Let's do it," he said.

Once the mustangs entered the trap, they would go to the far reaches of the valley, giving the vaqueros time to close the gate the mustangs had entered. The older horses would be culled along with others that had not recovered properly from wounds. The drive of the mustangs could be as long as forty miles or more in either direction. The vaqueros would start the mustangs slowly and gently with riders moving them along.

The next morning, everyone took two lariats with them as they rode out to hunt for branches and brush to use to build fences. It was going to take a lot.

To everyone's surprise, Razor looked as if he had done this all his life. In fact, he not only caught a large piece of driftwood on the first try, but he was also the first to throw his lariat.

Enrique and Roberto had suggested that they lay the brush three rows wide on the ground then put two rows on top of that. One row would then be added to the top. After the first three lines of brush were laid from the river to the valley entrance, Razor gathered everyone around. It had been a long day of hard work.

"Everyone knows what to do to get our trap ready," said Razor. "Enrique and I will be going to look for some of his cousins to help. We will leave at daybreak in the morning and go to the Villa de Jonas. We may have to go as far as the Ciudad de Chihuahua, but we will return as soon as possible. I know all of you saw rattlers we disturbed today, and some had their dens destroyed. They will be out looking for a new place to den up, so be careful."

Chapter 11

The Two Banditos

Early the next morning, Finder, Walks, and Roberto saw Razor and Enrique off. Finder told Razor he had done enough dry firing to load his weapons. Razor told him they were loaded. A smile crossed Finder's face. Razor and Enrique had loaded their saddlebags with ammunition, jerky, and other food the night before.

Razor had discussed with Enrique the importance of secrecy about what they were doing. Catching mustangs was not against any law, but he didn't want any outside interference. They could barely see when they headed southwest down the river. They stayed along the river until it disappeared into the desert.

Several herds of mustangs were seen along the river but none in the desert. It was around noon when the river disappeared into the desert. "Are there no mustangs in the desert?" asked Razor.

"They are desert mustangs. There is a limited source of water, and the stallion in each herd is as protective of the water as he is of his mares. In fact, there are more fights over the water than there are over the mares. If they lose the water, they must move back into the mountains."

"It is difficult for a stallion to service more than fifty mares. In the mountains, young studs will start stealing from a herd when the count of the mares nears fifty. Often a mare will willingly go with a younger stud if they are not being serviced. In the desert, the size of the herd depends on how much water is available. Often the mares will drive off weaker horses if the water source is limited. We are lucky to have plenty of water in the Rio Casas Grandes."

Enrique had wanted to go to the Villa de Jonas before undertaking a long trek to Chihuahua. If his cousins were not there, some of his family might know where they were. They hoped to reach the Villa de Jonas before dark.

As they entered the small village of Jonas, it seemed that everyone in the village rushed out to greet them and many called out Enrique's name. There were many smiles and lots of laughter.

Razor enjoyed their happiness. The only way he would be happy again was to confront Ralph Marlow and Raiman Callaway. If he had to kill them, so be it!

From two doors down, a whistle came and a hand waved. "That's Juan Mendoza and his brother Armando behind him. That's who we are looking for," Enrique said.

Razor was introduced to all as a friend. They had no doubts that he had lived in Mexico all his life even though his name was Razor Sharp. His Spanish accent and his mannerisms could not be done by a foreigner.

These were poor people in the village, but everyone put on a feast for Enrique and his friend. Boiled chicken and peppers were served with rice. After the meal was finished, Enrique and Razor finally were able to speak with Juan and

Armando alone. After discussing the job with the two men, without disclosing where it was, both were eager to have a long-lasting, full-time job.

Juan spoke up. "Señor Sharp, could you use one more vaquero? He is our brother Antonio. He is strong, loyal, and a good vaquero. He will be here tonight and will jump at a full-time job."

Razor's hand moved up to his throat, and he replied, "Absolutely, but please call me Razor." This was not at all Mexican custom, but because he was younger than all his men, he would feel better about it.

Early the next morning, Razor, Enrique, Juan, Armando, and Antonio rode out. They planned to be back at their encampment in the ruins by nightfall.

Finder brought Razor up on their progress during the two days he was gone. They had completed the bottom two rows of fencing and had started on the top tier. Their progress had slowed for having to go farther to find brush.

The next day, Razor, Juan, Armando, and Antonio hauled the brush to the fence, and Finder, Walks, Enrique, and Roberto would place the brush on the top row. By noon the fence was completed.

At the entrance of the trap, brush gates were to be placed on both sides of the fence. Each gate would be fifty yards long and would be pulled in place by the vaqueros and their horses. The gates would be three rows wide at the bottom, two at the middle, and one at the top. The only difference would be that they would be laced together with rope. A cinch rope around the bottom bundles would be left with a loop tied at the end of the rope for the vaqueros to tie onto. The gate away from the direction of the drive would be closed. The gate where the horses entered would be dragged in place as soon as the last horse entered.

Breaking the horses to saddle and branding them would take place in a corral that was to be built farther inside the valley.

By the end of the day, the gate nearest the camp was pulled into place and tied to the center fence and into a large cedar tree protruding out of the cliff. It was pulled back open for easy passage to the other side.

They headed back to the camp for food and rest for the night. Walks was out front as usual. He came running back toward them. "Razor, there are two Mexican banditos at the camp. They have their bandoliers full of ammunition. I looked for others but couldn't find any sign of others. I'm sure they are alone."

"Walks, go back with Enrique and Roberto and see if they recognize them. We want no trouble. Stay out of sight. It's good that no others are with them, but there may be others nearby. Come back as soon as you can."

Thirty minutes later, Walks, Enrique, and Roberto returned.

"We know them, Razor," said Enrique. "They are a sorry and dangerous lot from the Rio Santa Maria area. They have a hideout there. They are in a gang of fifteen or so. The gang came to Villa de Jonas twice last year demanding to be fed. The first time they came, all of us who could work were off working. The only people there were women, children, and elderly men. They were told there was no food. They immediately killed three goats belonging to a friend of ours.

He complained, and they killed him. Three months ago, these two came with five others seeking food. They were loud and drunk on tequila. They fired several shots into the air and ground. That time Roberto and I, along with six of our cousins, had just rode in from the northern range of Chihuahua. After we killed two of them and wounded two others, they escaped. One of the ones at the camp was one of those two who had been wounded during that raid."

"What do you think they want here?" asked Razor.

"I don't know, but whatever it is, it's not good."

"Do you think they would recognize any of you?"

"I don't know, Razor. We can't take a chance on them leaving here alive. They would come back with their gang of banditos and wipe us all out just for our weapons alone. After the death of our friend in their first raid, Roberto and I sought out the *federales* in Chihuahua to tell them of the killing. They were aware of the gang. Their leader was the notorious Paco Espinosa. Espinosa was so vicious Juan "Cheno" Cortina, the "Red Robber," kicked him out of his gang. Then Espinosa took his gang back to the south of Chihuahua on the Rio Santa Maria. The federales said that Espinosa's gang would kill their own mothers for a peso or a bottle of tequila. They also told us they thought they had found their hideout on the Rio Santa Maria and were hot on their trail. They may have found their hideout and broken up the gang by now," said Enrique.

"Come around, everyone. We will have to plan this as we go. Walks, do your thing and disappear. Come in at your discretion. Everyone spread out, and I'll take the point. I hope our show of force will suggest to them that they take no action against us now. We don't want them to leave and get help from other banditos. When we get in position near them, I want all of you to stay out of their sight, except Finder and me. From cover, keep your rifles aimed at them. I'll confess to not speaking or understanding Spanish. So be careful. Talk to me in Athabaskan, Finder, without looking at me you might sign me. Follow me and let's be careful," said Razor. "As we approached, the banditos stood and waved. They each had a broad smile, rifles in the crooks of their arms, pistols on their hips and one behind their belts in front. Each carried a large knife on his hip opposite the gun. In Spanish they spoke. "Hello, my friends. We are hungry, may we eat with you?"

They seemed nervous and worn-out. Razor kept his right hand close to his Colt and opened his left hand upward as a gesture of not knowing what he had said. He turned to Finder and asked in the Eastern Athabaskan dialect what he had said. "Tell him in broken Spanish to slow down and repeat what he had said."

After feigning not understanding and having the banditos repeat again, Finder got across to them that they could not speak Spanish or English well but continued to pretend to not understand what they were saying.

Still speaking in the eastern dialect, Finder said, "Razor, let's move Enrique in and let him talk to them in Spanish. We will tell Enrique to get as much information from them as he can."

"That's good, Finder. Just be ready in case he recognizes Enrique."

Finder called Enrique in from his cover and told him what they wanted him to do. When Enrique called out "Mis amigos," the two banditos seemed to relax. They gave no indication of any recognition of Enrique.

"Relax, they will feed you. What are you doing here?" Enrique asked.

The two looked at each other. "Don't worry, the gringo or Apache understands no Spanish. They are also very dumb," Enrique said in a snide tone of voice.

"We are on the run. Our leader has been killed by the federales, and we're trying to get back with the rest of our gang."

"Where did you come from?"

"The Rio Santa Maria area."

"Are you telling me my good friend Paco Espinosa has been killed?"

"You knew Paco?"

"Did either of you ride with Cheno Cortina?"

"No!"

"Well, I did! I was there when Cheno ran Paco off," Enrique said.

"What are you doing with this outfit?" one of the banditos asked.

"Everyone must be somewhere. I'm only here looking for something better."

The banditos looked at each other and gave each a nod then turned back, looking at Enrique. "Want to join us?"

"Doing what?"

"Before morning, we are going to take this bunch down. We'll take all their weapons and money and try to get back with what's left of our gang. Since you rode for Cheno Cortina, you might come in handy if we need to join his gang."

"That sounds interesting, let's go inside the chow hall and talk. I'll ask the gringo to have someone bring our food inside when it's ready."

Razor had heard every word of the conversation. He listened to Enrique as he told him in Athabaskan to have someone bring their food inside.

"I'll have Walks and Finder bring in the food." He signed Finder to find Walks and what he wanted them to bring to the table.

"Enrique, move away fast from the table when Walks and Finder move in with the food. Be ready to get out of the way!" When the banditos sat down, they both pulled their pistols from their belts in front and placed them on the table in front of them. They weren't aware that they had seven guns pointing at them. Razor and the others had entered the eating area. The banditos were feeling smug. They had a new confidant and were in no hurry to enter a gunfight. They would eat and come back later at night after forming a plan with Enrique.

A short time later, Razor heard Walks and Finder laughing. They entered the room with two large baskets. Razor had signaled for everyone to stand and clap as they entered. Enrique had stood and moved away from the table where the banditos were still sitting. When both Finder and Walks feigned tripping, they spilled the baskets in front of the banditos. There was no time for the banditos to reach for their guns or try to run. The rattlesnakes struck at their every move. Screams of terror filled the room, then there was total silence.

It took Walks and Finder only five minutes to round up the ten large rattlesnakes. All signs of the two bandito's presence were removed and buried. Their ammunition was confiscated.

Razor held a meeting about what had happened. He made sure everyone knew what the banditos had planned for them. "I don't think any more of their gang will show up here but stay alert. We did what we had to do. We shall never speak of this again.

"Enrique, you have some explaining to do. Where did you come up with the idea of telling them that the Apache and gringo were very dumb?"

Enrique hesitated and began to squirm. He finally got out, "Boss, I didn't mean it. I was just play-acting."

Chapter 12

Fort Fillmore, New Mexico Territory

By noon the next day, the other gate was finished. It was dragged into place and attached to the center fence and cliff. It was then pulled out of the way and left against the cliff, ready to be closed when the mustangs were inside. All ropes and knots were checked on both gates so there would be no problems when it came time to close them.

The small single-row brush drift fences had to be put in on both sides of the center fence. This fence started at the river a hundred yards from the center fence. It drifted back to the center fence a hundred yards before reaching the gates. If all went as planned, the mustangs would drift to the opening of the valley and into their trap.

Razor called Finder and Enrique to go with him to select the location of the corral, while the rest finished the drift fences. The whole eight hundred acres were searched, and a location that pushed up close to the western wall was chosen. This location was selected for the large concave stones along the face of the cliff that held water. Stakes were set and marked. The drift fences were finished, and everyone returned to camp.

After eating, Razor told everyone about his plan. "Juan, Armando, and Antonio will build the breaking corral and the shed. I want a separate twenty-acre corral and shed built beside the breaking corral to keep the more purebred horses. You all know the ones I'm talking about. It's for the one horse you would want to keep for yourself. It's amazing that after over two hundred and fifty years, there are a few that are near pure bred."

"We will protect their bloodline. On our return from delivering horses, we will bring back oats to feed the special-bred horses."

"You might find some old corral boards that are fit to use for a fence. If not, use wood from barn doors or the abandoned houses. You'll find stakes for the corral in the southwest area of the canyon. The corral sheds can be built against that wall."

"You may have to go to the mountains and cut cedar poles and use rope. Just make sure the corral is strongly built."

"I want Walks to spend his time scouting for the herds of mustangs on both sides of the center fence."

He didn't have to tell Walks to look for signs of Indians or outsiders.

"Finder, Enrique, and Roberto will be going with me to Fort Fillmore. We should be back in five or six days, and when we return, we'll be ready to start trapping mustangs."

It was a hundred miles to Fort Fillmore. Enrique and Roberto knew the way and had traveled it several times. Razor hoped to travel fifty miles a day. He knew he would be pushing it, but Finder, Enrique, and Roberto thought the horses were in great shape and that the trail was good, so there was an excellent chance they could make close to that many miles. They were to travel light and would eat only jerky on the way there. They each carried a small bag of oats for the horses. Water would have to be found along the way.

Enrique led the way. He followed the river to the northeast until leaving it a short way from the border of the New Mexico Territory. They came into New Mexico south of the Tres Hermanas Mountain and turned east to the West Potrillo Mountain. He pointed out a mountain lagoon holding enough water for several large herds. They spent the night near the lagoon. They continued at first light, going through the West Potrillo Mountain pass, sliding just north of Mount Riley and the East Potrillo Mountain to their destination.

Razor could not help but think of Bonnie Lou when they entered the area. Her father was now his enemy, but he would not let that interfere with his friendship with Bonnie Lou. Knowing Bonnie Lou, he was sure her friendship would be everlasting, regardless of what was going to happen in their futures.

Razor's hand moved to his neck, and he had to fight the urge to go into Mesilla and confront Raiman Callaway and Ralph Marlow immediately. He was not ready, but the urge demanded he work harder to reach the point of being ready. He would show them no mercy.

Roberto guided them to a cantina that also served food. It was only a block south of the Fort. Razor reminded them to not mention his name. The cantina not only served good food, it had a stable for the horses and rooms for them. A stable boy was instructed to care for the horses.

Razor took his first bite of food and froze. Sitting at the next table and facing him was José Solis. José had attended his classes for several years. The man looked up and directly at him and then looked away. Razor spoke to Finder in Athabaskan instructing him to sign Enrique and Roberto to eat in silence. Razor continued eating quietly and didn't look at José again. Razor knew he had grown taller and more muscular these last few months and was much darker in color. The hat had covered his eyes. He was convinced José had not recognized him. José left the cantina without another glance in Razor's direction.

Razor was up early the next day. He put on his suit and tie. He cleaned his boots and hat and met everyone in the cantina for breakfast. He had previously filled everyone in on his plan for the day. Razor would be unarmed except for one pistol. He wanted all his weapons, but it was the custom for those in town for business to be armed with only one gun. To do otherwise, one would be branded a gun slick or gunfighter, and he never wanted that recognition.

Enrique and Roberto left the cantina first. They were well armed with their Colt .45s and Winchester rifles. They acted to be in deep conversation and leisurely strolled toward the Fort.

There were vendors outside the open gate selling everything from watches to feathers. The two guards were walking back and forth in front of the gate, guarding entry into the Fort.

Razor left shortly after Enrique and Roberto, making an authoritative approach toward the gate. Enrique and Roberto were supposedly looking at the vendors' offerings while actually guarding Razor. Finder was leisurely following Razor at a short distance. The guards stopped Razor at the gate, blocking his entry.

"What is your purpose in the Fort, sir?" one of the guards asked.

"To see the quartermaster." "Do you have an appointment?"

"No." said Razor.

"The quartermaster does not see anyone without an appointment, sir."

"That's too bad. It's a little farther, but I guess I'll have to sell my horses to Fort Sumner." Razor turned away to leave.

"Wait! Wait! Wait! If you have horses for sale, I'm sure the quartermaster will see you."

"I'm not going to wait around just to see if he will see me. I want you to take me to see him now or I'm leaving."

"Sir, I'll take you to his office now."

Razor followed the fast-walking corporal. He walked into the quartermaster's outer office. The corporal addressed the sergeant at the desk. "Sergeant, the quartermaster needs to see this man." He looked up at Razor and asked if he had an appointment.

"No!" said Razor.

"The quartermaster sees no one without an appointment." Razor turned to leave.

"Sergeant, he has horses for sale," the corporal cried out.

"He will see you now, sir, follow me," the sergeant said.

The sergeant opened the door without knocking, and before anyone else could say a word, the sergeant spoke. "Sir, this is an emergency."

He turned to the vendor sitting across from the quartermaster. "Sir, you must leave the room. I'll find you and tell you when you may return."

"Major, please forgive me, but this man has horses for sale."

"Sergeant, leave this man, and go back to your duties. And make sure that no one disturbs us until we are through with our business," said the major.

"I'm Major Childers. I don't want to waste your time, sir, so I'll get right to the point. Geronimo has reportedly stolen every available horse in this part of the country. I don't normally buy stolen horses, but I'll now. It is necessary. I don't want to know if they are stolen. How many horses do you have?"

"First, Major, I don't deal in stolen horses. We hang horse thieves. The horses I'll be selling will have only one brand on them. The brand is registered in the branding book for the New Mexico Territory. Before we go any further, you will have to agree to never buy a horse with my brand on it from anyone but me."

"I agree. How many do you have?"

"How many will you give me a procurement document for?" Razor asked.

"Five hundred."

"At what price?"

"I usually pay only thirty-five dollars a head for saddle-broke horses, but now I'll pay you forty."

"We'll take the thirty-five," said Razor.

"How fast can you start delivery?"

"I'm coming a long way with them, but I can have the first hundred here in four weeks. Then I'll deliver a hundred every four weeks."

"I want them as fast as you can get them here. What name do you want on the procurement document, and how do you want to be paid?"

"Under my name, Razor Sharp. I want gold coin deposited at Wells Fargo in El Paso. I'll give you the deposit information when I deliver the first hundred."

"Your name sounds familiar," the major said.

Since it was not a question, Razor passed over the major's thoughts and replied, "Major, don't tell anyone where or who you are getting the horses from. I'm going to be busy delivering your horses and don't have time for every Tom, Dick, and Harry trying to buy horses from me. It would be best if you wrote out the procurement document yourself. That way only you and I'll know about it."

"I'll do that now." *Razor Sharp!... I know I've heard that name before,* he thought to himself.

"Here is your procurement document, Mr. Sharp. I appreciate you not jacking up the price. Please hurry and don't let me down. My future is at stake."

"You will not be let down, I promise," Razor said with a handshake and a look straight in the major's eyes.

I like this man, thought the major.

The major put his copy of the procurement document in his safe and then opened the door and ordered the sergeant to escort the gentleman out. He told hm to cancel all his appointments for the rest of the day. This was the first time in weeks that he had peace of mind. He thought back through what he had just encountered.

Mr. Sharp must be a very important man. He wasted no time and was so reassuring. I know he will deliver the horses because he will receive no money until the Army receives the horses. He must be wealthy to turn down the extra five dollars a head and having five hundred horses for sale. He is a good man to know, he thought.

Razor went straight back to his room. The others joined him shortly. By noon they were across the Rio Grande headed to El Paso. Razor set up his account with a token deposit at the Wells Fargo terminal. There were about four hours of daylight left. They rode north and crossed back over the Rio Grande after making sure they would be in the New Mexico Territory and not Mexico after crossing.

They started their trip back to the Rio Casas Grandes. The route was just north of the Mexican border and south of the mountain ranges until they crossed into Mexico. Then they headed south to Rio Casas Grandes. The round trip would take them about five days with time to spare.

They had noticed mustang tracks along the river for miles. When they were approaching the drift fence, they looked ahead and saw the gate pulled shut. The gate on the other side of the center fence was also shut. They pulled the entrance gate open, entered, and closed it behind them. They saw the corral and three horses in the distance and soon spotted riders. Juan, Armando, and Antonio approached and began waving.

The corral had been completed, and a shed was well underway.

"You should see the mustangs!" exclaimed Juan. "We saw a bunch of tracks going into the valley and none coming out. We decided to close both gates and see what we caught. There are sixty-three mustangs in the far back. They were wild as thunder until Walks and his horse eased through them. After they saw Walks' horse following him everywhere, they started settling down. This must be one of their grazing areas."

"They haven't tried to leave. They must have come in after we left yesterday. We left early to find more boards. Want to go see the mustangs?", Juan asked.

"Pick out the best twenty and we'll break them for our remuda," instructed Razor. "The corral and shed look good but is it strong enough to hold two mustangs at a time?" Razor asked.

Before getting an answer, he told them that they had to be on the road with one hundred and twenty saddle-broke mustangs in three weeks. "We need another breaking corral, don't we? Those extra twenty mustangs will cover the ten we need for our special use and the other ten in case we lose a horse or two. He also wanted to do more than he promised.

By noon the next day, the other corral and shed were finished. "Walks always shows up just as the work is finished." Finder laughed as he spotted Walks running toward them with his horse trailing.

Walks reported he had seen several hundred mustangs within fifty miles each way from the center line. He had crossed the river and scouted that side then headed north and found even more mustangs. He had not come in sight of anyone, nor had he seen any shod horse tracks across the river.

By six o'clock that evening, six mustangs had been saddle-broke and branded. Another set of branding irons was needed. Razor would send Finder and Walks to Deming and have two more sets made. He also had a special and private need for one iron himself. Finder and Walks left for Deming before daybreak. Twelve mustangs had been saddle broke and branded that day.

Finder and Walks returned late on the third day with the new branding irons. Razor kept one set for himself. The new corral and branding irons increased the count of mustangs they could break each day, as well as the number of horses they could break to eighteen or so each day.

A quick roundup was called when Walks reported a herd of sixty-one mustangs was within five miles of the drift fence on the north end. The east gate would have to be pulled open. The captured mustangs were in the far end of the valley, but they'd have to watch them carefully to keep them from escaping.

Razor, Walks, Finder, Enrique, and Roberto would drive the herd. Juan, Armando, and Antonio would stay hidden downwind until the mustangs were in the enclosure, then quickly pull the gate shut. Walks and his horse would follow them into the valley, and would spend time settling them down, a continuing routine for Walks and his horse.

Razor and his crew would cross the river and go east for three miles, turn north for about seven miles, cross back over the river, and slowly move in from behind. Mustangs have a great sense of smell and will move away from the scent of a human. They will always shy away from water, unless they're thirsty, because it offers nothing to eat, and it slows their movement. If they needed to flee, they would flee on land, not water. Only if pushed would they enter the river.

After about an hour, they saw the herd. The horses were moving away from their pursuers, eating as they went. When they reached the drift fence, they showed a little defiance, but when they saw the widening valley ahead, they seemed eager to enter. Each of the men attempted to count the horses, and most came up with sixty-one. Altogether, the total count would be a hundred and twenty-four in the enclosure.

"That's her!" yelled Razor. "My special horse!" He saw her as she pranced through the gate heading for the far reaches of the enclosure. Razor pointed her out to Walks, Finder, Enrique, and Roberto. "I don't want anyone to put a rope on her but me. She's my Sweet Pea."

Razor rode his bay horse into the enclosure and followed the herd until they stopped. He had his Sweet Pea in sight. He stopped and unsaddled his horse and retrieved a small bag of oats and a stiff brush from his saddlebag. The bay eagerly started to eat the oats from the bag he set on the ground. Razor begun brushing the bay down and rubbed the brush all over the horse. He weaved in and out between the horse's legs and hugged its neck and rubbed his nose and brushed his mane. From the corner of his eye, he saw the young mare taking it all in.

Razor put the saddle back on the bay, emptied the rest of the oats on the ground, mounted, and slowly rode away. Razor was only fifty feet away when he peeked under his arm and saw the young mare easing toward the oats.

Early the next morning, Razor returned with an extra sack of oats and placed them on the ground and backed away fifty feet and fed and brushed down his bay. The young mare eased out to the bag and started eating. The rest of the herd had eased away from Razor and the young mare. That evening, Razor repeated the process. This time he backed away only forty feet.

The next day, Razor moved off to a more secluded area. The young mare left the herd and came to the oats. That afternoon, Razor found the herd on the west side of the enclosure. The herd moved away to the northeast, and the young mare followed Razor, as he carried his oats into the twenty-acre corral for the special horses.

Chapter 13

Delivery of the Mustangs

It took an extra day and a half to break and brand the extra twenty-four mustangs. Early on the twentieth day after telling Major Childers he would have the hundred horses at Fort Fillmore, Razor had nine days to fulfill his promise.

The vaqueros had picked out four of the wildest mustangs. Two had been placed in each corral. Walks and Finder kept the horses from resting with their fake mountain lion cries and bear noises. They traded out every two hours. The horses raced around the corral, kicking and stomping all night, getting no rest at all.

The next morning at daylight, the horses were led away, each tethered with a rope around its neck held by four of the vaqueros. Walks, Finder, Enrique, and Razor pushed them from the side and from the rear. The herd moved out at a slow pace. The lead mustangs were holding back the herd. After bunching up for the first mile or two, the horses picked up their pace and the herd strung out following its leaders. A fast, steady trot was held for miles along the riverbank.

Just before leaving the riverbank, the herd was slowed to a walk and were not pushed, giving the mustangs a chance to drink their fill from the river and rejoin the moving herd.

Before leaving the river trail and crossing into the New Mexico Territory, Walks, Finder, Enrique, and Razor lassoed dead but heavy mesquite trees and dragged them behind the herd, wiping out their tracks. It was getting dark enough to cover the dust plume it was creating. The horses in the herd were trotting again and were led into the darkness. After they had passed the foothills of the Tres Hermanas Mountains, they were definitely ready to stop.

The mustangs had to be prodded to start their movement the next day. The four leaders of the herd no longer required ropes to retard their urge to run. They would follow the vaqueros. The tracks of the herd looked as if the herd came out of the mountains. The trot of the horses didn't create a high dust plume and the dust settled back to earth soon after the horses passed. The herd watered at the lagoon in the West Potrillo Mountain then were driven through the pass.

As darkness approached and the herd neared the Fort, the drive was slowed about ten miles out to lessen the possibility of a dust column. In total darkness, the herd slowly moved on toward the Rio Grande and crossed to the east side five miles south of the Fort.

The vaqueros dragged mesquite branches behind the herd for the last few miles then into the Rio Grande to hide the evidence that the herd had passed this way. Once they set up camp on the east bank of the Rio Grande, Razor freshened up and put on his suit and tie. Finder and Enrique joined him. They crossed over to the west side of the river and headed to the Fort. When they arrived, they were challenged at the gate.

Razor asked to see Major Childers.

"The Fort is closed for the night, sir."

"Private, I know you have your orders, but would you please find the officer of the day, for me?" Razor asked.

"I will, but it will do you no good." A few moments later, an officer appeared.

"I'm the officer of the day, sir. The Fort is closed, sir."

"Lieutenant, this is very important. Just wake Major Childers and tell him there is someone here who wants to talk to him about a hundred horses. I assure you he will see me."

"What is your name, sir?"

"That's not important. Tell him!" Razor said in a demanding tone.

"I don't want to get court-martialed for waking Major Childers at two in the morning," the lieutenant said.

"You may get court-martialed if you *don't* tell him, Lieutenant," Razor replied.

"Give me a minute. I'll see what happens."

In less than two minutes, the lieutenant returned. "Follow me, gentlemen, and hurry," the lieutenant said.

Razor was met at the door by the half-dressed major. "What's wrong, Mr. Sharp?" the major cried.

"Nothing's wrong, Major. I have one hundred and fourteen saddle-broke horses within five miles of here on the east side of the Rio Grande. Where would you like them at daylight?"

The major jumped around in glee. He grasped Razor's hand and kept shaking it in appreciation. "Mr. Sharp, my superiors doubted your ability to perform. I want you to spend the day with me and let me introduce you to them. They, too, will be pleased."

"Major, I appreciate your offer, but I've got to have a hundred more horses back here in four weeks."

"We will need to do a count. Just tell my men here where you want the horses. I have your signed bill of sale here with wiring instructions for the money. I trust it will be wired this morning.

"It will be wired this morning. I'll call out a company of troopers and take over the herd as they cross the Rio Grande. We can do a count as they cross. I'll be with them. Mr. Sharp, I can't tell you how appreciative I am of you. After you get the five hundred

horses delivered; I want to celebrate this successful venture with you."

"Thank you, Major."

When they returned to the herd, Razor had Enrique select ten horses from the remuda. He had previously prepared a bill of sale for each of the ten horses. They were for the friends who Razor had met in his language classes. He had drawn maps to the new owners' homes and provided a list of instructions.

It stated that these ten horses were a gift. They were never to be rebranded. The new owners could not sell the gift horses. If asked where they got the horse, they were to tell them that it was bought from Razor Sharp. If asked where Sharp was, they should say that they see him often around town and in the area. The new owners were to ride the Razor-branded horses all over the area and especially in Mesilla. They were to tie the horses to hitching rails around the stores and especially at the bank of Ralph Marlow. "Enjoy your horse. It is important to me that you do these things. Signed, Razor Sharp."

Razor handed the bill of sale with the instructions to Enrique. "Have Roberto help you. Be at the first house at daylight. If the person on the bill of sale is not present, leave the horse and bill of sale with a family member. I'll be here to make sure the transfer goes smoothly with Major Childers. We will go to El Paso as soon as you return."

The troopers arrived at daylight. Major Childers's smile could be seen for a hundred yards even in the dim light. Armando led one of the herd leader mustangs across the river and turned him over to a waiting trooper. The others followed in group of two and three at a time. Each horse was counted as it exited the river.

Major Childers spoke up. "The open razor brand will make a perfect place for our US brand. It will fit in nicely above the V of the open razor."

The count matched, and the horses were on the way to the Army's corrals for shoeing and branding with the US brand.

Roberto and Enrique arrived as Major Childers was leaving the river following the herd. He saluted them, and they returned the salute.

Razor and his crew headed off north, still on the east side of the Rio Grande. They gradually turned southeast when they were out of sight of anyone who might have been watching. As usual, Walks ran ahead to scout with his horse following behind. He spotted a large outcropping of rocks, which would be a perfect location for an ambush if it were not so obvious. He pointed it out to Razor and Finder in passing the rocks.

They rode into El Paso and spread out with Razor in the middle. There was something about Razor that made people want to look at him. He looked at them also but discreetly. El Paso was a rough and dangerous city. People were killed and robbed daily. Fist fights were abundant and were usually fueled by alcohol.

Razor withdrew enough gold to pay all the hands and buy needed supplies. They headed south and crossed over the border by way of the bridge, into Ciudad de Juarez.

Juarez was a much safer place than El Paso. El Paso was a jumping-off place for desperate people wanted for crimes. If they were wanted by the Texas Rangers, they could flee to Mexico or New Mexico from El Paso. If wanted by New Mexico law, they could go to Texas or Mexico by way of El Paso. If the Mexican federales wanted them, they went to El Paso.

Food in Juarez was superior to that in El Paso. Roberto and Enrique led them to their favorite cantina. *Cervezas* were ordered for all. Glasses were raised, starting with a toast by Razor: "For the successful completion of the first delivery of the mustangs to the Army."

It had been decided that when they returned to Rio Casas Grandes, Antonio was to go on to Villa de Jonas to hire a cook. They had eaten the first decent meal most had had in over a month. The new cook would change that.

They then went to the *mercado* where they bought clothes, candy, fruit and ammunition. The crew had more money than they had had in a long time and rewarded themselves for the many hours of hard work. Razor bought more colorful bandannas, which made him want to get back to work.

Razor's happiness was being measured with small accomplishments. Such as his Razor brand, his first procurement document for the mustangs, his first mustang delivery, a good meal, and the new bandannas. Finding his Sweet Pea also brought him a lot of pleasure. He would enjoy these small things, but he would never truly be happy until he destroyed the two who took so much from him.

Chapter 14

Comanche Encounter

When Antonio returned with the cook who had brought a cart loaded with pots, pans, and a cage of laying hens, they were all delighted. The cook was quickly nicknamed Huevo Duro, "hard egg" in English, for his demanding rules at the dining room table. He answered to the name with pride.

The new roundup was underway. Long hours were put in by everyone, and everyone worked as a team. Razor was spending time early each morning and late each evening with Sweet Pea, his special mustang. The young mare would see Razor brushing his bay each day. After a few days, the young mare wanted to be brushed. She jumped away when Razor first touched her with the brush, and he ignored her. She kept coming back, and now the mare insisted she be brushed as much as the bay.

Walks would butcher a Texas Longhorn once a week. Steaks, roasts, and stews were cooked daily. Those who were away from camp ate jerky, a dried meat that never spoiled.

The evening meal was a time to celebrate the day and accomplishments. After eating, the men enjoyed storytelling and reports of happenings. It brought fleeting moments of the joys of camaraderie to Razor, but the happiness was dampened by the thought of what lay ahead in his drive to destroy Ralph Marlow and Raiman Callaway.

Razor had been going off with Walks, still picking up tracking lessons and locating the next drive. The trek also put him a long distance from the camp. Razor didn't want any shooting around the area of the camp for fear it would attract unwanted attention, so these forays were an opportunity to fire his weapons. He even surprised himself with his ability to hit his targets whether quick drawing, standing still, or riding at a fast pace.

He often shot his rifle as a pistol or at his shoulder. He was always cautious in his surroundings, knowing that anyone in earshot might show up to see what was going on. It could be Comanches or banditos. He and Walks would scout the area for signs before he started shooting.

Walks and Razor were making a figure eight around their previous trail when both froze in their tracks. Walks signed that six unshod horses were now on their trail. Walks sawhorse droppings in the trail ahead. He picked up one of the stools, and steam escaped as he opened it. He signaled to Razor that they had been dropped in the last few minutes.

Walks whispered to Razor, "There will be more Indians in the area since this was a hunting party. Most hunting parties have twenty to twenty-five members. The hunting parties usually split into two or three groups to increase the area they could cover." Walks stated he didn't want any gunfire that would attract others if it could be avoided.

Instead of following the trail, they turned and backtracked on their own trail. This way they would be facing their pursuers, should there be any. They went past the area where their trail had been picked up and followed by the unshod horses. Razor led his horse a hundred yards off the trail and loosely tied him in a grove of thick mesquite.

Walks and Razor found suitable shelter on both sides of the trail and split up and waited. Walks' unbridled horse followed him at a distance.

Comanches! Walks saw them coming from fifty yards away. He signaled Razor to hold his fire. He wanted to see the Comanches' reaction when they realized one of them had been shot with an arrow. At twenty-five yards, Walks released his first arrow. Razor had his rifle aimed ready to fire, if necessary, an opportunity that came almost immediately. Walks' arrow went through the Indian's heart. His scream brought gunfire from the others as Walks disappeared.

Razor opened fire and killed two before the rest could turn their attention to him. Razor quickly changed his position before firing and killed another as Walks' arrow found the fifth. The sixth and last Comanche plowed his horse into Razor, knocking him to the ground and sending his rifle flying. Razor reached for his Bowie knife as the Indian flew off his horse with a tomahawk. Razor rolled to one side, slid the big knife high under the Indian's right rib cage into the Comanche's liver and lungs. He grabbed the hand holding the tomahawk and held it steady while the Indian bled out, which took only a short time. When the Indian quit moving, Razor removed the knife and slit his throat to make sure he was dead.

Walks rushed to him. "We've got to move and move fast. Let's hope we are running away from them instead of toward them," Walks said.

They had gone a mile before slowing and covering their tracks. They decided to try to stay hidden and without a fire for a couple of days. There was enough jerky to last several days. The last thing they wanted to do was leave a trail back to their camp. They found water in a small stream and filled their canteens. Now they needed to find a defendable hideout.

They found a bareface cliff that was facing north. It would give them protection from the south. The clay cliff had a high perch but no caves or overhangs. The perch gave them a clear view to the north, east, and west, and bullets wouldn't bounce off the cliff walls.

Later the next evening, Razor slipped back down to the creek for water. After filling the canteens, he started to stand. He froze a third of the way up and lowered himself flat to the ground. He had seen at least twenty Comanches heading toward him from the east. He had no cover. The only thing he could do was crawl away from the creek and stay flat in the open with only a few scattered bushes between him and the Indians.

Thoughts raced through his mind. Had they seen him? No! If they had, they would have charged him. Had Walks seen them? He hoped so, for if he had, he knew Walks would have a plan. Should he rise up and kill as many as he could then run? That's not a good idea for now.

He heard them dismount upstream. They were watering their horses, and he dared not move. He closed his eyes and only peeked through the grass. He had heard and believed that cautious people and animals could feel when they were being watched from cover or from behind. He himself had felt this feeling many times before.

From the middle of the Indians, one let out a bloodcurdling scream. A large Apache arrow that was shot from above but far away from the cliff raced through his body. The others raced toward the direction from which it came. They rode in circles, looking for a sign. There was none. No other arrows were shot. The Commanche warriors spread out farther and still found no sign or trail. Then they all moved east and were out of sight.

Razor had not moved throughout the ordeal of the Indians' search. The last circle the Indians had made got close to the trail he had taken to the creek. He still thought his best bet was to sit tight and not move a muscle.

As darkness swept over the area, Razor still had not moved even to take water from his canteen. He hadn't seen any movement or heard any sound since last seeing the Indians move out. He continued to lay silent for fear they might have left someone behind to seek their attacker, thinking the attacker might move with the cover of darkness. Later that night, Razor located Walks, and both moved back to the cliff.

Walks told Razor that he had seen the Comanche examining his arrow. He saw that the Apache arrow had struck fear in the Comanches. The White Mountain Apache occupied a large area that was nearby. They were a fierce enemy of the Comanche who dared not enter their territory. Walks was certain that after they found the Apache arrow, they had left for their own stronghold in fear that the shooter of the arrow had left to get help. Early that morning at the Rio Casas Grandes camp, Razor's horse showed up, concerning everyone. Finder and Enrique set out to track the horse.

Before nightfall, they found where Razor had loosely tied his horse. Later they found the blood and tracks where unshod horses had been loaded with the bodies of the fallen. Finder and Enrique waited in a fireless camp for daylight.

Early the next morning, Finder and Enrique caught up with Walks and Razor walking back toward the camp.

Later that night Razor lay in bed, thinking about the events of the past few days. He thought about his first killing. It concerned him that he had no remorse for killing the Comanches. Razor's mind was eased when he realized that he felt no satisfaction in killing the Comanches. It was simply something that had to be done.

Several years prior, he had read a book about people who were excellent target shooters but could not hit anything when people started shooting back. One reason why they could not hit anything was because they didn't want to shoot or kill anyone. The main reason was that they had not gotten to a point in their lives to realize that the person firing at them was attempting to kill them. Razor had gotten to that point and killed the Comanches because he knew they were trying to kill him.

This is something he needed to think about when he determined what was to be done about Ralph Marlow and Raiman Callaway. His mind wandered. He knew he would not hesitate to kill Ralph Marlow or Raiman Callaway if needed. After all, they had intended to kill him.

Razor felt comfortable that he could now defend himself in any fight if he were observant and not walk into a trap. It would not matter if it were an Indian, bandito, or white man. He would not depend on others to protect him. He would start venturing out alone.

As Razor was dozing off, a coyote started howling. The thought Razor had was that the coyote had satisfied his hunger for the day and was now looking for a mate. It woke him enough that he thought of Bonnie Lou and their relationship. It led him to think of his future mate. Ralph Marlow and Raiman Callaway had robbed him of any such pursuit until he settled with them. Before the beating had occurred, Razor had had many thoughts of howling.

Much thought and planning went into the next delivery to the Fort. There had to be a lot of talk as to where the horses came from. It had to be known that the brand would have been looked up in the New Mexico Territory Brand Logbook by now. A lot of talk would be centered on the question as to how Razor Sharp could come up with so many horses. The word from the troopers would be that the horses came from the east or northeast.

It was decided that no one would expect another delivery so soon and that it should be safe to use the same trail and tactics.

Preparations were complete for the drive. The remuda had been selected and trained from week one. The bill of sale had been made but was waiting on the final count. Ten other bills of sale had been made with instructions to the recipients.

There were now seven special horses in the corral. Razor was able to saddle his mare but held up on putting on a bridle or even a hackamore. Sweet Pea adjusted to every new experience put forth to her, but Razor wanted her to be older before he rode her.

The final count of horses was one hundred and thirty-one—a hundred and twenty-one for the Army and ten for Razor Sharp's special friends.

The drive started early. Late that night after the herd had bedded at the base of the Tres Hermanas Mountain, Razor selected a horse from the remuda that had not been ridden that day. He rode off with Walks running beside him and Walks' horse following. In his bedroll, Razor had one of his branding irons. After riding about five miles northeast, Razor stopped. Walks pointed out the star he wanted Razor to go toward. Razor knew the mountain ranges and their shapes. He should have no trouble reaching Mesilla. Walks turned and brushed off the trail back to the herd.

Razor rode hard. The herd would be at the Rio Grande the next night around midnight, and he had a lot to do. The next day he arrived in Mesilla an hour after dark. Most everyone goes to bed after dark, and this was true with Señor Hector Ramos. Razor had given him a horse and had taught him how to speak and understand English. Razor tapped on the door and said, "Señor Ramos, this is Razor Sharp. I need your help." Ramos came to the door with a candle in his hand. He was hesitant and unsure until Razor reminded him that he had taught him English and had given him a horse. The door then opened wide, and with a bowed head, Señor Ramos let him in.

Razor quickly explained to him that he needed to borrow his wagon for a short time and that he would bring it back around midnight. He also asked to borrow a large metal bucket. "Señor Ramos, don't tell anyone that you've seen me this night."

Ramos told him he would go to the barn and help him hitch up the wagon. He also offered his help for whatever Razor had to do that night. Razor thanked him but said, "It's a one-man job."

After leaving the barn with the wagon, Razor drove to a secluded area and stopped. He built a fire out of dry mesquite and burned it down to coals. Razor buried the branding iron deep into the coals and filled the bottom of the bucket with sand. Razor pulled the white-hot iron from the fire, placed it in the bucket, and covered the branding iron with the coals. He buried the rest of the coals, placed the bucket in the wagon, and sped off.

The first stop for Razor was Ralph Marlow's bank. The streets were deserted except for a large dog sleeping in the middle of the street. The wagon woke the dog. The dog's response was to lazily scratch his fleas, yawn, and stretch back out to continue his long nap.

Razor carried the bucket to the door, removed the iron, and branded the door. He wanted Ralph Marlow to know Razor Sharp had been there. He made sure the wood didn't catch fire. He stoked the iron back into the bucket and returned to the wagon.

Razor's next stop was to brand the gate of the freight yard. He wanted to send Callaway the same message.

After returning the wagon and bucket to Ramos, Razor cooled down the iron in a bucket of water. After drying it off, he rolled it back in his bedroll.

Razor then set out looking for his herd of mustangs. The herd was on schedule. The process of dragging the mesquite was underway. After checking with Finder, he turned and rode to Fort Fillmore. This time the guard led Razor straight to Major Childers' quarters. The orderly woke the major, and Razor was immediately received.

Major Childers greeted Razor with a worried look on his face. "Mr. Sharp, I've had a visitor that said he was owed money by you for the horses you sold me and demanded to know where you were."

"Major, ask Ralph Marlow to show you a note or any other document with my name on it for any transactions with him. If he does, I'll give you one thousand horses free. You have a copy of my signature!"

"Since you didn't know where I was, tell him I'm around the area and I've been looking for him to settle with him. Let me handle Ralph Marlow's demand. I'll take care of it. It has nothing to do with the horse business or money." Razor's hand moved to his neck. "I have one hundred and twenty-one of your horses across the river. Have your company of troopers there at daylight for the count. Don't be late. I've got horses to gather."

"Mr. Sharp, I didn't mean to offend you. Mr. Marlow is an important man in the area and—"

"Is a two-bit banker more important than I am, Major? If he is, I'll take my horses elsewhere! You think about it. If your troopers are not there by daylight, we will be gone before the sun peeks over the horizon."

"You are more important, Mr. Sharp. We will be there."

The count started before the sun rose and was finished in less than thirty minutes. The bill of sale was signed and vouchers were exchanged.

"Major, if you have a problem with me or our contract, I must know now. I live up to my commitments and back up my word."

"Mr. Sharp, I have no problem with you, and I am happy with our contract, and I look forward to more horses. You'll never hear another word from me concerning this matter. I'm sorry I was concerned."

"I want to remind you no one is to know when I'll be back or if I'll be back. For your own information, I'll be back in four weeks."

"Thank you, Mr. Sharp," the major said.

"Please just call me Razor, Major."

The major rode off to catch up with the herd and was relieved that he had not blown the contract. His thoughts ran deep concerning Razor Sharp. Here was a man not to cross. He was all business and to the point. He looked you in the eye when he talked to you. He wondered if he might have graduated from West Point. He had traits of a general.

Childers breathed a sigh of relief that he had been cut off before he mentioned the horses, he had seen around town with the razor brand. It was on his list to discuss, and it was none of his business. He had to be careful not to offend such a powerful man, even though he didn't look a day over twenty years old.

The word had spread about the horses, and Fort Fillmore had to send twenty of its horses to Fort Sumner. The major would try to squeeze another hundred head from Mr. Sharp. He had to protect this relationship.

Enrique and Roberto arrived just after the major had ridden off. All had gone well, and the ten branded mustangs had been delivered with the bills of sale and instructions intact.

Chapter 15

Vengeance

Ralph Marlow hired a group of desperados to find Razor Sharp after the hundred horses showed up at Fort Fillmore with a Razor brand on them. Marlow had seen horses with Razor's brand being ridden around Mesilla and had the riders questioned. They all told the same story. They were bought from Razor Sharp, and they saw him often around the area. This convinced Marlow that Razor was in the area. Marlow was furious that his henchmen had not been able to locate Sharp.

Now he had a Razor brand on the front door of his bank. It seemed like a childish prank to the townspeople, but to Marlow, it was a threat. Before he figured out what he would do to counter this threat, Raiman Callaway rode up. They met behind closed doors. Raiman told of his gate being branded and of his teamsters and guards refusing to remove the gate. They decided to file charges against Razor Sharp and sent for the marshal.

When Marshal Lester Block arrived, Callaway and Marlow told him they wanted to file charges against Sharp for branding the door and gate.

"Boys, remember when Sharp was dragged out of the barn at the freight yard that night, with signs of a struggle including blood splattered around? Remember the fight between Buster and Razor? Witnesses said Buster attacked Razor. You accused Razor of knocking Bonnie Lou down when Stew and others witnessed Buster throwing her to the ground. Raiman, your crew accused you and Ralph of the disappearance of Razor Sharp."

"Now I'm asking you. Where's the proof that Razor did it?" asked the marshal.

"What about the horses?" asked Marlow.

"What about them?" asked the marshal.

"Where did he get them? He didn't have any money. He had to have stolen them," Callaway said.

"I haven't heard of a hundred horses being stolen. Do you think a boy as young as Razor could steal a hundred horses?" the marshal asked.

Before anyone answered, there was a knock on the door. "Come in," Ralph said.

A clerk stuck his head in and said, "Thought you would like to know that the Army received delivery of a hundred and twenty-one horses this morning with the same brand that's on the front door."

"Who told you that?"

"A trooper who was in on the count."

"You have to arrest Sharp, Marshal," cried Marlow and Callaway.

"Where's your proof?" the marshal repeated.

Razor's crew had a smooth routine. The drive of the mustangs to the trap started a long distance away, but it was a slow, gentle movement that didn't spook the horses and was mostly handled by Walks and Razor.

Razor had continued his dry firing and took every opportunity to kill game for the camp. Any game was a welcome alternative to the plentiful beef. High-pronged antelope were plentiful, but the mountain lion attacking him was the most exciting. His horse had shied away from the movement. Razor turned to look over his shoulder and saw the mountain lion in midair, sailing toward him. He pulled his Colt .45 and shot him just before the animal reached him. It fell at the horse's feet. The bullet went in at his breast and crushed his vertebra on the way out. Razor's hand had gone to his neck, stopped on the scar made by Marlow's and Callaway's rope, and thought, *I am ready.*

The cook, Huevo Duro, raved over the mountain lion. "It is the best-tasting meat in the world," he said. He proved his point that night. All that was left were the bones, and they had been cleaned slick as a marble. Finder asked Duro for the bones then secretly removed the bones and head and wrapped them inside the skin of the animal. He located a large ant bed, stirred it up, and placed the skin and bones on top then placed brush over it.

The count was mounting, and they would be leaving soon. Fifteen special horses had joined Sweet Pea in the twenty-acre corral. Razor worked with his young mare daily. She was broke to lead with a hackamore and adapted to the bridle without fuss. Razor was now able to walk around and under the mare. She loved being brushed and having her nose and forehead rubbed.

Without the saddle on the mare, Razor rode his bay to the gate of the twenty-acre corral. "Armando, open the gate and let us out then close it. When you see us coming back, let us back in the corral." Sweet Pea followed the bay out the gate and continually stayed at the heels of the horse. Razor trotted the bay over the eight-hundred-acre enclosure. The mustangs in the large enclosure moved away from them. Razor picked up the pace and, after an hour, ran the bay back into the corral with Sweet Pea still at the bay's heels.

Razor again expressed his concerns about using the same route and tactics as the two drives before. He let every man in the crew express his opinion. The plan had worked to perfection so far. Everyone agreed to not become complacent with what they had been doing and to stay on heightened alert. Razor told them he would not be on the drive but would join them at the Rio Grande.

Before Razor left, Finder presented him with a hat band. It was made of plaited horsehair from the manes of several mustangs. Encased in the plaited hair were the two large fang teeth of the mountain lion. The two teeth were separated by two tail vertebrae of the mountain lion. The teeth and vertebra had been cleaned by the ants. The vertebrae were chalk white. Finder pointed out that Indians, especially Comanche, gave great respect to the bearer of such for the bravery taken to kill such an animal. Razor told Finder that he would wear it with great pride.

Razor rode into Mesilla an hour after dark. He went to the freight yard and looked it over. He tied his horse in the mesquite and went in hugging the shadows. Raiman Callaway was not around. A light was on in the office, and Stew was sitting there, doing freight bills. Razor entered with one finger over his lips, giving the international signal for silence. Stew turned and was startled. "What the hell do you want, stranger?"

"Mr. Stew, it's me, Razor."

"You can't be. Razor is just a kid."

Razor took off his hat and smiled. "I promise you, I am."

"Oh! Razor, this is hard to believe. We had thought you might be dead until your horses started showing up around here. Jacob has had his guards searching for you since you disappeared."

"Mr. Stew, where is Bonnie Lou?"

"Callaway sent her off to a boarding school in Santa Fe. She was speaking out about the lies that her father and Ralph Marlow were spreading about you, when everyone in town knew the true story. She wanted to go. She wanted to get away from all that and especially away from Buster Marlow."

"Is Buster around?"

"He's around. Trying to act tough. Won't work. Says his leg hurts too much. Says he will get you first time he sees you."

"I've been around. Don't think he's been looking too hard. Have you seen Miss Scott, the teacher?"

"I've seen her often, Razor."

"Do you still have my belongings, Mr. Stew?"

"I put them in a potato sack, saving them for you, Razor."

"Would you look her up and tell her I'm okay? I would like for you to give her my Latin book for safekeeping and tell her I'll come for a visit soon."

"Sure, I'll do that, Razor."

"Mr. Stew, I need your help. I don't want to get you in any trouble with Callaway but let me tell you what happened."

Razor told of his beating and the threat to kill him if he ever returned. He told of his rescue and showed him his rope scar. "Mr. Stew, I don't care if this story gets around, but I'll never mention it again. I have the scar on my neck to always remind me, and I'll never forget. After I settle with Marlow and Raiman, I'll not let it interfere with my happiness."

Razor feared for Bonnie Lou's safety. "I knew she hadn't lied about what happened with Buster."

Stew told Razor of the teamsters' and guards' refusal to let Callaway take down the branded gate. "Callaway has been showing fear since the horses started showing up, Razor. What can I do to help you?"

"Mr. Stew, I'm going to shoot straight with you. Marlow and Callaway unjustifiably attempted to kill me. Now that I've survived, they are denying my right to be in Mesilla or the Territory with a threat to kill me if I show up there. Now, I'm angry and vengeful. I don't plan to kill Marlow or Callaway, but they may die."

"What do you have in mind, Razor?"

"I'm going to brand them with my Razor brand. I'm going to beat them as they beat me and burn their necks with a rope. I'll leave a scar that's wider and deeper on their necks than mine is. I'm going to leave them ten miles out in the desert as they did me, but I won't leave them tied."

"After I do this, hopefully they will leave me alone. Marlow and Callaway were sincere about killing me if I returned. Well! Here I am. I feel certain Marlow and Callaway have people out looking for me. What I want is help getting Callaway and Marlow alone. I want them together. It could be night or day. I just don't want any outside interference. All I want from them is my pound of flesh and for them to leave me alone. If they don't, I'll kill them!"

"Razor, every hand I've got is on your side with this. Let's come up with something. I doubt that they would recognize you now. You have grown at least six inches and put on eighty pounds of muscle and are twice as dark as you were when Marlow and Callaway last saw you. I'll send them a note saying that a man is here now who knows where you are and that the man will tell them for two hundred dollars. They must come alone, because the man wants no one else to know that he is telling them where you are because he wants no trouble with Razor Sharp."

"I like it, Mr. Stew. I have access to a wagon. I'll hide it down the road where they left their carriage when they took me. I'll tie them up and run or drag them down to the wagon. I'll take them out in the desert so we can have our little talk," Razor said.

"It should work," Stew said. "I'll include in the note that I don't want any of the teamsters or guards to know that I am helping them find you, because they all like you. I'll tell them I am holding you here until they can get here, then I'll leave you alone with them."

"Mr. Stew, give me an hour to get the wagon in place."

Razor was ready. The wagon was in place. His horse was moved into the freight yard and tied behind the building. The two lariats were ready. He had rags to shove in their mouths, pig ties to tie the rags, hands and feet.

The messenger was on the way. Razor retrieved his branding iron and placed it in the coals of the heater that kept the coffee hot.

A buggy came into the freight yard and stopped in front of the office. Stew was meeting them out front as they exited the buggy. Razor was trailing behind. "Here he is, Mr. Callaway. I'll leave you alone with him."

"Thanks, Stew."

"It's nothing, Mr. Callaway, just want to help," Stew said as he walked away.

"You got the money?" asked Razor.

"Yes, we have the money."

"Let me get my map." Razor turned, grabbed one of his lariats, and threw it around them both. He jerked them to the ground, stuffed the rags into their mouths, tied their hands, feet, and removed their weapons.

The lariat was removed from around Marlow's and pulled tight around the Callaway's. The other lariat was placed and pulled tight around the neck of Marlow. Both were given instructions to roll over on their sides.

Razor retrieved the branding iron from the coals. Their eyes were as wide open as they could be. Their heads were shaking back and forth, screaming the muffled sound of "No!" Callaway was the first to receive the Razor brand. He had rolled over on his back, trying to kick Razor, who held him down with his foot. He pushed down on the branding iron and burned the brand through his trousers onto his hip. Callaway passed out.

The smell of burning flesh made Marlow throw up and pull the rag from his mouth. Razor crammed another in his mouth and tied it in before Marlow could scream. Razor placed the branding iron back in the coals.

"Marlow, don't be passing out on me like Callaway did. I want you to feel this. I usually don't brand worthless scum like you two, but Razor Sharp wants the world to know that he owns you two." He jerked tight on the rope and took the branding iron from the coals and repeated the process that he had done with Callaway.

Callaway had regained consciousness before Marlow was branded and looked at Marlow with tears flooding down his face. Callaway passed out again as the smell of Marlow's burning flesh reached his nostrils.

Razor held the branding iron in the rain barrel until it cooled and then rolled it back into his saddle blanket. He untied their feet and jerked them erect with the ropes around their necks.

Razor led them to his horse, mounted, and took off toward the wagon, jerking them both to the ground. He let them get back on their feet and told them they had to run or the lariat would hang them. When they reached the wagon, he pulled them in with the lariats and gave slack as they fell into the bed of the wagon. He left the slack in the lariat so they could breathe. He re-tied their feet and tied his horse to the back of the wagon and headed west. The bright full moon was shining. He had both lariats in his hands and pulled them often to make sure they were still attached.

Razor tried to take them to the exact location they had taken him, then he stopped and pulled them both out of the wagon with the rope and let them fall to the ground.

"Does this place seem familiar to y'all?" Razor asked. "I'm sorry, I forgot to take the rag out of your mouth. I want to talk to each of you."

"First, I want to introduce myself so you will know who you are dealing with. You probably don't recognize me, but I'm Razor Sharp!"

Fright filled their eyes. Each thought Razor Sharp was going to torture them further and then kill them, and they were helpless and could not defend themselves. The first thoughts in both their brains were, *why had we not gone ahead and made sure he was dead before we left him tied here in the desert thinking he had no way to survive?*

"I'll let you be first, Mr. Marlow. I'll take the rag out of your mouth, but you can't say a word until I tell you that you can speak. I want this to be fair, so I'll untie your hands and feet and let you stand up. You do exactly as I say. If you run or try to attack me, be ready to pay the consequences. You understand, Mr. Marlow?"

Razor untied Marlow's hands, and Marlow reached for the rag, and pulled it out. Razor stepped forward and crushed Marlow's upper teeth and nose with the heel of his fist.

"Marlow, you don't follow instructions well at all. I didn't tell you to take the rag out of your mouth."

A sobbing "I'll kill you for this!" came from Marlow's mouth. As soon as the words came out, he was back on the ground from two blows, one to each eye.

"Are you ready to listen and let me talk?" After nodding yes, Marlow was dragged to his feet with the rope.

"Marlow, you used a club to beat me while I was tied and on the ground. Then you kicked and stomped my head and left me tied up. You promised me that if I survived and came back to Mesilla, you would kill me. I'm not going to kill you now, and I'm not going to leave you out here tied up to die as you did me. I'm back to stay. Now I'm going to give you four weeks to leave the New Mexico Territory. If you are not gone by then, I'll chase you both down and kill you. If I find that you have hired others to kill me, I'll kill you both on sight. You need to get your son, Buster, out of the country now, because I might start looking for him as soon as I get back to Mesilla.

"Now, Mr. Callaway. The same goes for you. You too used a club, and I'll only use my hands. I'll help you to your feet, untie your hands, and take the rag out of your mouth."

As the rag was removed from Callaway's mouth, he fainted. Razor took his canteen and wet the cloth and brought Callaway back to consciousness. "Buster lied," Callaway whispered.

"You knew that when you were beating me with a club!" Razor said. He pulled him to his feet with the rope and knocked out his two top teeth and followed with two blows to his eyes and another to his nose to make sure it was broken."

"Callaway, the same goes for you."

"If I ever hear that you've muttered even a word of a threat against me, I'll hunt you down. I won't go easy on you as I have tonight. I'll personally hold you responsible for your gang of henchmen. They may all get killed, but if they or you harm or attempt to harm me, I'll come for you. If you make any statement or ask any questions to the Army about the horses that they are buying from me, I'll come for you. It is none of your business."

"It's only ten miles back to Mesilla. I'll leave you a canteen of water. Think about it. That's a far better break than you gave me. Pick up a long stick and rake it along in front, and you should find any rattlesnakes or scorpions that are waiting for you. This will give you a lot of time to think about what I said."

"Everyone by now knows that you both beat me with a club. I'll tell everyone that your beating tonight was in response to that. Your black eyes and broken noses should heal up in six or seven months. If you stand on your feet, your Razor brand should heal in six months. If you mess up, your next brand will be between your eyes. I hope the rope burn scars around your necks never go away."

Razor's hand had automatically reached to his own neck as he spoke. As an afterthought, he grabbed the rope on Callaway's neck, held his head steady, and dragged the rope back and forth around his neck to make sure there would always be a deep scar. He repeated the process with Ralph Marlow.

Chapter 16

Deaths of the Gringo Desperados

The story spread about someone beating Ralph Marlow and Raiman Callaway for the beating that they gave Razor Sharp. They both had been lying low and out of sight. Buster Marlow had disappeared, and no one had seen hide nor hair of him. There were rumors that he had gone into Mexico and was already in trouble down there for threatening to shoot someone. It was said that after the fight with Razor, he practiced using a firearm, saying it was not necessary to brawl and that he would never brawl again.

The marshal spread the word that Buster had lied about Razor Sharp, throwing Bonnie Lou to the ground and that Razor had started the fight.

The herd of mustangs had arrived on time and were met by Razor. He cautioned everyone to be vigilant, more so now than ever. He expected trouble. The count was completed, and the ten horses with the bills of sale and instructions had been delivered to the new owners. The major sought more time to socialize with Razor, to no avail as usual. Razor told him the one hundred and forty-eight horses remaining on his procurement order would be delivered within four weeks.

The crew moved out, heading north while still in sight of the troopers. They made their usual turn to the southeast. Walks appeared from nowhere, stopping the column of riders. Walks told them that he had picked up sign of six riders off the trail and found them in hiding at the large rock outcroppings that they had talked about before. "They looked like gringo desperados to me."

Razor listened intently to Walks. He had thought that the branding and the injuries he had given Marlow and Callaway would have ended this, but it might be just starting. He felt he was ready "I don't think they're there to rob us," said Sharp. "They are Marlow and Callaway's hired henchmen. I thought they might have found us sooner. I'm surprised that they chose the rock outcroppings since it's such an obvious location for an ambush."

A plan was quickly made. Walks, Finder, and Razor would leave the rest of the crew and make a large loop to the north and come back to the rock outcropping from the south. They would move slowly to prevent dust from rising. Roberto, Enrique, Juan, Antonio, and Armando would go slower and drag a small mesquite to create enough dust as seven riders would create.

They would start singing with slurred loud words, as if drunk, within earshot of the rock outcropping. Razor, Walks, and Finder eased in behind the rocks while the bushwhackers' attention was on the loud singers. All six of them were located and in sight.

The bushwhackers were taking aim when three shots from behind bounced lead off nearby rocks, sending them into disarray and panic. "Drop your weapons now or be killed!" Razor demanded.

Two raised their weapons to fire at him, and Razor shot them dead. The others dropped their weapons and raised their hands. Razor didn't like having to kill them any more than he did when he killed the four Comanches, but they had tried to kill him. Enrique, Armando, Antonio, and Juan rushed in and lassoed the remaining four and dragged them through the brush and cacti to take all the fight out of them. Then they were dragged back to the rocks and tied up as they cried in pain from the cactus spines.

With little coaxing, they confessed to being hired by Marlow and Callaway. Razor had each of them sign a confession to that fact. They had not committed murder and eagerly signed it.

The crew needed rest and decided to spend the rest of the day in the shade of the outcropping.

At midnight, they moved out with the two bodies and the four other bushwhackers, who were gagged and tied to their horses. They eased across the Rio Grande, skirted the Fort, and rode into Mesilla under the cover of darkness. The large dog was still asleep in the middle of the street and was awakened by the crew but again moved only to scratch his fleas. They rode around him and deposited the two bodies and the other four bushwhackers on the steps of Marlow's bank. They released the bushwhackers' horses and pinned the confessions on the four. Each had his individual confession and signature pinned to their shirts. A larger note was left so all could read what had happened but didn't give details on who killed the two. As Razor and his crew rode off, he looked back at the sleeping dog and for some reason thought of Aristotle. The dog seemed to have reached his goal in life by being happy, sleeping and not letting anything disturb him but his fleas. Even the scratching of the fleas was a natural reaction of being awakened. It brought a smile to Razor's face. This touch with happiness could not mask the realization that he would have to kill Raiman Callaway and Ralph Marlow. His conscience would be clear. He had given them a chance.

Next morning at dawn, the two bodies and the four tied bushwhackers were discovered. Within ten minutes, a crowd of more than sixty people had gathered, with more on the way, including the marshal. No one had released the four or removed the bodies of the two dead. Razor had several friends in the crowd, and they only smiled as they kept their thoughts to themselves, Marshal Block being one of them. The marshal wanted everyone to see what might happen to them if they attempted to harm Razor Sharp.

Razor and his crew arrived at Wells Fargo at two o'clock in the afternoon. As usual, he paid the hands and put off eating until they crossed the border into Juarez. After eating, Razor told them he had been putting off a journey that he was now ready to make. He would be leaving them here and would return to Rio Casas Grandes in about three weeks. He would have at least ten extra hands with him when he returned.

He asked Enrique if he would find some vaqueros, family or friends who wanted a full-time job.

"Try to hire at least ten and hire more if they are good vaqueros."

He gave Finder the money for supplies and Enrique money for extra food and other expenses.

"We will be delivering the hundred and forty-eight horses to the Army to complete our contract. I want my usual ten. We will deliver them to a different location."

Farewells were made, and Razor was excited. This journey to return to where his parents were buried had been constantly on his mind and he had pushed it back until now. He also needed to recover the heavy pouch he had hidden. He cautioned himself, *Don't let this interfere with my awareness of Callaway or Marlow.* His occasional pleasant thoughts of his dear friend Bonnie Lou would be done with caution also.

Chapter 17

Grave of Razor's Parents

Razor stopped at the *mercado* and bought a small shovel and headed back into Texas. He rode northeast out of El Paso, and nightfall overtook him well before he reached the Hueco Mountain range. He bedded down in a clearing in some chaparral. It was thick and thorny and had animal trails in and around it. Any movement by man or animals would give off sounds of movement and would alert him of any danger.

Being this close, he could not resist going to see some of the petroglyphs in the Hueco Mountains. Overhead in every cave and on every protected wall and boulders were huge drawings of animals, spirals, and warriors with their weapons. His understanding was that the petroglyphs were in all the caves and on every stone that could be reached by the ones who left them. It would take several days to see them all, and that's what he promised himself that he would do someday.

He continued his journey three hours after the break of day. He pushed hard, leaving the Hueco Mountains, and skirted the foothills on the west side, where he could water his horse and fill his canteens.

He could see the Jarilla Mountain fifty miles due north. He would not be able to reach them by nightfall, but he would ride on into the night until he reached the north side of the mountain, where he knew there was water. A half-moon was out, and he could see the great white sand dunes not far ahead. He took out his telescope and looked southwest and thought he could see the road that went to Mesilla. He decided to stay in the mountains, where it was much cooler, and leave before dawn in the morning. The half-moon would still be out then, and reflections from the white sands would reflect the light he would need to travel safely to his destination.

At the break of day, Razor rode past his destination as if paying it no mind. After a mile, he took out his telescope again and looked up into the west side of the Sacramento Mountains and foothills. He was satisfied he would have plenty of time to complete his task before any intruders could interfere. Razor dismounted, went back, and wiped out his tracks leaving the roadbed. He rode back south in the foothills until he saw his destination. Razor tied his horse out of sight of the road and removed the shovel. He paused at the edge of the small mound that marked his parents' graves and stood still until he cleared his emotions. He bowed his head, said a prayer, and for a few moments enjoyed thinking about his wonderful parents.

For some reason, he thought of Bonnie Lou's terrible father and felt sorry for her. He wished he could help her in some way. He promised himself that he would someday. Razor regretted that not killing her father would never be an option.

Making sure, one more time, that no one was near, Razor started digging. He had dug down over four feet and began to worry. He knew he had placed the small leather pouch here.

Had someone seen him drop it? The thought had just entered his mind when he found it. He slipped the pouch in his pocket and re-filled the hole near his parents' graves.

While smoothing out the fill dirt, he silently apologized to his parents for the intrusion. He covered his trail back to his horse and rode north along the foothills. After a couple of miles, he rode back to the road, stopped, and walked back to cover his trail that led him to the road. He then headed south toward Mesilla. When he came to the Jarilla Mountain east of the road, he left the road and again covered his tracks. He climbed high into the mountains, finding a freshwater stream and cooler weather. Razor made camp near the stream. He had found an area where, years past, a rockslide had uprooted a large tree, creating a hole in the mountainside that was surrounded by large stones. The area would be big enough for him and his horse. After watering the horse, he led him into the sunken enclosure and fed him his oats. He felt safe in building a small smokeless fire.

The removal of the leather pouch from the grave of his mother and father had been emotional, and he would have liked to have spent more time there, but he had not dared.

After eating some jerky, he pulled the pouch out of his pocket. It didn't seem as heavy as it did when he had placed it there nearly ten years ago. He was expecting gold because of its weight. He was not disappointed. He opened the pouch and removed a map and a large gold nugget. The gold was a single flat rough nugget, about two fingers wide, one finger thick, and three inches long. Razor had never seen a nugget before, only coins. But he knew it was a big one.

He unfolded the map. It was a survey map, and inside he found a folded letter. The letter was instructions he was to follow.

Find the sheet of paper in the last piece of furniture you and I made. Look inside the piece and push in on the top of the lower right panel, then push upward. You will see a piece of paper at the bottom. Pull it out from the bottom. It has two Xs on it. Place that piece of paper on top of this map. Line up the four corners and stick a pin in the middle of the Xs, penetrating the map. Destroy the piece of paper with the two Xs. Press several other holes in the map. Make sure you know the two that were located with the Xs. Look under the perforations made through the Xs to find the location of the treasure.

The armoire! thought Razor.

He read the instructions several times and kept coming back to "*look under the perforations made through the Xs.*" He read the instructions again then held it over the fire until he had to drop it.

Razor now knew where to find the treasure once the location was determined. He rubbed the gold nugget in his hands and remembered the instructions from his father—hide it. He was sure he was talking about the map and not the gold. Razor didn't need the money right now, so he decided to hide both. He slid the map back in the pouch and found a large rock nearby. With the shovel, he removed two feet of dirt from under the rock and placed the pouch in the hole.

He replaced the gravel under the rock. The large rock would divert rainwater away from the pouch.

He slept well that night. When he awoke, he scoped in all directions from his perch. Seeing nothing of concern, he made coffee and ate some hardtack and jerky then buried his campfire remnants and covered his trail down the mountain. He turned south toward Mesilla. He would not make it to Mesilla in one day and again decided to spend the night in chaparral along the way.

When Razor arrived in Mesilla the next morning, he was surprised to find the bank closed. He rode on toward the freight yard. Before going in, he looked around and didn't see much activity. He entered and found Mr. Stew at his desk.

"Are you okay, Mr. Stew? What's going on?"

"Razor, am I glad to see you! Callaway hasn't been around for quite a while. We heard he and Marlow were back, but both have disappeared since the two dead bodies and four guys full of cactus spines showed up on the bank's doorsteps. Also, the rumor is out that Buster shot and killed two Mexicans across the border and was seen in El Paso, drunk and packing iron."

"Thanks for filling me in," Razor said.

"Mr. Stew, I think Marlow and Callaway will be leaving the territory. They threatened me with death if I showed up in Mesilla, and I did. They hired six henchmen to do the job. The four who survived their attack on me confessed that they had been hired by Marlow and Callaway. If Callaway does show up, he might fire you."

"I don't care. I'm having trouble holding on to the workers. They know what went down with you and Callaway, and they don't like it one bit. I would have lost them ten months ago if there had been any steady jobs around, they would have all left."

"Mr. Stew, I have steady permanent jobs to offer but only if you come aboard as their foreman. Everyone would be paid as much as they make now. I would want you to do all the hiring and would expect you to hire the best hands. Will you do it, Mr. Stew?"

"I'm ready, Razor. The North American-Pacific Railroad has bought a right of way from Santa Fe to El Paso, and construction has already started. It's all on flat ground and will be built fast. The long freight hauling by wagons will be over soon, so there should be workers available when that happens. How many hands do you think you need?"

"I want twenty who can move out in five days. You can hire more if it is someone you don't want to leave behind. Here is two hundred dollars in gold coin to buy a wagon and supplies. We will be branding and driving horses. Then we will be working on a ranch. I'll be back in five days, be ready."

Razor mounted and headed toward the Rio Grande, looking for Raiman Callaway. When he got close to his mansion, he saw activity in the stable. Callaway's carriage was hitched and loaded with various valises, and he was untying a horse.

"Hold it right there, Callaway," Razor hollered. He didn't draw his Colt, but he was ready to respond if needed.

"Please don't kill me. I'm leaving and will never be back. The bushwhackers were Marlow's idea. He has already left. I didn't know it until this morning."

Callaway looked like death warmed over. His left hand went continuously to his hip, and he limped with every movement.

"Stop your whining, Callaway! A deal is a deal. I agreed to let you and Marlow stay for four weeks if I were left alone. You broke the deal, not me. Where is your wife?"

"She's left me. She left the day the bodies were left at the bank. She's in Santa Fe with Bonnie Lou. Neither ever wants to see me again. Please don't kill me. I'm nearly dead now. I can't sit down, and I try to sleep on my stomach. I am in constant pain with my hip and the rope burn on my neck."

"That's good news. I hope Marlow is having similar pains."

"Mr. Sharp, I was just leaving, and I am never coming back to the Territory. Please don't kill me."

"Callaway, I'm going to make one last deal with you. The only reason I have not already blown your head off is because of my friendship with Bonnie Lou. You leave, and if I ever see you again or if you ever attempt to see your wife or Bonnie Lou again, I'll hunt you down and kill you. You will not get a reprieve. Now, I need a place to stay. Give me the key to the house."

Razor watched Callaway's buggy cross the Rio Grande and head east. He was leaning away from the Razor brand on his left hip, and his left hand was trying to steady the cloth wrapped around his neck as he was hurrying away. Razor watched him go until his dust cloud disappeared then went to the front door and, using the key, entered. He searched each room, looking for the armoire. He paused when he entered what had to be Bonnie Lou's bedroom. *What a special friend she was*, he thought. He missed her. Her father's insistence that she was not to have anything to do with him didn't damage their friendship.

He planned to keep the nicer furniture as payment for the expenses he had incurred in burying his parents. He opened the door of an armoire and was disappointed to see it completely empty. He kneeled and pushed in on the top of the lower right panel then pushed up. The panel rose from the bottom, exposing a sheet of paper.

All that was on it were two Xs. He lowered the panel back in place. A needle from the sewing drawer would serve as a way to pinpoint the location of the Xs on the map.

He left the room and locked the door. He rode swiftly across the Rio Grande with the paper securely in his shirt then headed south to El Paso. When he reached El Paso, he crossed over the bridge into Juarez. He didn't find Buster or Ralph Marlow, but he was ready if he did find them.

At a local trading post, he bought twenty cast-iron molds of different sizes to cast gold bars and a hundred coin-sized molds. He bought two carbon steel rods and had the Razor brand cut into the end of both. Each had a different-sized brand. One was for coins, and one was for bars.

He crossed back over the Rio Grande with the molds in two potato sacks and headed north to the Jarilla Mountains. It would take all day and part of the night to reach them. He paced his mustang even though she was conditioned for long treks. He rode on into the night until he reached the Jarilla foothills. He gave his mustang all the water left in the last canteen then bedded down for the night. The trail into the mountains should be evident in the morning light.

Razor was telescoping everything in sight at daybreak. Seeing nothing to alarm him, he mounted and rode until he found his trail. He refilled his canteens and let the mustang drink his fill from the small freshwater stream he had found previously. He wasted no time in finding the rock that protected his leather pouch. He looked around for a few minutes, and seeing no one, he quickly dug it from under the rock. With the map laid out on top of the rock, he lined up the edges and punched a hole in the middle of the two Xs.

He lit a small fire and burned the paper with the two Xs. He studied the map and made several pinholes in a pattern that was easy for him to remember.

He studied the map again until he was familiar with it all. He slipped it back into the leather pouch with the large nugget and slipped the pouch into his front trouser pocket.

Skirting the Jarilla valley on the north and heading northeast toward the Pecos River valley took him to the east side of the Sacramento Mountains, where he turned due north. He continued north until he hit the Rio Penasco then turned due west and went up into the mountains. He had the map, but his memory rendered it unnecessary.

Razor's heart raced as he saw his family's house at a distance. It was perched on a plateau surrounded by large ponderosa pine trees. From there you could see for miles. When he reached the house, he hid the molds and chisels. He stood on the front porch and looked back down the mountain. The view was breathtaking. There was a small stream that ran from behind the house, which created a ripple of water that meandered down the mountain to the Rio Penasco.

The house could not be seen from the west, north, or south, only from the east. His father had told him of the many adventures he had while building the house. He was a furniture builder by trade and was determined to build their home as he would build a fine piece of furniture.

There were bear claw marks on the front door. He smiled, as he knew his father would, that the bear could not get in. His father had mentioned to Razor that no bear or Indian could forcefully get through the door unless they found the secret latch. Razor unlatched the door and entered.

No leaks or deterioration of the structure were apparent. Razor opened the shuttered windows and the other doors then looked for the house's most prized possession: his mother's books. After touching each of the books, Razor pulled the pouch from his pocket and removed the map. He spread it open and told himself, *the treasure is under the pinhole marked by the X. Under the pinhole is the floor. The treasure is under the floor.*

It took Razor almost an hour to find the trapdoor in the floor. If he had not known his father's work, he might never have found the steel-lined cavity. The first thing he saw was a stack of papers. Then stacks of nearly pure but rough gold nuggets that looked much like the one in the leather pouch. The nuggets covered the three-feet-by-four-feet floor of the cavity, which was about three feet deep. Razor examined them. Some had quartz attached to them, but most were clean. Razor folded the map and put it in his shirt pocket. He placed the pouch and nugget in the cavity and replaced the trapdoor.

Razor started going through the papers. One of the papers was of great interest. It was a note his father had written. The only thing it said was to go to the other X.

Lay on your stomach in the arroyo and look south. No mining required. Best after a hard rain. I found this accidently when it had been a convenient place for me to hide from several Indians.

The next item he found was a larger survey map and a document, a deed transferring 150,000 acres of land from a 350,000-acre tract of land from the heirs of the San Mateo Del Montoya Spanish land grant to Clayton Sharp; wife, Wynona Sharp; and son, Razor Sharp. Paid for with $160,000 of gold bars. The 150,000 acres ran from the ridge of the Sacramento Mountains on the west and halfway to the Pecos River on the east. The northern property line was the Rio Penasco that intersected the west and east property line. The south property line skirted the south foothills of the Sacramento Mountains and intersected the east and west property line.

Razor knew his father owned a lot of land but had no clue as to how much. The gold and papers had been safe for several years, so he decided to leave them where they were for the time being. He burned the paper referring to the other X, then locked up and headed to the other X.

It was located two hundred yards from the crest of the Sacramento Mountains, which was the west property line. There was a very small arroyo near the X. He lay flat in the arroyo, looked south toward where he thought the X should be. He saw nothing. A tall ponderosa tree was casting a shadow in the arroyo. He moved up a few feet to get out of the shadow and looked back…and then he saw it. He counted seven veins of gold protruding from the soft limestone, sandstone, and the hard quartz encasement.

When water from rain rushed down the arroyo, it had washed away the limestone and sandstone from around the gold veins. With no support, the heavy gold would break away from the main vein of gold encased in the quartz and left the gold on the ground or hung in the root system of the giant ponderosa pine tree. He took a large rock, reached into the root system, and grabbed the end of a piece of gold still attached to one of the gold veins. It was encased in the quartz. He tapped on it with the stone. After several taps with the stone, a piece of gold that weighed over a pound came off in his hand.

When it rained, the flow of water, from the top of the ridge into the arroyo, was just strong enough to wash away the sandy debris and some quartz down the arroyo. It was not strong enough to wash away the heavy gold.

The gold had not been harvested in over nine years, and it was far more than Razor could haul away. He put the large hunk of gold in the bottom of his saddlebag and continued to fill the two bags with the loose nuggets from under the root system. After loading the two saddlebags, he left the rest of the gold where it lay. He was convinced that no gold had washed farther down the arroyo but gathered several samples of soil and paned it. He found no traces of gold. He was certain his father had filed no claims since he owned the land, and neither would he. The last thing he wanted was a gold rush. He covered all sign of his presence then left, heading back toward Mesilla. His plan was to check with Mr. Stew then go to El Paso and deposit the two saddlebags of gold in the Wells Fargo bank.

Chapter 18

Razor Buys the Bank

Razor checked Callaway's house on the way back into Mesilla. He saw no evidence that it had been disturbed since he'd been there before. When he rode by Marlowe's bank, he saw a large sign directing people to pay their debt to the bank at the hardware store. Razor went to the hardware store and was told that the marshal was trying to sell the bank and use the money to pay off the depositors.

Razor went straight to the marshal's office.

"What can I do for you?" the marshal asked.

"Well, you probably don't recognize me, but I'm Razor Sharp."

The marshal jumped to his feet and declared, "I'll be damned if it isn't you! Razor, I've been worried about you. I don't know if you ran Marlow and Callaway out of town, but we are in a bind with the bank closing. Joe Brine, the bank teller, came to me early this morning and told me that when he opened the bank vault this morning, all the money was gone, and Ralph Marlow was nowhere to be found.

"Joe locked the bank doors and came to me and gave me the keys. It's obvious to me and the judge that Marlow stole all the money when he left. The business owners who had their money deposited in the bank don't know what to do without their money. I'm trying to sell the bank to get enough money to refund all the depositors' money so they can stay in business."

"How much money do you need, Marshal?" Razor asked.

"Around a hundred thousand dollars to pay everyone off. I don't know how we are going to do it."

"If you will give me the bank and give me the accounts receivable, I'll pay off all the depositors. I'll open the bank and accept deposits and will lend money like any other bank. I could be open in five days."

"Razor, do you have that much money?"

"Yes, I do. It will be in gold coin when I pay off the depositors."

"Razor, I want to do it, but I've got to get the judge's approval, and the first thing he will want to know is where you got the money."

"Marshal, I'll tell him it's honest money, and other than that, it's really none of his business. I just thought I could help the town out by keeping the depositors from going broke and having to move out. I need to know if the judge wants my help, for I've other things to do."

"Razor, sit tight. I'll go to his office now and get his approval."

"I can give you only twenty minutes, Marshal. Then I need to be gone."

In less than fifteen minutes, the marshal returned. "I have the agreement. I made him put it in writing."

"Now, I need the key to the bank. I have a deposit to make. Would you please find the bank clerk and tell him I need the combination to the vault. I'll offer him a job while he's there."

Razor went to the bank carrying his heavy saddlebags. He opened the door, went in, and waited for the clerk. When the clerk, Joe Brine, showed up, he opened the large safe and showed Razor how to change the combination on the lock.

He had the clerk stand outside while he unloaded his saddlebags and changed the combination. Razor reached in his pocket and pulled out a twenty-dollar gold piece, gave it to the clerk, and told him to get all the door locks changed out.

"Give all the keys to the marshal to hold for Miss Scott. Keep the change, Joe. Do you want to keep your job here at the bank?" Razor asked.

"Sure do!" Joe responded.

"I want to make you an offer. Miss Scott will be in touch with you to give you instructions as to what to do." Razor and the bank clerk left the bank together, and Razor raced to Callaway's freight yard.

"Mr. Stew, how many hands did you hire?" Razor asked.

"Twenty-five. There were five others I would have liked to hire, but you said twenty."

"Hire them! Send someone to Deming and have the blacksmith make three more sets of branding irons for me please. Make sure that Roberto, Enrique, and I get those sets."

"Mr. Stew, Callaway and Marlow seem to have left the Territory, and I have taken control of the bank. Miss Scott will be running it for me. Tell Jacob that I want two guards on duty at Raiman Callaway's house around the clock. I'm sure that he has left the Territory, and his wife has moved to Santa Fe to be with Bonnie Lou. I don't want someone stealing everything they left."

"Mr. Stew, can you get three wagons and teams ready to roll? I want Jacob to go with you and take all his available guards. He is to carry extra ammunition and two hundred empty burlap bags. Carry tarps, rope, and plenty of oats for the horses. Don't forget to water the horses before leaving. After you cross the Rio Grande, you will have no meaningful water until you reach the Rio Penasco so carry several barrels of water. Pack enough jerky and hardtack for five days. We will not have time to cook.

Hire at least five men and be ready to pull out in thirty minutes. Bring your whole remuda and all your teamsters. You will need to travel the rest of today, all night, and tomorrow morning. Go straight to the southeast side of the Sacramento and hug the mountain until you reach the Rio Penasco. I've traveled this route the last few days and have not seen anyone but be alert."

"With the three-quarter moon, you will have enough light to travel. Rotate the crew in and out of the wagons for sleep and rest. Rotate horses in and out of the remuda as needed. I'll meet you at the Rio Penasco and lead you to your destination. Mr. Stew, keep track of the charges for the wagons and horses. I want to make sure Bonnie Lou is paid for their use, since she and her mother actually own them."

Razor left in a hurry and rode to the schoolhouse. He knocked on the door with his hat in his hand, waiting for an invitation to enter.

"May I help you, sir?" Miss Scott asked.

"Hello, Miss Scott, I'm Razor Sharp."

The teacher lost her composure. She threw her hands to her heart and rushed toward Razor and threw her arms around him and cried tears of joy. The class stared in amazement and amusement. She turned to her class and introduced Razor as a former student and declared a recess for the class.

"Miss Scott, I'm in a big hurry, and I need your help."

"Razor, you know I'll help you any way I can."

"Well, I'm sure you've heard that Mr. Marlow left town with all the depositors' money. I've agreed with the judge and Marshal Block to buy and open the bank. I'm on my way to get the money now. I must have the bank open in four days. I want you to contact Joe Brine, who was Marlow's clerk and teller. I don't know if I can trust him and where his loyalty would lie, and I need your opinion on that."

"I know Joe. He was one of my best students. I think he would be a good employee, and I'll find out where his loyalty would be."

"Would you go over the books with Joe and help get the depositors paid back as soon as we open?"

"I will, Razor, even if I must close the school. If the depositors don't get their money back, there probably won't be a school. Razor, you've made me so happy and proud of you."

"Thank you, Miss Scott."

"Here is a hundred dollars' worth of gold coins and the new combination to the bank vault. Marshal Brock will have the new door keys for you. We'll want to go to the sign painter and have a new sign painted. Here's what I want on it." Razor handed her a sheet of paper that said, 'Razor Sharp's Depositors' Savings and Loan Bank of Mesilla, New Mexico Territory,' with 'Manager: Miss Mary Ann Scott' printed in smaller letters underneath and with the Razor brand burned in each corner."

"Oh my! Razor. You want me to be the manager?"

"Only if you want the bank to reopen, Miss Scott. If you won't be my manager, I won't open it," a smiling Razor said.

"Razor, I know the town would rather have a bank than a school, so I'll accept."

"Ask Mr. Stew to have his crew put the sign up. Keep the change from the hundred for other expenses you might have."

Razor stopped at Pedro Gonzales's house on the way out of town. He was a recipient of one of Razor's free horses. After greetings, Razor asked to borrow his horse for a few days.

He filled his six canteens from Pedro's well and stopped at the Rio Grande and let the horses have their fill and then headed to his home is the foothills of the Sacramento Mountains. By this time, Razor's horse knew the trail. Razor scoped the trail as far ahead as he could and searched for dust clouds farther in the sky. He closed his eyes for long periods of time, and when he opened them, he was still on the trail. He took advantage of any high points in elevation to scope what lay ahead and his behind.

This time Razor thought he might have overfilled his plate. He didn't have a hundred thousand dollars of gold coin. He couldn't tell the world he would be paying off in gold nuggets and create a gold rush so he would have to hurry.

He watered the horses sparingly with water poured from one of the canteens into his hat and changed his mount as needed. He rode through the night. The cool desert temperature was a blessing. By daylight Razor had reached the east side of the Sacramento Mountains. The air was cool, and a soothing wind flowed off the mountain. Razor had two full canteens of water. He gave it all to the two horses.

In five hours, he was home. A quick look around confirmed there had been no intrusions. He loved the thought of home. He had to be ready when the wagons got there. He removed the trapdoor and laid the papers aside. He took a blanket and placed about fifty pounds of gold on it. He pulled it to the porch and stacked it. It took ten trips to empty the concealed container. Razor covered the gold with a blanket and returned to replace the papers in the container. He closed and latched the hidden trapdoor. He looked around, remounted, and then rode down the mountain.

The horses had just finished watering when he rode up. Shouts and applause rang out from the crew when they saw Razor. This was the first time they had seen him in nearly a year. Razor recognized them all and knew them all by name. He gave them recognition by pointing or waving at each. When he saw Jacob Walters, he shook his hand, and thanked him for all his support. Razor raised his hand, asking for quiet among the crew.

“Men, we don’t have enough time for me to tell you all that’s going on. I’ll tell you that this will soon be your home. We’ll build bunkhouses to sleep at least sixty hands. You had better practice up on hitting the spittoon because I’m not going to clean the floor for you." Laughter broke out from everyone.

"The food will be good, and there will always be plenty of it anytime you want it. I know everyone is tired, but we must be back in Mesilla two days from now. Mr. Stew can fill you in on the details. Mount up and follow me." Shouts of approval followed.

The gold was placed evenly in the two hundred gunnysacks and loaded into the three wagons. The horses watered in the stream. The water barrels and canteens were refilled upstream from where the horses watered. The wagons pulled out with several men asleep in them.

"Mr. Stew, the wagon tracks are to be dragged once we leave. Have Calhoun build a forty-acre corral next to the barn. I'll have a special use for it. I have a few things I need to do here. I'll catch up with you before nightfall."

Razor took a different path to the other X. He would be going often and didn't want to make a trail. He used caution when entering the area of the arroyo. He again filled his saddlebags with the large gold nuggets. It would take numerous trips just to collect the nuggets already lying on the surface beneath the washout. He would take these with him, but when he got settled in, he would refill the chest under the trapdoor. Then he would convert the nuggets into gold bars and haul them by wagon to the bank.

Just before dark, he caught up with the wagons. He turned his horses into the traveling remuda. He found an empty place in a wagon and crawled in with his saddle and saddlebags. He was asleep within seconds of lying down. The wagons had never stopped rolling.

Before daybreak, Razor found Mr. Stew. “I’ll be leaving the wagons, Mr. Stew. I’ll see you at the bank in Mesilla.”

A few hours later, Razor was rested, and his two mustangs had been watered and fed. The packhouse carried the saddlebags of gold. By ten o’clock the next morning, Mesilla was in sight. Razor swung farther south to bypass Mesilla. He was headed to Fort Fillmore to see if he could exchange some of the nuggets for gold coins.

Chapter 19

Killing at the Bank

Razor was received immediately by Major Childers. He met him at the door with a big smile.

"Major, the rest of your horses will be here as promised. But I'm not here to discuss them, and I need to get right to the point. I need your help. After I tell you what I want you to do, and if you can't help me, tell me who I need to talk to who can help me."

"Razor, I'll help you. Tell me what you want."

"Major, let me show you something." Razor dumped the forty pounds of gold on the major's desk. "As you can see, the nuggets are clean. I have another bag just like this in the bank at Mesilla. I need a hundred thousand dollars in gold coins today and will pay twenty percent more than that with clean gold nuggets."

"Razor, I hope you are not depending on the gold nuggets that were in the bank. The bank's closed down."

"Major, I now own the bank in. I plan to open it in the morning and have given my word that I would pay off the depositors in gold coins. It would be tomorrow before I could get to Wells Fargo in El Paso to exchange the gold nuggets for the coins, and by that time, I would have broken my word."

"If I had the coins today, I would give you the eighty pounds of nuggets. My help at the bank could then pay the depositors tomorrow morning when the bank opens. I'll have more gold nuggets at the bank before nightfall, and I'll go to El Paso tonight with enough gold nuggets to buy the hundred thousand dollars of coins. I would deliver them back here to replace your coins and pick up my gold nuggets, less the twenty percent charge owed you for the loan of the coins. Will you or could you do this?"

"Razor, I'm sure I can get this done. I'll tell the commanding officer. I'm sure he would insist on a company of troopers to go with the coins from here and pick up the nuggets in Mesilla and bring them back here. They could escort you and your gold nuggets to El Paso and bring the gold coins back here then take your nuggets back to your bank. You have been a vital vendor for this fort. Sit tight, I'll get this done."

The marshal removed the spectators from around the door of the closed bank and ordered everyone to stay across the street as Razor and the troopers reached the bank. Stew was taking the gold nuggets into the bank vault.

"Mr. Stew, have someone return Pedro Gonzales's horse to him. I borrowed it when I needed another and didn't have time to get one of my own. Give him this twenty-dollar gold piece and my thanks for the loan. I also want twenty guards to stay all night here until Jacob can figure out a schedule for day and night. Have them all get some sleep and be back here before dark," Razor said.

"Yes, sir," replied Stew.

Miss Scott was there with Joe Brine, weighing and counting each nugget.

"Where do you want the hundred thousand dollars of gold coins?" Razor asked.

Smiling, she said, "Just throw them down anywhere. Just kidding! I'll have Joe stack them as I count them."

Razor loaded the saddlebags full of nuggets and gave them to the lieutenant. "This is the other half of the collateral for the coins."

"I've got to have a receipt for that, Lieutenant," said Miss Scott.

Razor loaded more than enough gold nuggets to buy the gold coins from Wells Fargo.

"Miss Scott, you will be here tomorrow to open the bank, won't you?"

"A team of horses couldn't drag me away, Razor."

"I'll be back before three o'clock tomorrow afternoon," Razor said.

Razor and the troopers were in El Paso, sitting at the door of the Wells Fargo office when they opened, and were back at the Fort by two o'clock. The one hundred thousand dollars of gold coins were transferred, and Major Childers and the commander of the Fort, Colonel Charles Stubblefield, insisted that they were not going to accept any payment from Razor for borrowing the coins. They were glad they could help Razor and the town of Mesilla.

Razor and the troopers arrived back at the bank at three o'clock. The gold nuggets were returned to the vault, and the troopers left.

"Miss Scott, I must see Mr. Stew first, then I'll be back here to see how everything went." Razor left the bank looking for Stew. He had gone only two blocks when Joe Brine ran out of the bank screaming.

"Mr. Sharp, come back! Buster Marlow has got Miss Scott, threatening to kill her! He wants to know where you are so he can kill you! He has his arm around her neck, choking her! He says that she's giving his money away and that the bank belongs to him!"

"Joe! Where is he holding her?

"Behind the teller's cage!"

"Joe, give me your key. I'll go in by the side door. You go find the doctor and get him here as fast as you can. Then tell everyone to stay clear of the bank, including the guards."

Razor pulled his .45 Colt, checked it, and slid it loosely back in the holster. He took a deep breath then eased the side door open. He saw Buster and heard him ranting.

"He was always your pet! I want you to see me shoot him, then I'm going to kill you for giving my money away!"

Razor saw Buster's gun jammed into Miss Scott's side. He thought, *to shoot me, he would have to remove the gun from her side and point it at me. He wants her to see me killed, then he will kill her. That's all the information I need. I can do it.*

Razor had not drawn his gun when he called out Buster's name. Buster turned, moving his gun away from Miss Scott, then Razor pulled his gun and shot Buster between his eyes.

Buster's head snapped backward and then he wilted to the floor, releasing Miss Scott and his gun on the way down.

Razor raced to her side and quickly walked her out the front door. The doctor and Jacob were there, and Razor asked the doctor to take care of her.

"I'll take care of her, Razor!" said Jacob.

"Has she been shot?" asked the doctor.

"No," Razor said.

"What about the other one?"

"He doesn't need a doctor; he needs an undertaker. You both take care of her while I finish up here. I'll come for her at your office, Doctor."

Razor noticed the special interest Jacob seemed to have in Miss Scott. Marshal Block had heard the commotion and had started to the bank. Before he got there, he had heard the end of Buster's rant and Razor calling out Buster's name, then the shot.

"Razor, I'm sorry it came to this. I know Buster gave you no choice.," said the Marshal.

"This whole thing started over Buster Marlow. It won't end now until Ralph Marlow is dead. I feel that it is my responsibility to end it before some innocent person is killed."

"Razor, I know you have to do what you think you have to do. If I run into him before you, I'll try to take care of him. If you do have to kill him, you will get no fuss from me."

"Marshal, I don't want him put in jail. I don't want to worry about him getting out."

"We're on the same page, Razor. If I find him, I promise you he will never be put in jail. I'm just glad Buster didn't shoot Miss Scott or you. I'll get the bank cleaned up for you, and I'll get him buried."

"Thanks, Marshal, I really want to be the one who finds Marlow. I made him a promise. I'll get Mr. Stew to send over a couple of men to help clean up."

"Razor, come by my office before you leave town. I have something I want to give you," Marshal Block said.

"I'm going to the doctor's office to check on Miss Scott. I'll be by shortly," Razor said.

As Razor entered the doctor's office, Miss Scott rushed to his side. "I tried to talk some sense into Buster's head, but he wouldn't listen. I know you did what you had to do. I'm so thankful that you came. He would have killed me."

"Miss Scott, are you okay?"

"I'm fine, Razor. I'm ready to go back to the bank. I've got a lot of work to do."

"Miss Scott, the marshal, Mr. Stew, and a few of his men are cleaning up over there. Let's stay here a while. Jacob; you stay also. Miss Scott, tell me how everything went this morning with the depositors."

"Oh, Razor! It went great. No one withdrew all their money. They are leaving their accounts open, and we even opened several new accounts. They trust Razor Sharp. Everyone was happy, and I had the most fun I've had in a long time."

"Have they hired anyone to teach at the school?" Razor asked.

"They're looking. The town knows how important the bank is to them. They trusted me today with their transactions and even asked if I was going to continue working for the bank, and I assured them that I would be. They had rather have me at the bank looking after their money than teaching the kids. A few expressed their feeling that it would be easier to hire a new schoolteacher than it would be for you to find a banker."

"Miss Scott, I'll have Jacob hire ten guards to protect you and the bank."

"Razor, that won't be necessary. The people of this town will protect their money and me."

"A lot of gold and money is going to be coming in and out of the bank, and I had already thought of the need for the ten guards. They will be on guard around the clock. Any decision on Joe?"

"Joe is totally loyal to you and me. In school, he was one of my best math students. There is no one I'd rather have than Joe.

Let's go back to the bank," Miss Scott said. "There may be more depositors there by now."

"Come in, Razor," said Marshal Block. "I've had this on my mind for some time now, and this is something I want to do. The US Marshal's office has the authority to appoint special deputy US Marshals. These are people of high standing, ones who have proven to have courage and determination to take actions to protect themselves and the community. You are one of these rare people, and I want to give you this deputy US Marshal's badge. You can wear it as needed or anytime you want. I know of no one worthier to wear this badge."

"Well, thank you, Marshal. It will truly be an honor for me to wear it!"

Chapter 20

Marlow Hires Coraza

Ralph Marlow had settled into the compound he had bought in the southern part of Juarez. He had erected an eight-foot adobe wall around the perimeter of his property with shards of glass protruding from the top. His bank guards had gone with him, protecting him and the money he had stolen when he fled to Mexico. Marlow had paid them well for their services. Once they collected their money and got Marlow securely into the compound, they quickly returned to Texas and went their separate ways.

All the guards wanted to get as far away from the New Mexico Territory as fast as they could. They didn't want to get tangled up with the fact that Marlow had stolen all the depositors' money. The guards had always been on the side of the law. The amount of money paid them to take Marlow to Juarez and the thought of being unemployed made the decision easy. All of them had taken Marlow's offer to get him to Mexico, and each had planted a seed in their brains that it was a continuation of their job and not bank robbery. Marlow now had to find security for his compound. With his abundance of money, he felt he could do this but needed guidance. He got the word out he was looking for a *segundo*. Of the twenty who showed up looking for the job, he settled on Caliente Coraza. Marlow didn't hire him because his name meant "Hot Armor" in English but because of his knowledge of how the federales and *la policia de la ciudad* worked. They both had to be paid protection money. Coraza would furnish all the extra security he needed.

Coraza was as fast with a gun as he was with words. Always clean and well dressed, he was comfortable with the law and the men he would be hiring. In some circles, he was known as a shrewd businessman. In others, he was known as an assassin.

Marlow had been busy counting his money when he got the news from Coraza that Razor Sharp had killed Buster. Marlow slumped in his chair.

"Coraza, how many men can you gather to go into the New Mexico Territory and stay until they find and kill Razor Sharp? I'll pay one thousand US dollars to the man who kills him and five hundred dollars to every man who goes with you."

"When do you want us to go?"

"Now!"

"Give me three days and I'll have twenty men ready to ride. I'll need a thousand dollars for ammunition and food. I've never seen Razor Sharp. What does he look like?"

"You won't have a problem finding him, but you might have a problem killing him. All the gringos I hired couldn't do it. He attracts a lot of attention wherever he goes. He wears colorful bandannas around his neck to cover the rope burns I gave him. I should have killed him then."

"Looks as if you are going to have rope burn scars around your neck. Did Razor Sharp put them there?"

"His gang did! Coraza, I'll give you five thousand dollars if you bring me his head and neck—with the rope burns."

"Marlow, I'd cut my own mother's head off for that kind of money. I'll have my crew in the Territory by tomorrow."

Early the next morning, Coraza left with twenty rough men. Their only association with the law was running from it. Most were proven assassins using different methods to accomplish the same results. Coraza knew most of them personally or knew their reputation.

Half of the twenty men crossed the low river crossing down from the river from the bridge. They crossed into Texas one or two at a time five minutes apart. The other ten rode west and crossed into the New Mexico Territory on the west side of the Rio Grande. The ten who crossed using the low river crossing met up five miles out of El Paso and crossed back over the Rio Grande and met up with the others who had already arrived in New Mexico Territory. They pitched camp and passed their time drinking coffee and cleaning their weapons. Coraza had ridden ahead to Mesilla to try and locate Razor Sharp.

Sharp had not been that difficult to find and would not have been hard to kill. There were other things to consider: his escape after killing Sharp and cutting his head off with his neck attached.

"Mr. Stew, this is what needs to be done. First, Jacob needs to hire twenty loyal hands to be guards at the bank. It is to be guarded twenty-four hours a day, seven days a week. I want you to buy twenty tons of oats and store it dry in the freight yard. I'll pay Bonnie Lou for the storage. I want Jacob to have ten of his guards go with me in the next three days. Have each of them carry several day's supply of jerky. We will be back in about ten days."

"In nine days, have wagon master Calhoun take one wagonload of oats to the east side of the Sacramento Mountains and distribute small piles of oats in the eastern foothills of the mountain. The rest of his wagons are to be loaded down with tools and supplies for cutting and hauling logs to construct the bunkhouses and dining halls. Mr. Stew, can you stay at the freight yard, so I'll know where to find you?"

Razor mounted and rode to the Fort. Major Childers and Colonel Stubblefield were eager to see him. They had heard of the shooting. Razor knew they wanted details but were too polite to ask for fear of offending him. Razor suggested that Marshal Block would be glad to fill them in on all the details. He had come to inform them he would be delivering the rest of the horses in fewer than ten days. He asked that they hold the final payment until he got back in touch and to give the receipt for the horses to Water Finder. When he returned, they would talk about selling more horses to them.

Razor returned to Mesilla and left with Jacob and the ten guards headed to Rio Casas Grandes. Ten miles out of Mesilla, Jacob and Razor questioned the cloud of dust that was headed west along the Mexico border. "Someone is in a hurry," mentioned Jacob.

"Hope they change direction and head into Mexico. There is nothing in the direction they are going unless they plan to run into us."

"Those are my thoughts also, Razor. Let's make a plan."

"Jacob, one of the Lipan Apache Indians who found me in the desert walks and runs everywhere and seldom ever rides a horse. His name is Walks with Pride. For the last nine months, I've walked and trotted as far as fifteen miles numerous times with him. I'm going to dismount and catch up with whoever it is before dark. I'll report back to you before morning. I'll take only my Winchester, extra ammunition, Bowie knife, and my telescope. I'll take one canteen of water and some jerky. I think they are trying to get to the East Potrillo Mountain before we do. Don't ride in until we talk. I'll come to you."

"I think you might be right. We need to know what we will be riding into, but I hate for you to go alone."

"I'll find out, Jacob. I don't need any help."

Razor gathered the few things he would be taking while riding and stowed his two colts. Never stopping, he handed the reins to Jacob, slid off his horse and laid on the ground until Jacob and the guards were about a mile away.

Razor stood slowly and straightened his canteen, knife, and ammunition. He telescoped in all directions, making sure he hooded the glass when facing the sun. Satisfied, he picked up his Winchester and placed the telescope around his neck, accidently rubbing the rope burn. This triggered the determination to kill them all if they were Marlow's henchmen. He was certain that Marlow would know by now that he had killed Buster and that Marlow would waste no time in trying to kill him.

When Razor had a large mesquite stand between him and the large dust cloud, he would run all out. When in sparse cover, Razor stooped near the ground and walked at a slow grazing pace. He was getting closer and needed a good place to stop and telescope the area. He saw a large mesquite that was sitting on a slight knoll. There were enough leaves to shield the glass. He would be looking into the sun, and shadows of the leaves were a must. Razor leaned the Winchester against a lower limb and took a small sip of water. He laid the canteen aside and held his hand over the glass in the end of the telescope until he was certain the end of the scope would be covered by the shadows of the leaves.

He counted twenty-one *bandoleros*. They were traveling in a V formation to prevent having to eat dust and enable everyone to shoot outward without hitting each other. Each of the riders wore a bandolier to carry their ammunition except for the rider at the head of the V formation, presumably their leader. They were headed straight toward the East Potrillo Mountains. Razor had no doubt that they had been sent by Marlow to kill him.

Razor located Jacob's dust cloud five miles northeast and headed that way. It took him eighty minutes to reach them.

"There are twenty-one of them," he told Jacob. "They are bandoleros. I'm convinced they were sent by Marlow to kill me. There is no other reason for them to be here. I've been thinking on the way back and want to run something by you. I would like to have one man find a dead mesquite tree and pull it toward the south end of the East Potrillo Mountain, stirring up dust. He will stop eight miles from the mountain and spend the night. I want him to light a couple of campfires and move away from the fires to sleep. At daylight, I want him to continue to move toward the south end of the mountain, pulling the mesquite. By the time he has traveled a mile, we should be in position to wipe them out. We will stay here until nightfall and move out toward the middle of the mountain range. In the morning, the bandoleros will be busy getting in position and watching the dust cloud. I'll move around until I find them, then we will move into our position. I want to kill their leader first. What do you think?"

"Razor, that's a good plan. I can't think of a better one, but I want you to remember that we will be outnumbered two to one. We need to kill a bunch of them before they know what has happened. I've never liked to bushwhack anyone, but we don't have a choice here. I know you want to kill their leader, but don't linger. He isn't their leader because he is dumb and slow on the draw. Don't think he has to be facing you for you to kill him. The buzzards won't know or care where he was shot."

"I understand, Jacob."

Even though he understood, he, too, hated to bushwhack anyone. He wanted this over with. He thought about being outnumbered two to one and cringed at the thought. Before Jacob had pointed this fact out to him, he had intentions of calling out their leader. He visualized that the others would stand and wait for the outcome. *How stupid could I be?* he thought.

The next morning, thus far, things were going as planned. Razor and Jacob had located the bandoleros, and the dust cloud was rising in the southwest, moving toward the mountain. The bandoleros soon picked up the sight of the cloud and rejoiced that it was heading toward their trap. While they were concentrating on the dust cloud, Jacob and Razor repositioned their crew closer to the bandoleros. Their leader was barking orders and moving in and out through the ranks of his gang. Razor was close enough to hear all the orders.

"I'll give the order to fire, their leader was saying. "We want to kill them all at the same time. There are only twelve of them. Start from the left. I want two of you shooting at the same rider. The next two, shoot the rider beside him and on down the line. We will all fire at the same time. I'll take the last two at the end of the line by myself. Keep firing until you know they are all dead. Sharp will have on a colorful bandanna. Don't shoot him in the head or neck. I've got to cut his head off below the neck and deliver it to Marlow. He wants to see the rope burn scar on his neck to make sure Sharp is dead. Stay in your positions and relax. Try to stay still and quiet. You know how sound travels in the desert."

Razor had confidence in Jacob's nine guards. They were intelligent and followed instructions. The guards could all sign and knew what was expected of them. Razor didn't know how many of them could understand Spanish but wished that they all could understand what the bandolero leader had told his men.

Jacob's crew had also been told the order in which they were to shoot the targets below them. Razor was confident that their first targets would be dead with the first volley of shots. When the bandoleros had settled down, Jacob's guards sighted in their first target. Their second target was next to their first. The word *Now!* was the signal to fire. Razor had his sight on the back of the leader. Just before the signal to fire was given, Caliente Coraza turned and looked straight up into the eyes of Razor Sharp. The word *Now!* was given and Razor pulled the trigger.

The guards and Jacob had killed their first target and immediately had started on their next. Of the first targets, only Coraza was alive. When Coraza had turned to look up at Razor, the bullet went in his left shoulder, shattering his arm and slowed down as it went into his upper chest. Coraza dropped his rifle and reached for his Colt with his right hand as he rolled to the ground and raised the Colt to return fire at Razor. Before Coraza could pull the trigger, Razor's second bullet rushed into Coraza's heart, and his third crashed between Coraza's eyes.

Razor didn't waste any more time on him as he fired at moving targets until nothing moved below. It was all over in less than ten seconds. The bandoleros had only gotten off four wild shots that hit nothing.

Razor was wondering what made their leader turn and look at him? No sound had been made. Razor knew it had to be the leader's feeling he was being watched. It could have created a disaster for Razor's crew. He realized he had made a mistake staring at the back of their leader. He pledged to never make that mistake again. He knew better. "Razor, I understood what their leader told them. I'd like for you to tell the rest of the crew what their leader said," Jacob said.

After reciting the conversation between the leader and the bandoleros, they all seemed pleased with themselves.

"Let's get the horses and clean this mess up. We'll lasso their feet and pull them back into Mexico. It's only about five miles. We'll destroy their weapons," said Jacob. After salvaging the ammunition and leaving the bodies in Mexico, the crew covered their tracks by dragging mesquite limbs all the way back to the mountains.

"Razor, the sooner we can kill Marlow, the better," Jacob said.

"That's something I want to do by myself, Jacob."

"I know you do, but the next time, he may send a hundred men after you, and the guards and I may not be around."

"I know! I'll put it on the front burner of the things I must do."

Chapter 21

Comanche Raid at the Strange Tumbleweed

Razor and his men had been in Mexico only a short time when they saw standing in the trail ahead of them a regal horse without a saddle or bridle looking straight at them and refusing to move. The guards were alert, looking in all directions with weapons drawn.

"No one shoot!" Razor shouted. "Walks! Come out here before you get shot."

"I could have killed all of you. Taking you off one at a time from behind with my bow," Walks was saying as he approached with a grin on his face. He was introduced to the guards, and then Walks took off running toward the trap, with his horse following close behind.

Razor was introduced to the new bunch of vaqueros from the Villa de Jonas. One of the new vaqueros was a master farrier. He had all the tools to trim and place horseshoes on horses that would raise its pads off the ground to prevent bruising. There was a total of forty special horses, including Sweet Pea, that were first to get their shoes.

Roberto reported they had saddle-broke more than three hundred mustangs and had more than two hundred in the trap that needed to be broke and branded.

"We'll put the other sets of branding irons to work and have the guards pitch in on the branding. Let's be ready to move the herd within four days."

"After we deliver the hundred and forty-eight mustangs owed to the Army, the new crew with Enrique and Walks will return here and continue to gather, break, and brand the horses. The rest of us will drive the remaining mustangs, including the special ones, on to the ranch. The special mustangs, including Sweet Pea, will have their special corral when we get them to the ranch. Let's get a good night's sleep and hit it hard in the morning," Razor said.

On the fifth day, they moved out with the herd. Razor had packed biscuits and a couple of longhorn steaks cooked that morning along with oats for the horses. He rode the bay and joined the special mustang herd. Sweet Pea stayed by his side each step of the way until Razor left the herd with his bay and a packhorse then crossed the border into New Mexico. Walks had to put a hackamore on Sweet Pea to hold her back.

Razor headed to Mesilla, switching out the horses as he went. He made it to the East Potrillo Mountain foothills and turned north into the mountain. Before dark, he stopped along a small stream and took time to scope out the territory. He made a small smokeless fire and fed the horses while he waited for the coffee to boil. He had not eaten anything but jerky on the way, but now he ate the biscuits and steaks, washing it down with coffee. He put out the fire and buried the remnants deep. He scoped the area again, staked out the horses in cover, placed his weapons and scope nearby, and finally lay down to sleep.

At dawn, Razor was awake but didn't move. He sensed something in the air around him but couldn't determine what it was. He would stay still until he figured it out. Someone or something was watching him! Whatever it was wasn't nearby or the horses would have nickered. Razor slowly moved his head and studied his surroundings.

It was not uncommon to see a tumbleweed, some three feet tall, move across the desert floor. They rolled and bounced along until a cactus or mesquite limb grabbed and held them until a gust of wind snatched them loose so they could continue their journey to nowhere. But something was unusual about the one Razor had been watching. It bounced along but didn't roll. The wind was flowing off the mountain to the east. The tumbleweed was moving west toward him. Razor didn't want to take his eye off the tumbleweed that was moving toward him but had to know if there were others.

Razor found his telescope without taking his eye off the strange tumbleweed. Without raising his head or scope, he was able to sight in on the tumbleweed. He watched for a few minutes, and nothing moved, nor did he see anything behind the weed. Was he looking at the wrong tumbleweed?

Suddenly, he did see movement. It was a Comanche! The Indian had moved his bow to get a better grip on the tumbleweed he was hiding behind. Razor could see no other weapons and was out of range for this Comanche and his bow. He had to stay out of range and locate the rest of his party and find out if they had any weapons besides a bow and knife. He moved the scope off the tumbleweed and looked for any others. He counted seven. Razor made a fast plan. He would shoot into each of the tumbleweeds as fast as he could. If one was wounded, he would move on to the next tumbleweed and go back and shoot at any movement he noticed. Razor had his Colt ready if needed. If the Indians allowed him, he would reload his Winchester. Replacement shells were in easy reach and others were available in his pockets if he had to move. He could only pray that none of them had a rifle.

Razor casually stood with his canteen to his mouth and the Winchester in his hand, looking down at his targets. He ran through his mind the order in which he would shoot. When Razor was ready, he would drop the canteen and shoot into the seven tumbleweeds.

Razor's first shot was fired before the canteen hit the ground. After the seventh shot was fired, he went to his knees and quickly reloaded his Winchester. He knew he had killed at least two and severely wounded two others. Now, there seemed to be movement everywhere. Razor didn't shoot at the two wounded ones but at three Comanches racing up the mountain, trying to get in range with their bows. Razor hit the one in the lead. His body was driven off the side of the mountain all the way to the foothills. The other two disappeared as if swallowed up by the earth.

Razor also disappeared after moving down the mountain toward where he had last seen the two remaining Comanches. Finder and Walks both had told him that he could not outrun a Comanche, and the only way to survive was to let them come to you. To make it easier, he was told to go as fast as he could toward the Indians and find a place he could hide before they got there. Preferably it would be a place that they could see him from only one direction.

The hiding place he found wasn't perfect, but it would have to do. He could be seen only from one direction, but he was giving up the ability to move about. Razor swept his tracks away and settled into a dry arroyo. Past waters had cut under the bank on the downhill side space for him to get under the embankment. Anyone going up the mountain had to turn around and look back down the mountain to see him.

The two remaining Comanches were hurrying up the mountain to where they last saw the shooters. They planned to pick up his trail there and follow him until they found him and killed him. White men always ran from Comanches. There was no reason to think Razor would be different.

With his cocked Winchester within easy reach, Razor waited with his Colt .45 in his hand. He heard the Indians running up the mountain behind him. He was ready, but he was not expecting what happened. The two Comanches hit the overhanging washed-out bank that Razor was hiding under at the same time. Their weight made the bank collapse on top of Razor, driving his left hand down on top of the Winchester and sent the two Comanches sprawling into the arroyo.

Razor fought to get out from under the weight of the bank as one of the Comanche rushed toward him. He didn't know where his Colt was, and his Winchester was half buried. Somehow, he was able to dig down where the rifle lay, find the trigger and pull it. The bullet entered the Comanche's chest, and he lost his footing. Razor grasped the hand that held the knife and upon death the hand surrendered the knife to him.

The other Comanche was hesitant about rushing Razor. While Razor was pinned down under the fallen Comanche and the rock and dirt from the fallen arroyo bank, the remaining Comanche scrambled to locate his bow and arrow.

The only weapon Razor had use of was the knife in his hand that had been surrendered to him by the dying Comanche. Razor quickly freed his arm and drew the knife back over his shoulder. When the Comanche stood and was drawing the string back to send the arrow flying to take Razor's life, Razor launched the knife. The knife cut the string while passing the bow on the way to the Comanche's heart. The Comanche dropped the bow and grasped the knife that was buried to the hilt. The knife's blade was wedged between two ribs, and the recipient could not budge it loose before dying. He bled out chanting the warrior's death wishes.

Razor dug out the Winchester and Colt from the fallen embankment. He rushed back to his camp, cleared and cleaned his weapons. He would have loved to have some coffee but because he didn't know if other Comanches were lurking nearby he needed to move out as fast as he could. He hated killing the Comanches but felt he had had no choice.

Razor put his hand on the rope scar on his neck. One thing for sure, killing Ralph Marlow wouldn't bother him at all.

Razor hastily retrieved his horses and packed up. He led them to the small creek for water and moved off the mountain cautiously. Razor saw on the desert floor the bodies of the two Comanches he had wounded earlier. He headed to Mesilla. Razor wanted to race away but slowed the pace. Stirring up a dust cloud or tiring the horses wouldn't be advisable. Not knowing if the Comanches he killed had other parties in the area made it imperative that he be cautiously aware of his surroundings and there was always a chance he would need to rely on the speed of his horse to save his life.

Upon arriving in Mesilla, Razor called on Miss Scott and Joe at the bank. The guards greeted him by name. He was surprised to see the front door of the bank painted bright red, and in the middle of the door, the Razor brand was painted white. A large flowerpot was on each side of the door with tall red rose bushes growing in each one. Inside the bank were several potted plants and vases of fresh-cut flowers. They brought a smile to Razor's face, and he thought that his mother would have loved them.

Razor's smile matched that of Miss Scott's when she saw him. "I've had an awful lot of women coming in, opening accounts instead of keeping their money under their mattress or in a buried fruit jar. They seem to enjoy coming here," said Miss Scott. "But I think they really want to catch a glimpse of you, Razor."

"I bet you had several single men coming as well," Razor said, grinning. It was the first time he had ever seen Miss Scott blush.

"Razor, the judge and Marshal Block want me to pin you down on a date that they can have a party to celebrate you saving the bank."

"You know that's not necessary. I didn't just save the bank for them; I needed a bank myself."

"But you furnished all the money to return to the depositors' accounts. The town would have been ruined if you hadn't. Razor, you have come a long way from the time you rode in here on that freight wagon. The folks just want to show their appreciation. Let them do it, Razor!"

"You pick the time, Miss Scott. Give me a week's notice."

"How about next Saturday?"

"Sounds fine. I'll be here."

Razor sent word to the major that the horses would be ready to be counted the next morning, and he would come to see him in a couple of days. Razor spent the night in his favorite sleeping place in Mesilla and left for home early the next morning. When he arrived, he made sure Calhoun had put the oats out as directed. He told him to have Mr. Stew ship him two more tons of oats and put them out as needed.

Calhoun helped Razor stake out the location for the building that would house the large forge. It would be a blacksmith shop during the day. The building would have all the tools that a good blacksmith would have. The forge had a steel rail structure overhead to be used for attaching a melting pot. The pot could be lowered or raised in the forge then transferred to molds on the molding table. Here the melted gold would flow from the tilted pot controlled by a long handle attached to the ears of the pot. The pot, handle, and the molds would be hidden in a false wall that Razor would build.

The entrance and rear door would be hanging on a heavy-duty steel rail. The steel latch would look and operate as any other but could be switched by a hidden lever to prohibit entry to anyone. The location of the blacksmith shop would lay north of Razor's barn, which was about fifty yards from the house. The kitchen, dining hall, and the first bunkhouse would be built farther southeast.

In the woods behind his home, Razor started marking timber that was to be cut for the buildings. He also marked trees that needed thinning. These were to be cut, peeled, and stacked with spacers between each pole and left in the mountains. The logs for immediate construction were to be dragged to the building sites and peeled.

Razor left Calhoun and his crew with plenty of work to keep them busy. He took time out to go to the hiding place for his gold and loaded his saddlebags. He placed the content under the floor in the hidden chest then left to return to Mesilla in time for his appreciation ceremony. About a fourth of the way to Mesilla, Razor saw the dust created from more than three hundred and fifty mustangs. He watched with pride as they passed and was pleased that they each carried his Razor brand.

Razor saw a commotion occurring back in the herd. It was Sweet Pea breaking from the herd and racing toward him. Razor raised his hand and signaled the vaquero chasing her to stop. He dismounted and moved away from his horse and greeted Sweet Pea with outstretched arms. Sweet Pea pranced around him, nodding and neighing, showing her affection for him. Razor wrapped his arms around her neck and returned her affection. He remounted the bay and rode off toward Mesilla with Sweet Pea tight by his side.

Razor waved at the vaqueros as they passed. He was proud of this moment of happiness, but the unfinished business with Ralph Marlow cast a shadow over his mood.

Razor went straight to Fort Fillmore to see the major. This time the guard at the gate let him enter unchallenged. He slipped a hackamore on Sweet Pea and tied her to the hitching rail with the bay and packhorse.

"Major, would you have your troopers deliver the gold coins for the last delivery of horses to my bank in Mesilla?"

"Of course, I will, Razor. I'll do it today. In fact, I have had horses requisitioned from six other forts and could use more if you have them."

"Major, I am doing my last roundup now. I don't know how many I'll have, but I'll let you have half of them if you want that many."

"I do want them, Razor."

"I don't know when I'll get them here, but half will be yours."

"Do you want a procurement document?"

"Major, your word is good enough for me."

"I know your word is good also, Razor."

Razor rode into Mesilla and was greeted by everyone he passed. This had not lulled him into being careless. He was on the lookout for Ralph Marlow, especially since Marlow had had time to learn that his last effort to kill him had failed.

He had often asked Marshal Block if he had heard any news about where Marlow might be. He had heard two reports that he was in or around Juarez, Mexico. No one had reported him being seen in El Paso or Mesilla.

The guards greeted him as he approached the bank. He was even welcomed with applause by a couple of customers as he entered.

Miss Scott rushed to him. "Razor, they butchered four steers and have them on the spit. They built a stage for the speakers and band and will attach a large dance floor. They are going to shut down Main Street tonight and drag the stage in place for the all-day feast and party tomorrow. People are coming from El Paso, Mexico, and even Santa Fe."

Santa Fe? That's where Bonnie Lou lives. I wonder how my sweet friend is doing. I haven't seen her for so long!

Razor went to the freight yard and found Mr. Stew. "Mr. Stew, I want to leave my Sweet Pea in the stable. Would you ask Jacob to put a guard on her."

"I've heard about that mare. She is a beauty."

"I'll be taking her to the ranch after the shindig. Give her plenty of oats and always fresh water. Put her in a corral during the daytime and back in the stable at night, if you would."

"I'll see that she is well taken care of," said Stew.

Razor told Mr. Stew the things he wanted done after the first bunkhouse and the kitchen were built. "I want to build a town and call it Mustang. What do you think of that for a name?"

"Would you find a surveyor and hire him and his crew on a permanent basis. Also, would you start looking for a herd of around a thousand white-face heifers, no steers."

"I think we can make that happen, Razor," said Mr. Stew. "Just give me a few weeks."

Razor went to the barn where he relaxed and made plans while he played with Sweet Pea. Early the next morning, he washed in the horse trough and put on his best clothes. He wished now that he had taken the time to buy some new clothes. Everything he owned seemed to be too small.

With Sweet Pea in a stall so settle her down, he left, riding the bay into town. Sweet Pea let everyone around her know that she wasn't happy being left behind.

Razor had to walk the last two blocks to the bank because the streets had been blocked off and were full of people. Razor was greeted from all directions. He didn't recognize many of the people, but Nell Simmons was one person he did know. He smiled to himself remembering her asking the class, "Golly, doesn't he have anything?"

And I had told her, "No! But I will someday."

The judge, mayor, and a representative of the governor of the Territory spoke giving praise to Razor for saving the bank. Colonel Stubblefield spoke highly of Razor for his honesty and trustworthiness. He told of him turning down an extra five dollars a head that the Army offered for his horses because they were in a bind. "He is a great and honorable man."

Razor thanked everyone for their comments and expressed his gratitude to Mr. Stew, the teamsters, and the guards for their help in raising him. "Jacob Walters was the one who led me out of the gypsum sand dunes and still goes out of his way to make sure that the bank and Miss Scott are safe."

He thanked Walks and Finder for taking care of him until he could take care of himself. Razor also gave special thanks to Miss Scott for her help in school and now at the bank. He thanked Marshal Block for looking out for him most of his life. Then he cheerfully said, "I'm hungry! Let's eat and listen to some music!"

Razor was swarmed with glad handers and friends. Every time he looked around, he saw Nell Simmons inching closer to him. He ignored her and moved away. Nell would speak loudly when greeting her friends. Razor knew she was trying to get him to look at her. When he did look her way, he intentionally looked over her head and didn't make eye contact. After an hour of Razor ignoring her, Nell could stand it no longer. "Razor, don't you remember me?" Nell asked.

"I'm sorry, I don't think so," Razor said.

"Razor, I'm Nell Simmons."

"Oh, yes, Nell, I remember you now. You are the girl who asked the class, 'Golly, doesn't he have anything?' I'm glad you're here. I just want to tell you that now I have *everything*!" Turning, Razor walked away. He wished Bonnie Lou were here.

The music and dancing continued until dark. Everyone seemed to have had a good time, except Nell.

Monday morning, Razor went to the telegraph office. At noon, he left with three telegraph codebooks. He gave two to Miss Scott.

"I would like you to learn telegraph code and then teach it to Mr. Stew and Joe," Razor said.

Chapter 22

Army Warning of Apache Wolf Pack

Mr. Stew went with Razor and Sweet Pea to his home to check on the progress of the construction. They saw numerous mustangs on the timbered mountainside eating the oats and lush grass. The special horses were in their corral next to the ranch house. The small stream flowed through the property, one of many streams throughout the mountains that provided fresh water for the horses. The other mustangs they saw were still herded up in thirty to fifty horse herds.

"Mr. Stew, we're going to start our breeding program that will bring back as much as possible the purebred Barb, Arabian, and Andalusian horses. I want four twenty-acre corrals built out of heart red cedar and a special two-acre corral within sight of my front porch for Sweet Pea. We will hold the special horses in the forty-acre corral that Calhoun and his crew built, until we get the new corrals built. We don't think we have many that are purebred of each type, but we do have a start. I think Sweet Pea is as near to a purebred Andalusian as we might find. I have Roberto and Eduardo looking for the purest blooded Andalusian stud they can find. They have several in mind. We'll breed Sweet Pea to the best they can find. It will take a few years for the different breeds to form, but it will be worth the effort."

"A surveyor will be showing up soon to stake out the new town on the edge of the foothills and prairie. It will be ten miles from my home. They will also survey a straight line to Mesilla for a telegraph line that will connect the ranch and town to the Western Union Telegraph office.

"I have made an agreement with Western Union. I'll pay for the materials and construction of the line and hire an operator for when the telegraph office is normally closed. I'll learn the code and teach the code to others at the ranch. That way we can be in touch around the clock. The twenty-five-foot poles, stacked in the mountains, are for construction of the line. And we'll be sending wagons to Denver to pick up eighty-five miles of telegraph wire and insulators."

With the help of Mr. Stew and Calhoun, Razor staked locations to build retainer ponds on the major creeks and arroyos in the foothills on the east side of the Sacramento Mountains. The ponds would be dug by mule skinners using their Fresno scrapers and dynamite when necessary.

All the logging was being done on the south end of the mountain several miles away. Only mature and defective trees were cut for the construction of the buildings. The defective trees were being cut to create more space for healthy, stronger trees to grow. Any portion of the defective tree that could be used was salvaged.

Razor rode off, heading south this time. When he was out of sight of the townspeople, he turned and headed north to the X. It wasn't that he didn't trust Mr. Stew or Calhoun. If he were the only one who knew of the gold, he had only to worry about himself making a mistake.

When he had arrived at the site, he tied his horse in a thick grove of young ponderosas and slowly moved into the arroyo on foot. He couldn't resist taking the large rock and breaking another big chunk from the vein of gold that was encased in the sandstone, limestone, and hard quartz. He filled his saddlebags with the loose nuggets, covered his tracks, and headed back to his horse.

When he was within two hundred feet of his horse, he stopped short and shuddered in his tracks. A surly black bear stood on his hind feet and was growling and clawing at the air.

He had left his rifle in its scabbard on his horse and the Colt .45 would probably only make the bear mad.

His next move, if the bear attacked, would be to drop to the ground and charge. Razor had read enough about black bears to know a human could not outrun one. He thought of climbing a tree, but unlike grizzly bears, black bears could and would climb trees.

Razor had no alternative but to stand his ground. He raised his saddlebags containing forty pounds of gold over his head. Holding them as high as he could, he made a growling sound and began shaking the bags side to side. The bear repeated his performance and then trotted off. It paused once and looked back to see the strange creature still waving its odd head back and forth.

Weak in the knees from the bear encounter, Razor was delighted to step into his saddle and put his hand on his rifle. He vowed to never again leave his rifle in its scabbard while he was in the mountains. He returned home and deposited the gold under the floor in the hidden chest.

When Razor arrived back in Mesilla, Miss Scott informed him that Nell Simmons had dropped by the bank several times, making disguised inquiries about Razor's well-being. "She keeps wanting to know when you might be available to discuss some banking business with her," Miss Scott said with a grin.

"You tell her you take care of all my banking business and that you are sure you can help her," Razor said, smiling.

"I told her that, and she told me she would do her banking business only with Razor Sharp and huffed out of the bank."

"Miss Scott, you must learn to do business with these young women. Besides, I'm sure you would do a much better job of it than I would," laughed Razor.

"By the way, Colonel Stubblefield wishes to see you as soon as possible, Razor."

"Okay, I want to check in with Marshal Block first. Then I'll go to the Fort."

The marshal's office was near the bank, and Razor could see that he was in. "Marshal Block, have you heard any news about Ralph Marlow?" he asked.

"Glad you stopped by, Razor. I had an informant tell me less than an hour ago that Marlow had slipped into El Paso two days ago and was trying to recruit another gang to hunt you down. Word got to Sheriff Will Partlow about his presence, and he set out to capture him. Apparently, Marlow is paying off a lot of snitches because he slipped back into Mexico before Will could round him up. Razor, you need to stay alert. Marlow has a lot of money and is willing to spend it to take you out."

"I realize that, Marshal. I think my best approach to this situation is to go on the hunt for him instead of waiting on endless attacks Marlow sets up."

"I wondered why you hadn't already done that," Marshal Block said.

"Marshal, I've been mighty busy. I've got it on my list. Guess I need to put it on top."

"That's what I would do. I'm not supposed to go into the state of Texas as a marshal. I'm restricted to the New Mexico Territory unless I'm asked by the Texas Rangers. They don't want me stepping on their toes, I guess. You just be mighty careful, Razor."

When Razor arrived at the fort, he was given an immediate audience with the colonel and Major Childers.

"Razor, Geronimo was rumored to be in the area two weeks ago on a recruiting trip. We have an informant who told us that several young braves from the Mescalero Apache tribe went with him when he left the area. Chief Elk Horn of the Mescalero Apache tribe forbid his son, Wolf Pack, to go."

"Wolf Pack thinks he has lost face with the braves who went and the family and friends they left behind. Chief Elk Horn has lost many of his young braves that have been killed in Geronimo's many battles with the white man, and we think the chief is ready for peace.

"We think Wolf Pack is now recruiting his own raiding party and is going to try to prove his bravery. We think he's the one who attacked the fortified wagon train last week near Tularosa. We are going to try to capture him before he gets killed by a white man. If he does get killed, not only would we have Elk Horn on the war path, but Geronimo might also come back to help him. Razor, your crew of guards is a formidable force to be reckoned with. We wanted you to know the situation we are faced with."

"You are closer to where Wolf Pack will probably be raiding than we are. We don't want you or your men to go out and try to capture Wolf Pack. We just want you to know what is going on and for you and your men to be on alert. We would expect you to help anyone who was under an attack from any Indian."

"Colonel, Major, thanks for the information. We will be alert and on the lookout for Wolf Pack."

"Any news on the horses?" asked the major.

"No, but I plan to go and see. I'll send you a message when I know something."

Razor found Mr. Stew at the freight yard. He told him about Wolf Pack and asked that he get the word to Calhoun. "Mr. Stew, emphasize that under no circumstance is Wolf Pack to be killed unless it is a life-or-death situation on our end. I want the guards to do nothing but guard. Are there any guards who you had who are not working for us now?"

"No, we hired them all."

"If Jacob can find more, have him hire them. I don't want gun slicks. I want people who will be loyal to our brand and will pull the trigger when necessary."

Razor knew that Mr. Stew understood what kind of people he wanted. He just didn't want him to forget, and he would repeat it often.

Early in the morning of the second day, Razor saw a high dust cloud in the southwest. It had to be the herd of mustangs.

"Mr. Stew, send word for Calhoun to send half his crew to the southeast corner of the Sacramento Mountain tomorrow night and hide out of sight at the edge of the mountain. I am convinced that Wolf Pack will see the dust column and will at least go see what is causing it and probably attack. Wolf Pack could also use the mountain to hide in knowing the herd would pass close by. Tell him to try to capture Wolf Pack and try not to kill him. I'll be with the herd."

Razor went to the Fort and told the major that the herd would arrive in less than three hours. "Major, the herd will be coming from the west," Razor said. He didn't express his thoughts about Wolf Pack. "If it's okay with you, we will have the vaqueros cut out half the herd on the way by the Fort and keep the rest moving and let them water in the Rio Grande as they pass through. I'm going on with the herd to the Sacramentos. You can do the count yourself and send the payment to the bank."

"That will work for me, Razor. Thanks, and stop by soon and we will visit.

Chapter 23

Wolf Pack's Attack

Razor joined the herd and talked with Finder, Walks, Enrique, and Roberto about the possibilities of being attacked by Wolf Pack and his war party. Razor thought the party would be small but had no way of knowing until it happened. He also thought it would be close to the Sacramentos. *I'm glad the special horses are not in this drive. I would be worried to death of the possibility of losing any of them,* Razor thought.

Apaches were great warriors. They were patient and seemed to have the ability to come out of the ground under your feet in open territory where there were no trees, rocks, or bushes. They also had the ability to disappear in the same environment. They could do the same in the mountains, and the mountains could be used for an attack on the herd.

He told Finder, Walks, Enrique, and Roberto that Calhoun and half his crew, which consisted of guards and teamsters, would be hiding in the mountains as they approached with the herd. "It is important that Wolf Pack is not killed. Finder, you tell all the guards. Enrique, you and Roberto tell your men. We will hold the herd on the east side of the Rio Grande, and tomorrow we will let them have their fill in the river before we pull out. We will travel all day and night and approach the southeast end of the Sacramentos by early morning. Your men can sleep in their saddles, but come daylight, they better be awake."

Calhoun and his men were spread out high in the foothills. Their horses were tied and guarded a half mile up the mountain. As morning approached, Calhoun could see what he thought would be the herd at a distance.

The cloud of dust was being held close to the ground by the cold air of the desert. It had created a fog-looking effect on the herd. Instead of the herd being strung out as usual, it seemed as if it was being held back in front and was being driven from the rear. This would make it more difficult to cut out a portion of the herd and drive them away.

Most of the vaqueros were in the rear and on the west side of the herd. If attacked, the plan was to stampede the herd to the east side of the Sacramentos. When they all had passed the south end of the mountain, the vaqueros were to ride into the timber of the foothills as far as they could. They would then abandon their mounts and make their way on foot to join Calhoun and his crew. When the mustangs tired, they would make their way into the cover of the timbered mountain. There they would find water and oats. With water and oats, there was no reason for them to leave.

Out of the corner of his right eye, Calhoun saw a slow movement. *Horses! Where did they come from?* They were moving slowly toward the herd. After a closer look, he saw something clinging to their far side. Indians! He signaled down the line for everyone to get ready and that each would try to take out a different horse. The count of the horses was sixteen. Everyone sighted their intended target but would not fire until Calhoun fired the first shot.

When the first shot was fired, everyone followed suit. The horses in the herd were stampeded and pushed around the end of the mountain. To everyone's surprise, at least twenty other Indians had been hidden from Calhoun and his men. They raced in, firing at the vaqueros at the end of the herd and Calhoun and his men, who were in the foothills of the mountain.

The herd was the least of the vaqueros' problems. Their plan worked. What they had not planned on was thirty-six Indians. They were also surprised that there were so many who had rifles. This might have been a blessing in disguise. The Apaches were deadly accurate with their arrows. Many had not had rifles long enough to learn to shoot or care for them properly.

The vaqueros had followed their instruction, and after all the mustangs cleared the south end of the foothills, they started moving up the mountain. Now they were regrouping and inching their way back toward Calhoun to make a line of defense.

Razor was with the vaqueros. He was not sure how he could recognize Wolf Pack. After they linked up with Calhoun, they made a quick count of everyone. Two of the vaqueros had flesh wounds, and one hurt his knee when he jumped from his horse to scramble into the timber. This would have been a disaster if Calhoun and his men had not been in place and had not realized that Indians were hiding on the blind side of their ponies.

More ponies than Indians were killed. Seven were hurt and some were unable to leave their downed ponies, which had fallen on them. All sixteen of the ponies that were carrying their riders on their sides, were killed. Two other horses that followed them had also been killed. Eight dead Indians were counted.

Razor's crew occupied the high ground, and the Indians were down below. Razor wanted to put an end to this now. For all he knew, other Apache could show up, possibly even Geronimo.

Razor signaled for quiet. In perfect Western Athabaskan dialect, he called out "Wolf Pack!" He received no answer. "Is your brave leader not with you? Wolf Pack is known in the white man's world as the one who will become the chief of the Mescalero Apache, and I must talk to him.

"My name is Razor Sharp. My father's reservation is close to Chief Elk Horn's reservation. We have always lived in peace with the Apache. I extend a truce to you so we may talk of peace."

"Wolf Pack has been wounded. He lies under the first horse shot," came the only reply.

"Go to all your wounded and help them. No one will harm you. Razor Sharp has spoken."

The Indians moved out one at a time as their courage increased. The Indian who first reached Wolf Pack stood and called out that Wolf Pack wanted Razor Sharp to come to speak with him.

Razor knew that most Indians kept their word, and the Indians were at a disadvantage with their position being below Razor and his men. He felt comfortable going down to speak with Wolf Pack.

"Wolf Pack, I am Razor Sharp. How badly are you hurt?"

"My leg is broken," said Wolf Pack. "And my right hip is out of place."

"Do you have anyone with you who knows how to set the leg and get your hip back in place?" asked Razor.

"They know how to set the broken bone, but no one knows how to get the hip back in its socket. You wanted to talk, talk!" Wolf Pack said.

"I want to be friends with the Apache. We have a mutual enemy, the Comanche. The Comanche killed my father and mother. Many of the Comanche are being driven out of Texas, and we are going to be seeing some of them come here."

"I want Wolf Pack to get well. I'll do everything in my power to protect the Apache from the Comanche. You need to be well to protect your people from the Comanche."

"I also have a plan to protect the Apache from the white man. I told you my reservation was next to Elk Horn's reservation. My reservation was bought from those who owned the San Mateo Del Montoya family Spanish land grant. My ownership of this land is honored by the Territory of New Mexico and the United States of America. I can come and go from my reservation if I go peaceably. I can invite anyone I want to be on my reservation, and I can refuse anyone I don't want to be on my reservation."

"The law of the Territory and the Army of the United States will protect me from intruders. Wolf Pack, you and your father can have the same protection for your reservation. The white man is here, and many more are on their way. Let me help you claim the Mescalero Apache reservation for you and your tribe. You would have the same protection from the white man that I have. All you have to do is live in peace."

"You can do this, Razor Sharp?" Wolf Pack asked.

"Yes, but you must let me get your hip back in place and set your leg."

"You can do that also, Razor Sharp?"

"I can and I will. I will not question your bravery but will tell you that it will be painful. Tell your braves what I'll be doing and that there could be cries of pain."

"There will be no cries of pain, Razor Sharp."

Razor had two of Wolf Pack's strongest braves assisting him in getting the leg bone back in the hip socket. A six-inch-diameter sapling, two feet long, was cut and peeled. With Wolf Pack lying on his back, the sapling was placed between his upper thighs. One of the Indians held the sapling in place, and the other held his broken leg steady. Razor kneeled on the outside of Wolf Pack's left thigh, reached across, and grasped the lower portion of the right thigh and pulled it toward him. The round sapling pushed out on the upper thigh bone, and Razor pushed the thigh upward with the ball on the joint sliding into the socket. He then set the broken bone. He cut the tail off his shirt and tied it around Wolf Pack's upper thighs to prevent his upper leg from coming back out of place. Wolf Pack closed his eyes and relaxed. "Thank you, Razor Sharp."

Sharp and Wolf Pack worked out a plan. The wounded leader would send all but four of his men back to the tribe. He assured them that he would be safe and protected by Razor Sharp and would return to the tribe as soon as he could travel on a travois. Razor had his crew build a stretcher, and, for the time being, Wolf Pack would be carried to Razor's home, twenty-five miles away, by the four braves who stayed behind.

After picking up another load of gold from the upper X location and putting it in the chest under the floor, Razor traveled to Fort Fillmore and met with Colonel Stubblefield.

He told him about the Apache attack and the wound that Wolf Pack had received. He presented the peace agreement he discussed with Wolf Pack.

"Colonel, I have promised Wolf Pack that I would help defend the Mescalero Apache against the Comanches and the white man if he and Elk Horn would commit the tribe to live in peace on the proposed reservation. For me to fulfill my promise, I need to buy the western part of the Sacramento Mountain range all the way to the great white sands from the US government."

"There would be fifty-two thousand acres in that tract. I already own the east side of the mountain and the prairie halfway to the Pecos River. This particular property would be a western buffer between the white man and the Mescalero Apache. I can pay gold for the property."

"Colonel, my mother and father are buried on this property. I not only need that property for a western buffer, but I don't want to disturb my mother's and father's graves by having to move them over the mountain. The United States government does not need this property, and they could spend the money I would pay for it to buy more horses."

"Razor, I'll tell them of your proposal, including the land purchase, but, Razor, the politicians of the government will have to handle the negotiations henceforth."

"Colonel, the government has been handling the negotiations, and look where it has gotten them. If they would put it in writing, I can get a lasting agreement with the Mescalero Apache."

"Give me two days and I'll let you know what I can work out," said the colonel.

"Your friend Nell is still looking for you, Razor," said Miss Scott, when she welcomed him into the bank. "What do you want me to tell her?"

"Tell her you think I might be in love with Bonnie Lou."

"That might drive her completely insane," laughed Miss Scott. "Have you seen Bonnie Lou or talked to her of late, Razor?"

"No, but I am going to have Mr. Stew locate her and her mother. I owe them money."

Razor asked Mr. Stew to contact Mrs. Callaway in Santa Fe. He planned to offer to pay Bonnie Lou and her mother twice the value of the house, wagons, equipment, stock, and the freight yard. Mr. Stew was to advise her he was not worried about getting a bill of sale or deed from Callaway. "If Callaway has a problem with my ownership, I can take care of that at that time."

The two days were up, and Razor was eager to talk with Colonel Stubblefield about his proposal.

"Razor, the politicians are insisting that the Army take Wolf Pack into custody and use him as a bargaining chip in negotiations with Chief Elk Horn," said Colonel Stubblefield.

"Is the bargaining to be used to get a meeting with Elk Horn?"

"That's part of it, Razor."

"Colonel, Wolf Pack is in my custody. He has my word that I'll protect him from the Comanche and the Whites. I won't turn him over to the Army or anyone else. If you can stall your superiors for two weeks, I promise you I'll get a meeting set up with Chief Elk Horn."

"I'll insist that you be present with the one official of the government who will make the decision on a peace agreement. I'll lead you and the government official to the site of the meeting and will guarantee your safety. I also insist that I sit in on the meeting, and I'll express my opinion."

"Razor, I'll do what I can, but remember, if I can't pull this off, I must try to take Wolf Pack into custody."

"Colonel, Wolf Pack is a free man. He may leave my custody anytime he wishes. Using Wolf Pack as a bargaining chip is a bad idea. The government wants peace with the Mescalero Apache. What better place could they start than a face-to-face meeting with their chief?"

"I agree with you, Razor. I don't see how a meeting with Elk Horn could be turned down. Go ahead and set it up. If I'm ordered to take Wolf Pack into custody, I'll search for him in the wrong direction."

A week after Wolf Pack had been injured, he had recovered enough that he could travel on a travois. The day before, Razor had sent a messenger to Mr. Stew with a letter that he was to deliver to Colonel Stubblefield in one week. The letter stated the meeting was set for six days from when he received it and that Mr. Stew would lead them to the secure location.

As ordered, Walks cut out eighteen Razor-branded mustangs. He gave the mustangs to Wolf Pack for the braves who were killed. Two of the horses were used for packhorses, and one was used to pull the travois. Walks, Finder, Razor, and three of the Apache herded the horses, and one Apache pulled the travois with Wolf Pack aboard. It was sixty miles to the Apache campsite. Pulling the travois turned the two-day trip into three. Other Apache were encountered during the second day. Some had raced ahead to tell Chief Elk Horn the good news.

Razor had spent hours before and during the trip talking to Wolf Pack about his plan for a meeting. Wolf Pack pledged his support. Elk Horn was told, by the braves that were sent back by Wolf Pack, of Razor Sharp's ability to speak the Apache language. He also knew Razor had helped Wolf Pack with his dislocated hip and freed his braves to return to the tribe.

With Wolf Pack's support and Elk Horn's perceived trust in Sharp, an agreement for the meeting was made. The gift of the eighteen mustangs didn't hurt. Razor Sharp guaranteed Elk Horn's safety. The meeting would take place in four days at Sharp's home. Elk Horn could have all his braves escort him as far as the Rio Felix. Then Razor, Walks, Finder, and four braves that Elk Horn would select would be at his side to and from the meeting.

The meeting was a total success, including the land purchase. All of Razor's guidelines were accepted. Elk Horn surprised Razor, Colonel Stubblefield, and the government delegate when he stated that he would forbid any of his braves from joining Geronimo.

"I have lost too many members of my tribe."

Now, Razor thought, *I must concentrate on finding and killing Ralph Marlow!*

Chapter 24

Santa Fe, New Mexico Territory

Word spread over the southwestern states and territories about Razor Sharp being instrumental in bringing peace in the New Mexico Territory with the Mescalero Apache Indians. Everyone wanted to know Razor Sharp.

Shortly after the peace agreement, Sharp received a message from Colonel Stubblefield wanting him to stop by the next time he was in Mesilla. Two days later, Razor called on the colonel.

"Razor, would you tell me all you know about the Pala Duro Canyon south of the panhandle of Texas," asked the colonel.

"Colonel, I've never seen it, but I have read about it. It's in the open plains south of the panhandle. There is not a mountain or a hill within a hundred miles. It's 120 miles long, 20 miles wide, and 800 feet deep. Why do you ask?"

"Callaway's horse and carriage were run off the prairie into the canyon. His body was found at the bottom by an Army patrol. They don't know if he accidentally drove it off the edge, intended to drive it off, or was forced off by someone."

"It has been rumored that Quanah Parker frequented the Palo Duro Canyon with his Comanche warriors for years," explained Sharp. "He used it as a resting place. The Comanches could have found him on the prairie and easily driven him off."

"Razor, I have a letter and death certificate here on Callaway, signed by a Captain Phillip Masters. It says they buried him where he lay. There are directions as to where the grave is, but Captain Masters strongly advises not trying to move him. I know you're a friend of his daughter. Would you mind delivering this to his wife and daughter and let them know what has happened to him?"

"His daughter is a loyal friend of mine," said Sharp. "I have other business I need to discuss with her mother and will deliver this news to them. Thank you for thinking of me to deliver this message. I am the one who should do it. Bonnie Lou is the first friend I ever had."

After leaving the fort, Razor went to Mesilla and contacted Mr. Stew at the freight yard.

"Have you contacted Mrs. Callaway?"

"No! I've sent her a telegram and asked the telegraph office to try to locate her. They were going to let me know when they did."

"Raiman Callaway is dead," said Sharp. "He was found at the bottom of the Palo Duro Canyon several days ago. I'll soon be leaving for Santa Fe to find Bonnie Lou and her mother."

Other things kept interfering with Razor's promise to himself to find and kill Ralph Marlow. He knew how important it was. He was now again putting it off. This procrastination could be deadly and not in his favor.

When Razor returned home, he instructed Calhoun to get together with Mr. Stew and start hiring a crew to dig all the holes and set the poles for the telegraph line. He told Calhoun if they needed money for wages or supplies to get it from Miss Scott.

"Walks, Finder, Enrique, Roberto, and I'll be gone for fifteen to twenty days. If you need me, get in touch with Miss Scott, and she can find me in less than a week. I'll also stay in contact with the telegraph office in Santa Fe, and you could leave me a message there."

Early the next morning, Sharp and his four companions left with two packhorses, two extra horses, and Sweet Pea prancing at Razor's side. Walks led the way, running with his horse close behind. It pleased Razor to see that Walks branded his horse with the Razor brand.

They would spend the night with the Apache at their camp in their new reservation. By noon the next day, they saw several Mescalero Apache smiling and waving while on their way to visit Wolf Pack and Elk Horn. They were pleased to see Wolf Pack recovering from his wounds and Elk Horn so relaxed.

"Peace is a wonderful thing. Thank you, Razor Sharp," said Elk Horn.

They left the camp at first light and cut through the valley separating the Capitan and Sacramento Mountain ranges. They hit the wagon road next to the great white sand dunes then turned north and headed to Santa Fe. They arrived the sixth day after leaving home.

Santa Fe was a bustling place. There were a lot of well-dressed people. This enticed Razor to seek out a haberdasher and get a new suit. It had been some time sense he had seen Bonnie Lou, and he wanted to look nice and clean for her. He wouldn't want her to be embarrassed being seen with him.

They turned into the first public stable and rousted out the hostler. They all jumped in and unsaddled the packhorses, saddles, and gear. The hostler helped them stow their belongings in the tack room, and they all returned to the horses, washed and brushed them down, then put them in separate stalls. Sweet Pea was put in a stall next to the tack room.

It was natural for any hostler to look at the brand on horses. It was also natural that they never say or ask anything about the brand to the rider. The regal look of the horses held the hostler's attention more than anything else. It was hard for him to take his eyes off them. The hostler had never seen the Razor brand before but had heard of the owner of the brand, Razor Sharp.

When he recognized the brand, he immediately picked Sharp out of the five. All of them were dirty with travel grime. His men showed respect toward Razor. He stood erect and would look you straight in the eye, as if he was genuinely interested in what you were saying.

"Mr. Sharp, if there is anything I can do for you, let me know," asked the hostler.

Razor smiled and was pleased that the hostler figured out who he was. "That's kind of you, sir. There are a few things you can help me with. Make sure the horses get plenty of oats tonight and turn them into the corral first thing in the morning. I'll pay extra for the horses to be in a corral with just them in it. They are familiar and protective of each other and especially the small mare."

"I'll do that!"

"We will be here a few days, and I want to pay you some of the money in advance. Look me up at the hotel across the street when you need more. Don't skimp on the oats and keep a special eye out for my Sweet Pea."

"I heard you call her that. I'll make her my buddy."

The men looked no different from any other group of cowboys that had been on the trail for six days, but they were different. Their near purebred horses looked better than any others in the territory. Everyone who saw the group knew that there was something special about each of them and not just Sharp. These were proud men. They were proud of the brand they rode for and proud of Razor Sharp.

Razor was a little disappointed that there were no messages for him at the Western Union office. He decided to take his men to buy clothes before they checked in to the hotel.

Razor bought a new black low-crown hat that he could hardly wait to wear. After they all bathed and changed into clean clothes, they walked to the large square in the middle of town. A large circular path downtown was the site of the nightly "*paseo,*" a Spanish custom practiced in countries with Spanish influence. Everyone—young people, older people, families, even little children—took pleasure in their nightly walk around the square on the promenade and simply enjoyed each other's company. It was fun to watch, but first the men wanted to eat a nice meal.

There were several restaurants to choose from. They settled on one that had several young goats cooking over hot coals in the open air outside the entrance. The carcass of each was rubbed with salt, garlic, and red peppers. They ordered two. Pieces of the *cabrito* could be pulled from the bone with ease. It was excellent.

Razor looked dashing in his low-crowned hat and the colorful bandanna around his neck. The rope burns were still visible but would have been much worse if Finder had not doctored them with the juice of the *Opuntia* cactus. The colorful bandanna covered the rope burn and always gave a flare to what he was wearing. The low-crowned hat fit right in.

Razor thought of Bonnie Lou often. Of late, knowing he would be seeing her soon, he had been thinking of her more and more and was looking forward to seeing his best friend.

Razor had not joined his men as they strolled along the storefronts. He crossed the street and stood several yards off the path that circled inside the square and watched the promenade. The girls walked in one direction, and the boys walked in the opposite direction. After several times around the circle, and with flirtations of each in passing, the moment they came for arrived. They stepped off the walkway and had conversations under the watchful eyes of their parents, elders, and friends.

Razor got caught up in their happiness. This was the first time in months that he had relaxed. He had never been in love but had read of this custom that occurred around much of the world. The only girl that he had ever thought about was Bonnie Lou. He ignored the many smiles he received from the girls on the path.

He showed apathy to each but could not prevent his heart from beating faster when he saw one of the girls who gave him a nice smile. She had olive skin and the beauty and grace of a true Spaniard. Another young lady made his heart beat fast but not as fast as it did when the previous girl had smiled at him. Why would one catch his interest more than the other and some not at all? He had never experienced this before. He liked the feeling but didn't know what to do about it. He rejoined his men and returned to the hotel.

The hostler wasted no time telling everyone he knew that Razor Sharp was in town. He invited them to stop by to see the horses he was boarding for him.

The hostler pointed out the young mare and took pride in telling everyone her name. "These are the finest horses I've ever seen," the hostler boasted.

The ones he told gathered other friends to go by for a look. By eight o'clock in the morning, at least a hundred people had stopped by to look at the horses and hopefully get a glimpse of Razor Sharp and his young mare, Sweet Pea. The news of Razor Sharp being in town spread fast.

People who usually stayed inside most of the day came out into the street, trying to get a glimpse of the man who brought peace to most of southeast New Mexico with the Apache. They knew he had also saved the bank in Mesilla and sold the Army over five hundred horses, with his Razor brand on each, for five dollars less than the Army offered.

As Razor and his crew were finishing breakfast, two well-dressed gentlemen approached their table. They introduced themselves as staff members of New Mexico's Territorial Governor, Alfred Hays. "The governor would like to have a meeting with you before you leave town," one of them said.

"Tell the governor that I have some personal business to take care of first. Then I'll look forward to meeting with him. I do not know how long the business will take, but I'll contact him as soon as possible. Please give him my kindest regards."

Bonnie Lou had thought of her friend Razor Sharp often. Her thoughts had never developed into words in the past because of her parent's feelings toward him. As soon as she heard about Razor being in Santa Fe, all that changed.

"Mother, I want to talk to you about Razor Sharp."

"Bonnie Lou, you are forbidden to ever mention that name to me again. He is a murderer."

"Mother, there is no proof of that. Everyone has a right to defend himself. If you don't want to listen to me, I'll make this short and to the point. Razor Sharp is in Santa Fe, and I am going to find him. He is a dear friend who you and father have treated terribly."

"Bonnie Lou, I forbid you to do that!"

"Forbid all you want, I'm going."

Bonnie Lou was only a short distance from the square. She would start there. She spotted a large crowd of onlookers milling around the entrance of a restaurant. She approached the crowd and stopped when she saw them moving out of the way to let someone through. It wasn't Razor. This guy was much taller, darker, and…and "Razor Sharp!" she screamed.

Razor turned to see Bonnie Lou rush toward him and leap into his outstretched arms. The crowd came alive with applause. Razor ducked into the city marshal's office, taking Bonnie Lou with him. After introducing himself to the deputy, he explained that he needed a quiet and respectable place to talk with Miss Callaway.

"I can let you have a jail cell reserved for women only. We don't have anyone in it now. If you leave my door open, it should be fine."

Razor looked at Bonnie Lou as she nodded her head. "That will work for us," Razor said.

Bonnie Lou brought Razor up to date on everything concerning her life, including her mother forbidding her to look for him that day. Razor did the same concerning his life except for the near-death beating he had received from her father and Ralph Marlow.

"Bonnie Lou, I have cherished your friendship. I am here to help you and your mother. Would you take me to her? I have something I must share with you, and your mother must be present."

"Razor, I don't think mother would ever meet with you."

"Do you think she would recognize me?"

"No! That's a great idea."

"Bonnie Lou, take me to her, and I'll do all the talking."

When they arrived at the front door, Razor asked that Bonnie Lou be strong about what he had to tell them. She responded by reaching over and squeezing his arm.

"Mother, there is a gentleman here who says he must see you." She stepped back and let Razor walk in.

"Mrs. Callaway, I have been sent here by Colonel Stubblefield of the United States Army. I have some bad news for you both. I have in my hand a death certificate for Mr. Raiman Callaway."

"Did Razor Sharp kill him?" Mrs. Callaway screamed.

"No! Sharp had reasons to kill him but refrained from doing so because of his friendship with your daughter."

Bonnie Lou sobbed, and Mrs. Callaway comforted her.

Razor told them circumstances of the Army finding the body. "The Army's recommendation is that the body is not removed because of the danger of a Comanche attack and the dangers of getting in and out of the canyon itself."

Razor's heart went out to Bonnie Lou. He understood the difficulty she had with her father, but her sadness about his death was understandable.

"Mrs. Callaway, this may not be the right time for me to bring this up, but Razor Sharp wants you to know what I am about to tell you. Sharp is a very wealthy person and is a dear friend of your daughter. He has authorized me to make an offer to you and her."

"Keep in mind that he can buy or build freight wagons and has hundreds of horses. He will buy all the wagons, horses, freight yard and the home in Mesilla that you and Bonnie Lou have and will pay you and Bonnie Lou twice what they are worth. A railroad is being built, as I speak, from Santa Fe to El Paso. The long-haul wagon freight business will soon be over. If you both want to take him up on his offer, he will pay you while he is still in town."

"He can't buy my daughter's love."

"He has her friendship. Love has nothing to do with it. He wants to help her. If you don't want his money, he can give it all to her, and she can help you if she wishes."

"Would you take me to see Razor?" Bonnie Lou asked.

Before Razor could answer, Mrs. Callaway said, "I'll take his offer."

"I'll pass that on to him. Do you agree also, Bonnie Lou?"

"Yes!" she answered.

"He will be in touch with you this afternoon, and yes, Bonnie Lou, I'll take you to him."

When walking away, Razor told Bonnie Lou how sorry he was over the loss of her father.

"Razor, it was not necessary for you to offer me and my mother twice what everything was worth. She has plenty of money. It was mother's money that my father spent for everything. I think it was the reason he was so tight with the money. Mother was always putting pressure on him to make more."

"Bonnie Lou, I'm going to pay you and your mother separately. Your half will be yours and yours alone. I have calculated the value and will set up an account in your name and deposit the money for you only. I'll give you the deposit slip this afternoon. I need nothing from you but your address. From your mother, I'll need a bill of sale for the equipment and horses and deeds for the land, house, and freight yard."

"I've missed all the conversations we had when we were in school together. Hopefully we will have time someday to continue them," Razor said.

Mrs. Callaway was instructed to be at the Cattlemen's Trust Bank with Bonnie Lou at 3:00 p.m.

"Now, Mrs. Callaway, if you will sign this bill of sale and the deeds, I have $20,000 cash for you and a $20,000 deposit slip for Bonnie Lou's account here in this bank."

"Sir, I'm supposed to get all the money. I'm Bonnie Lou's mother!"

"Mrs. Callaway, you are not getting Bonnie Lou's half. If you don't want the $20,000 for your property, Bonnie Lou can keep hers, and we will forget about buying your property."

"But you said you would pay me twice what it was worth."

"You are mistaken. You were told that you and Bonnie Lou would be receiving twice what it was worth. Sharp has accomplished what he wanted to accomplish and that was to take care of his dear friend. He does not need your property." Razor rose from his chair to leave.

"I'll sign. Give me the money."

The banker witnessed the transaction and said, "I thank you, Mr. Sharp, for your business."

Mrs. Callaway was so shaken and angry about having Sharp's identity kept from her that she could not rise from her chair.

Razor contacted the governor's office and set up a meeting with the governor for the next day. He stopped by the stable and played with Sweet Pea for a while. He truly loved that horse. The thought came to him that there were very few things that he loved. He loved his mother and father, his friendship with Bonnie Lou, and his books. Everything else he just liked or appreciated. He liked his friends and appreciated beautiful sunsets. Things like that.

Razor found his crew, and they ate at a different restaurant on the square. The square was always a festive site. Many ate at tables in front of the café. Mariachi bands would stroll by, stop, and play their songs for tips. The number of excited sightseers wanting to see Razor Sharp had waned during the day.

Razor again elected to watch the promenade, while the rest of the crew wandered around seeing the sights. This time it was known who he was. Now they all smiled. His heart raced even faster when he recognized the two girls who had made his heart race the night before. He decided he had better leave before he embarrassed himself. The first girls who made his heart race the day before left the walkway and headed toward him, then another did the same.

In broken English, one of them asked his name. In perfect Spanish, words rolled out of Razor's mouth with all the grace and refinement of a true Spaniard. She smiled even more broadly. The second girl entered the conversation, and others swarmed in to listen. The promenade had all but stopped. He offered apologies for interfering with their promenade and explained that he enjoyed watching. He insisted he would leave if they didn't continue.

Everyone but the two who left the walk first moved back into the leisurely walking. Razor asked them many questions about themselves. When he finally left their company, his heart was still beating fast. It beat just a little faster when the first girl smiled at him or asked him a question. *That's odd,* he thought. *I must figure this out before I get myself in trouble.*

He met with the governor the next day. The governor gave him a warm welcome and talked to him about the peace treaty with the Mescalero Apache. He questioned Razor about his assurance that the peace agreement would last.

"Governor, the peace treaty will last as long as we keep the white man out of their reservation. My vaqueros and guards are loyal to our brand. We will block any encroachment from the south and east. The great gypsum sand dunes are a natural deterrent from the west. The Army has agreed to protect them from the north. Elk Horn and Wolf Pack want peace. Geronimo knows he is no longer welcome on the Mescalero reservation for recruiting purposes and will have no reason to come to their reservation."

"Mr. Sharp, if we have peace with the Apache for six months, I want to give you a celebration party here in Santa Fe. You deserve recognition for a job well done. Saving the bank in Mesilla was also greatly appreciated."

"May I send you a list of people I would like invited?" Razor asked, with complete confidence that the agreement would work out.

"Of course!"

"That will be two weeks before Christmas. I'll stay and celebrate Christmas in Santa Fe," Razor added. As he was leaving the capitol building, he stopped in his tracks. At about a hundred feet away and down a long hallway stood the most beautiful girl he had ever seen. She was dressed fashionably, giving the aura that she was someone important. She was with a boy who looked to be her age and an older man. All of a sudden, she turned her head and their eyes met. She had a slight smile on her face before she had made eye contact with him. She held the eye contact for a second then turned away with the same slight smile still on her face. Razor stood and watched her walk away with her friends.

His thoughts went back to the promenade and his heart racing over the two girls who talked with him. That was child's play compared to this. What had just happened to him was like being hit by a lightning bolt.

He had to talk to her. Where had she gone? He looked everywhere. *She did look me straight in the eye and smiled. Did I make her smile? What made her turn and look at me? Okay! She already had the slight smile on her face, but I could have caused it.* Razor knocked on several doors and asked about the three to no avail. He questioned his sanity. *Did this really happen?* He rushed out of the Territorial capitol building and looked everywhere. He looked over the town for the rest of the day. It must have been his imagination.

Razor checked on Bonnie Lou before leaving Santa Fe. Her mother was angry about the whole thing. She showed little remorse about her husband's death. She hated losing control of Bonnie Lou. She had not changed her mind about Sharp. Bonnie Lou was sad about the death of her father but was proud that she had stood up to her mother concerning her best friend, Razor Sharp.

Razor had told her about the telegraph line he was putting in at the ranch. She promised to telegraph him at least once a week after it was up and working.

He and the crew left early the next day for home. His eyes continued to look for the bolt of lightning that had struck him.

Chapter 25

Mustang, New Mexico Territory

They had spent the last night of their return trip to Mustang in the Apache camp of Elk Horn. Wolf Pack's leg was mending, but it would take a long time before he would be able to walk. He made Razor promise to come to him at least once a month until he could ride again. He wanted to know more about the white man's customs.

Construction of the town had gone well while he was gone. Mustang, New Mexico Territory, had been surveyed with stakes set and plats made. Razor planned a party and asked Huevo Duro to plan the menu, and, with some extra help, he would cook for a hundred fifty people. Sharp held a meeting with all his employees two weeks before the party. He described the type of town he wanted.

He wanted his employees to move their family members to Mustang. He hoped that they would come to see it as home, marry and have children there. If any of them wanted to run a store, he would give them the property and loan them money to operate and charge them a very low interest rate. During a special meeting of residents, he passed out plats of the lots in the town. A church and schoolhouse lot were marked, and one lot had been claimed by Razor Sharp's Depositors Savings and Loan Bank of Mustang, New Mexico Territory. The lot across the street was for a jailhouse and city marshal's office. The plat was marked with the kind of stores that would be built. For fire safety, the lots were large, and no store could be built closer than fifty feet to one another.

Timber for construction of stores would be free to the employees, but only marked trees could be cut. A sawmill site consisting of fifty acres was located five miles out on the prairie. No lumber from this mill would be shipped anywhere but the Mustang area. In addition, strict fire rules would be enforced.

The employees would have first choice on the lots. If an employee didn't want to own a store but didn't want to live in the bunkhouse, they could select a lot marked resident and build a home there. The lot and timber would be free also, and Razor would loan the money to build the house free of interest if they continued to work for the Razor brand.

"Next weekend, Miss Scott from Razor Sharp's Depositors Savings and Loan Bank of Mesilla will be here to help you with your loans." He would have Jacob Walters escort her in.

"We will have some outsiders here looking around. Some will be troublemakers. The citizens of Mustang will need someone with authority and ability to handle any situation that could occur. I want to nominate Jacob Walters as Mustang's town marshal. All of you know Jacob and know he will be fair with everyone and will do a great job. All in favor, say 'Yes.'" Not a single voice said no.

The hardware store was the first store claimed. Then the stable, restaurant, hotel, blacksmith, grocery, laundry, and clothing.

It had been a long day, but he called Jacob aside and shared his thoughts. “Jacob, a new town attracts a lot of men who come for no other reason than to test the strength of the town. Some will test it until resistance is shown then move on. If no resistance is shown, the town will spin out of control when word gets out that a person can do anything he wants to do there. The town fills up with riffraff until the good people leave. The Roman Empire existed by brute force. This force was accomplished by numbers of combatants. I don’t want to conquer neighbors as the Romans did. I envision Mustang as being a town that’s fair and welcomes everyone but has enough brute force to resist those who want to test the strength of the town.”

“Razor, we’re on the same page. I too have thought of this,” said Walters. “We have the people in place, and I’ll have a plan to handle any situation that needs handling, with brute force if necessary.”

“I knew you would. I just wanted you to know I agree with you and will support you.”

“Thanks, Razor,” Jacob said.

Always in the back of Razor’s mind was that lightning bolt connection he had made with that pretty young woman in the courthouse hallway. He wanted to claim her as his wife. Somehow, he knew she was the one.

He should be happy with all the progress going on around him, but he wasn’t, at least not completely. He blamed himself for not having found the young woman, and there was still Marlow to take care of.

By the time the party started, every lot had been claimed by an employee. Jacob claimed the highest residential lot on the west side, looking down on Mustang.

Razor took Miss Scott, with Jacob accompanying them, to his home to show her his mother's books. Thrilled, she asked Razor, on the spot, if she could move to Mustang and run the bank there. She wanted to be close to the books so she could read them all. She said that Joe Brine would do an excellent job as manager of the Mesilla bank, and she would have time to hire and train an assistant while her bank was being built in Mustang.

"Joe would not need as much protection as Miss Scott, and she would be safer in Mustang anyway," Jacob pointed out.

Razor wanted to keep her happy and agreed. He was smiling inwardly. He was happy that Miss Scott wanted to be close to his mother's books. With a slight smile on his face a thought came to him. He was sure being close to Jacob never entered her mind.

Razor had a plan for the sawmill. He made a fast trip, with Walks and Finder, to see Elk Horn and Wolf Pack. They sold them on the idea that the Apache could work at the sawmill and be paid with gold. They could buy food, clothes, hardware, and lumber in Mustang. There would be a millwright, but they would work under the supervision of Walks or Finder. A millwright was found and hired. Construction of the sawmill would start immediately.

Some of the vaqueros brought their families all the way from the Villa de Jonas for the party. Most of them stayed on afterward, planning to make Mustang their new home.

Razor met with Mr. Stew and wagon master Calhoun. A decision was made to immediately leave with twenty wagons and go to Rio Casas Grandes and load up granite stones from the many fallen walls. They would salvage all the wooden doors and windows that were available. They were to make sure they loaded up the purple *Opuntia* cacti that they would transplant around Mustang for future use.

Not only would the teamsters go, but most of the vaqueros and half the guards. They would return with the last roundup of mustangs. The granite stones would be used to build the bank and jail. Razor gave the warning, "Watch out for the rattlesnakes. I don't want to lose any of you to snake bite!"

Razor's mind was always on the lightning bolt that had struck him. He knew he was in love. He knew he would be able to do much more with his life if she were with him. He would look for her when the governor gave him his appreciation reception in Santa Fe.

Razor also had Ralph Marlow on his mind. Killing his henchmen had slowed Marlow down, but killing his son, Buster, had to have poured coal oil on the fire. Sharp had given much thought to why Marlow had not had someone attack him by now, and he decided that Marlow could be healing from the many wounds he had inflicted on him. Marlow might have had time to heal enough to try for revenge. He would keep his eyes open.

Chapter 26

White-Faced Cattle

Stew's search for a thousand head of white-face heifers led him to the Rocking C Ranch near Abilene, Texas. He had contacted the ranch foreman, Rocky Lane. They were starting a roundup in a week and would be thinning their herd. He invited Razor down for a look. Rocky planned for Razor, Enrique, and Roberto to board the train in El Paso. They were to get off in Lorain. The men would be met by Rocky.

They left their horses in the public stable near the train station, then boarded the train. Razor sat in a window seat on the terminal side looking forward. The train jerked forward and started moving east. Razor was thinking of the lightning bolt that had entered his life. When the train was pulling out of the station, a young man, a young woman, and an older man were walking toward him on the train platform. The girl had a pleasant smile on her face and turned and looked toward Razor. She looked away, then her head snapped around and she looked directly at Razor as the train sped out of the terminal.

It's him! she thought. *What are the odds of this happening?* She turned and raced back down the platform, chasing the train as it pulled out of sight. She put her hands to her face and cried. *I know it's him, I know he is the one,* she thought. She turned to the older man and said, "Luke, I don't know where you should start, but I want you to find out who he is."

After she told him of the two sightings, Luke spoke, "Amanda Gale, that's a lot of territory to cover, and me never having seen him will make it more difficult."

"I know you can do it, Luke. You can do anything," Amanda Gale said.

Her twin brother, Paul, spoke up, laughing, "Amanda Gale, do you want Luke to shoot him, throw him in jail, or bring him to you?"

"No, Paul! I want Luke to find him, I'll handle the rest."

Razor also did a double take. When he turned back to look again, he saw her looking at him. He thought of jumping off the train, but as fast as the train would be going when he got back to the door, he could break his neck.

If he did jump off and wasn't injured or killed, the time it would take to get back to the terminal, she would probably be gone. His heart was racing. He asked himself, *What were the odds of this happening? I know she had seen me, and I know she knows I saw her. I must find her. We both know we are meant for each other.*

All of Razor's thoughts were centered on how fast he could get back to El Paso. When they arrived in Lorain, Rocky was waiting with three strong-looking horses. In Razor's, Enrique's, and Roberto's minds, was the thought, *They are not as good as our mustangs.*

Razor asked about the train schedule going back to El Paso.

Rocky told him of the every-other-day schedule.

"I must return on the first train back," said Razor.

"We can ride a mile up the track and leave our signal for the train to stop here in Lorain," said Rocky.

On the way to the ranch, Rocky talked about the Rocking C and the white-face cattle. They started the herd seventeen years ago. They had been so successful they bought an additional fifty thousand acres and added it to the ranch. They had sold off all the cattle that were not of the white-face breed.

Razor told Rocky about his mustangs and of his plan for them. It was common knowledge that most mustangs had superior bloodlines compared to everything else commonly marketed. The purification of the bloodline would make them even more desirable.

After a good night's sleep and a big breakfast, the two men went to the range to watch the roundup. Each had a lariat on his saddle. There was an abundance of unbranded mavericks. After watching a few minutes, Razor's lariat snaked out and grabbed a heifer. She looked to be a full year old and unbranded.

"Do you have a thousand of these you would sell?"

"Sure do," Rocky replied.

"How much?" Razor asked.

"Thirty dollars"

"You brand with my brand?"

"If you have the irons."

"I have the irons."

"Would you drive them to me for thirty-five?"

"No! But I'll brand them, water and feed them before putting them on a train and deliver them to El Paso for the thirty dollars," Rocky said.

"Rocky, how many bulls do you think I'll need to start with?" Razor asked.

"A mature bull should be able to service twenty-five to thirty-five heifers."

"I think I'll go for forty bulls. I want to make sure all the heifers get serviced this first year. Do you have that many to spare that were not born in your herd?"

"I'm sure I do. They will have a foreign brand with the Rocking C brand two inches above. We can put your brand two inches above the Rocking C."

"At what price?

"I'll sell you the mature bulls for sixty dollars each."

"We have a deal," Razor said. "I want you to ship the bulls four days after the cattle. It will make for a smoother drive if we don't have the bulls mixed in the herd to mess with."

"How long will it take you to cut out and brand a thousand head?" asked Razor.

"We should have them ready to ship in about three weeks. We will water and feed them in Lorain before we load them. They will be in El Paso within ten hours or less after loading."

Razor, Roberto, and Enrique unrolled their bedrolls and handed the three sets of branding irons to Rocky.

"Where do you want the money sent?" asked Razor.

"Ranchers Preferred Bank of San Angelo. Assign it to the account of the Rocking C Ranch."

"I'll leave Roberto and Enrique here to help you with the roundup if you want. Just feed them."

"I sure need them. I'll feed them at least once a day." Rocky laughed.

"That will be plenty, that's more than I feed them some days," said a grinning Razor. "I'll plan to be back here in eighteen days to check on the progress and will fund your account when I return. Could you arrange to have the train stop in Lorain and have a horse there for me?"

"Sure," said Rocky.

"I'll have grub with you, and then I'll be drifting back to Lorain to wait for the train tomorrow morning. I've got some thinking to do, and this will give me plenty of time to do it," said Razor.

Razor could not get back to El Paso fast enough. He would look there for his lightning bolt. When he arrived, he had no idea where he should start looking. He had only been gone two days and was in wonderment of the activity in the city. *Where did all these people come from*?

Razor soon realized that the railroad construction from Santa Fe to El Paso had just now reached El Paso. The roadbed had been made and cross ties laid. At a distance, he saw hundreds of men carrying rails from flat cars. The rails were laid on the ties and spiked to the ties as soon as they were set. Razor watched the rhythm of the workers as the train neared. Like magic, in less than twenty minutes, the track was tied into the line that would take you to Dallas. A celebration occurred at that moment. Razor had no time for this; he had to search for his lightning bolt.

Amanda Gale enjoyed celebrating with her family after the last spike was driven, and the line was connected to the existing line in El Paso. She still had the slight smile on her face but was a little sad that he was not there to help celebrate. She had to find her young man.

Razor stayed two nights in El Paso before he gave up his search and decided to go to Juarez and have a good meal. Razor could think of nothing but his lightning bolt, which was dangerous. He should never forget the danger that could be nearby until Ralph Marlow was killed. He needed to hunt down that slithering snake.

Razor had ordered his food and sat alone against a wall, pensive and quiet. He was jarred back to his senses when he heard the name Marlow. His brain kicked in, and his hand moved toward his gun. He looked everywhere he could without turning his head. After a moment, Razor shifted his chair to be able to see everyone in the room. Ralph Marlow was not present.

He concentrated on the conversations around him. There was an argument going on about an offer to ride with Marlow and hunt down and kill Razor Sharp.

The argument was getting louder. Razor held his head steady, looking from under his hat. Two were saying it would not be worth it because Sharp had too many friends in Mexico, and there would be retaliations for the killing. They also pointed out that Marlow was a crook and might not pay. One said that Marlow would be crazy to have Sharp killed in Mexico. If he did, the Mexican federales would kill or drive him out of Mexico, then Marlow would have no place to go. If he kills him in the States, he can flee back into Mexico. Everyone agreed that Marlow would try to kill Razor on the north side of the border.

Razor ate when his food arrived but casually kept his hand near his gun. His eyes were on everyone, and his ears hung on every word. "Marlow could not pay me enough to even think of killing Sharp. He is a good hombre," said one. They all seemed to agree.

Razor finished his meal. He realized how careless he had been thinking about the girl instead of Marlow. He had given Marlow a beating, killed most of his henchmen, scared him out of Mesilla, and killed his son. Razor knew Marlow being on the run for bank robbery would not diminish his hatred toward him or his capacity to do him harm.

He had put much thought into what he was going to do. He left money on the table to pay for his food. Razor stood with his back to the wall. His left hand raised and touched the rope burn, and his right hand was lowered and rested on his gun. In a calm voice and in border Spanish, Razor spoke. "I could not help but hear your conversation concerning Ralph Marlow and Razor Sharp."

Everyone turned and looked in the eyes of a dominant, strong man.

"I think you are wise to not get involved with Ralph Marlow. I know Marlow and Razor Sharp. Sharp taught me Spanish. He has taught English to anyone who wanted to learn at no cost to them. Many came from Mexico to learn. He has given horses to his Mexican friends in Mesilla. At the age of fifteen, Sharp was dragged into the desert by Marlow and his friend Raiman Callaway, and while Razor was tied up, they beat him until he lost consciousness. They left him there tied up to die."

"Sharp will not be an easy man to kill. He has many friends such as I who would give their lives for his safety." Razor rested his hand on the handle of his gun and calmly said, "How many friends does Ralph Marlow have who would do the same?" No one in the room moved or said a word.

"Just as I thought. If you associate with Ralph Marlow, you never know when one of Sharp's friends may be near, and it could easily cost you your life. You are all wise men. Do not do anything foolish. Tell your friends what I've said. There are others in this room who feel the same as I do. Think about it."

Razor turned his back on everyone and eased out the door. He had not heard a sound come from the cantina. Razor rode out of Juarez and headed for Mesilla and his favorite bed.

Back in Mesilla, Razor received a pleasant surprise from Miss Scott. She and Jacob were going to marry.

"That devil beat me to it." Razor laughed.

"You know, Razor, if you had asked me, I would have said 'yes,'" laughed Miss Scott. "Jacob and I'll just have to adopt you," she said.

"You have already done that," Razor said.

Razor returned to Mustang. He was very disappointed in not finding his lightning bolt. He felt he would be safe thinking of her while he was in Mustang but not so in El Paso.

Razor made a visit to the X each day for fourteen days. He was careful to use a different route each time. He put the gold in the chest under the floor, filling it to the top. There were still nuggets attached to the roots and lying on the ground, well hidden from above. There was an abundance of gold still attached to the main veins that were free of quartz and an untold amount encased within the soft limestone, sandstone, and hard quartz.

Chapter 27

Whoa! Watch Out!

The wagons returned to Mustang with the *Opuntia* cactus, stones, doors and windows. Six hundred mustangs had been left at Fort Fillmore, and six hundred had been dropped off in the Sacramento Mountains. Forty more special horses were put in their corral next to the ranch house. Five hundred of the six hundred mustangs that were left in the Sacramento Mountains were less than a year old. Twenty single women, forty children, several wives, and other family members of the vaqueros were brought to Mustang with the caravan from Rio Casas Grande and Villa de Jonas. The guards and teamsters also started moving their family members to the promising new location.

Razor had Mr. Stew recruit a personal cook for him out of the bunch. He also asked him to deliver two wagonloads of coal to his blacksmith shop as soon as it was finished.

The surveyor added one hundred more residential lots as requested by Razor. Construction started on the blacksmith shop, the jailhouse, and the bank. Razor informed Mr. Stew that he wanted a telegraph terminal in the bank as well as his home.

Razor decided to return to El Paso a day before catching the train back to Lorain in hopes of seeing the young lady of his dreams. He would keep an eye out for Marlow and her.

He knew she was the one for him, and he knew that she felt the same. Why else would she smile at him and look at him straight in the eye? Well, she really didn't actually smile at him. She already had a slight smile on her face both times he saw her. She might have looked at him because he looked at her. Still, he must find her.

Razor left his horse in the public stable near the train station. He was disappointed as he boarded the train to Lorain. He would again sit in a window seat on the terminal side facing forward in hopes he might see her again on the platform. Razor had already decided if he did see her, he would jump off the train regardless of whether he broke his leg or whatever. As the train neared the end of the platform, he was disappointed that he had no reason to jump.

As Razor left the train in Lorain, he saw a horse with a Rocking C brand in the corral. He saddled up, tied his bedroll on, and departed for the ranch.

The roundup was going well. Roberto and Enrique were glad to see him and told Razor how impressed they were with the young stock they had been branding.

After the branding started the next morning, Razor hailed Rocky.

"If it is okay with you, I'll ride down to San Angelo and have the money transferred and bring you back the receipt."

"Sounds good to me," Rocky said.

Meanwhile back in Mustang, Jacob was about to be confronted with a situation he had planned for. When the train started running between Santa Fe and El Paso, the Overland Stage Line lost all its freight and passenger business to the railroad. They moved several of their coaches and opened a line from El Paso to Tucumcari. The Line established stops and layovers in Mustang, Roswell, and Fort Sumner. Drummers selling their wares were the most frequent passengers on the new coach lines. Soldiers' wives and gamblers made up the rest.

The Mustang stable became very profitable as the stagecoach line was using the stable for its horses. With the new coach line came a few undesirable passengers. City Marshal Jacob Walters, or one of his deputies, were on to them like stink on manure and sent them on their way. Word got out if you didn't have any business in Mustang, don't go there.

Word reached Jacob over the telegraph, that the Texas Rangers ran ten cattle rustlers that were headed toward Mustang out of El Paso. An informant had told the Rangers that the rustlers thought Mustang, being a new town, would be an easy target. By the time the rustlers arrived, Jacob had thirty seasoned guards, thirty tough teamsters, and twenty vaqueros waiting their arrival.

Jacob had all others evacuated to the foothills to keep them out of harm's way. The ten rustlers rode cautiously into town with no one showing resistance. Jacob stepped out in front of them and held out his arm, signaling them to stop.

"What the hell do you want?" bellowed their leader. All their attention was on Jacob.

"I want you to look around you."

They looked and saw what had silently moved in behind them. Thirty horsemen all wearing a star had their weapons pointed at them. Behind them were thirty teamsters also wearing a star and with their weapons pointed at them. The twenty vaqueros wearing their stars had their lariats in their hands ready to spring into action. All were riding mustangs with the Razor brand.

"Now I want you to drop your weapons or be killed. Don't make the mistake of fumbling your weapons. Be slow and easy about it."

One went for his weapon and was shot out of his saddle. Before he hit the ground, he was lassoed and dragged away. The other nine were lassoed and pulled to the ground. They were hog-tied and all their weapons were removed.

"Have Miss Scott telegraph the Texas Rangers and ask them to come and pick up their rustlers," the marshal said.

Razor was headed to San Angelo to pick up his money. He enjoyed riding alone. He stopped later that afternoon and camped out on the North Concho River, north of San Angelo. He would go to sleep thinking of his lightning bolt.

The break of day came, and he was approaching San Angelo. For some reason, he felt that she was somewhere close by. Now he knew he was going crazy. The town was busy with lots of freight wagons and carriages moving about. You had to pay attention what you were doing, or you could get run over.

Razor was between two freight wagons when a third wagon was cutting in on him. It made him look over at the wagon to make sure it didn't run him over, when his eyes darted across the street at a girl on a horse. She was wearing denim jeans and a cowboy hat and a gentle smile on her face.

Razor's heart nearly jumped out of his body. It wasn't from the wagon crowding him but the girl. His lightning bolt could not be here! Why would she be here? If she were here, she wouldn't be in jeans and wearing a cowboy hat. Razor looked back to see if he could catch another glimpse of her. She was gone, and there was no way to get on the other side of the street fast enough to see where she had gone. It wasn't her anyway, but he wished it were. It was just wishful thinking on his part.

The girl's attention was drawn across the street. Her heart nearly jumped out of her body. Not because of the wagon nearly hitting the cowboy, but the cowboy looked like the young man she had seen in the New Mexico capital and in the rail car in El Paso.

Why would he be here? If it were actually him, would he be dressed like an ordinary cowboy? She looked back to see if she could get another glimpse of him, but he was gone, and there was no way for her to get on the other side of the street in time to see where he had gone. It wasn't him anyway, but she wished it were. It was just wishful thinking on her part.

Razor found the telegraph office and sent the telegraph to Miss Scott to transfer the money. He also told her to get in touch with Mr. Stew and for him to have ten vaqueros at the train station in two days to help drive the herd back to the ranch. He waited to get the receipt from the Western Union confirming that the money had been received and transferred to the Ranchers' Preferred Bank and into the Rocking C account.

Razor spent the rest of the day riding around San Angelo, looking at the sights. He drifted south, stopped, and looked at someone's townhouse. The barn was bigger than the house. He didn't know why he had been drawn there, but it was a pleasant feeling. He rode west and hit the Concho River, turned north, hit the main street, and went back east to the hotel. He had a leisurely dinner and retired to his room at the top of the stairs and went to sleep thinking of his lightning bolt. He left early for the ranch and arrived at dark. He gave the receipt to Rocky.

Rocky and Razor talked into the night about ranching, cattle, and horses. Razor told Rocky of their town, Mustang, and invited Rocky to visit him there. Razor told him that he should have a telegraph line at his ranch by the time he returned and would send him a wire giving his location number. "Check with Western Union the next time you are in San Angelo," Razor said.

Cattle cars had been ordered previously, and the herd was moved to the corrals in Lorain. The cattle were rested, fed, and watered. They were packed tight in the cars to prevent them from falling and getting trampled by the others. The train pulled out of Lorain at dark, and ten hours later, they were being unloaded, fed, and watered in El Paso.

Armando and Antonio had led the other eight vaqueros from the ranch and arrived the night before to help in the herding of the cattle. When the train arrived, they rejoiced in telling Razor the story of the rustlers. The Texas Rangers spread the story to all the newspapers in Texas, New Mexico, Colorado, and Arizona. This amount of force would certainly be a deterrent to desperados thinking that Mustang would be an easy target for their misdeeds.

When Razor was getting off the train, the man watching the cattle unload was asking himself, *"Could he be the one?" He could be.* He didn't want to spook him. He had done his research on Sharp. He learned that he was as trustworthy as could be and his word was as good as gold in the bank. Razor rescuing the bank and bringing peace with the Apache was something everyone knew about him. Only a few in the Territory and Southwest knew of Sharp saving his bank manager from being killed by killing her attacker. They also didn't know that Sharp had killed two of the five who had tried to kill him and could have killed them all but spared their lives. Sharp was also silent about Marlowe and Callaway beating him nearly to death and leaving him to die.

These were traits Luke admired, and Amanda Gale would also. She would have to find out these things by herself because he would not tell her, and he was sure that Sharp wouldn't either. He knew now why Amanda Gale was so attracted to him, if he had, indeed, found the one she wanted him to find. If not, she should change her mind and forget about the other guy and get after Razor Sharp.

"Mr. Sharp, my name is Luke Shaw. Rocky Lane told me of you and your herd of mustangs.

"Nice meeting you, Mr. Shaw."

"I've heard a lot of good things about you, Mr. Sharp, and would like to know you better."

"Please call me Razor, Mr. Shaw."

"Razor, I will if you will call me Luke."

"Okay, Luke," said Razor.

Razor knew the man standing in front of him was someone that he too wanted to know better. He wanted to give him all his attention but couldn't resist looking around to see if his lightning bolt or Marlow were nearby.

"How do you know Rocky?" Razor asked.

"I do security work for the Rocking C. Now I'm looking to buy six mustangs for two seventeen-year-old twins and their sixteen-, fifteen-, fourteen-, and thirteen-year-old brothers. I understand you sell mustangs to the Army. For extra money, would you let me buy six of your mustangs and handpick them?"

"I would love for you to handpick them, but I'll not accept extra money for you doing so. I'm proud of my mustangs and want them distributed throughout the southwest. All the mustangs will have only one brand in place when I sell them. I suggest that future brands be placed two inches above the V formed by the open razor brand. I'll sell them for the same price I charge the Army, which is thirty-five dollars."

"When can I see them?"

"We have a three-day drive to my ranch. Would love for you to tag along or you could come up later."

"I want to tag along," Luke said.

Roberto, Enrique, Razor, and Luke had breakfast together, while Armando and Antonio started the herd north. The restaurant was across the street from the railroad terminal. Razor was the first out the door and had stepped to his left to let Luke out to join him.

"Whoa! Watch out!" Razor pushed Luke aside as he reached for his two Colts and fired one. A bullet was on its way to Razor's head as he dove to the ground and was rolling to get up as he fired at the second gunman. He dove behind the horse watering trough. The two gunmen now lay dead. Luke had fired and killed a third that was aiming at Razor. Luke ducked behind a rain barrel. All the firing was being directed at Razor. Luke, being higher than Razor, had a better view of the situation.

He saw three more gunmen. One was at the northwest corner of the terminal, while the other two were behind an outbuilding. Water was spewing from some of the bullet holes shot in the horse trough. The water was stopping some of the bullets, but the water would soon be gone. Razor had to move.

Luke signaled Razor to be ready to run. Luke stood and hollered at the gunmen with both of his Colts belching fire. All three turned their attention toward Luke as Razor rushed toward the gunmen with both Colt .45s blazing, hitting all three. Luke also hit all three. All six of the fallen gunmen were gringos.

Razor noticed a horse at a distance leaving a cloud of dust that was racing toward a low river crossing back into Mexico. It had to be Ralph Marlow. Killing Marlow was going to be put on top of his list of things to do.

"Luke, thanks for your help. I apologize for getting you involved in my problem."

"I want to be your friend, Razor. What are friends for if not to help them in tight places?"

Thoughts raced through Luke's mind. He realized Razor's actions were the same as he had taken throughout his own life. Luke's first thought was that he had to introduce this man to his boss and that this strong man is the one Amanda Gale needed in her life. She would never be happy with anyone who was weak, regardless of how good-looking they were. Amanda Gale was seventeen and had never had a serious courtship. Most men were intimidated by her. He knew Razor would not be intimidated by anyone.

A small crowd started gathering on the street. "Razor! Let me take care of this for us. I know the sheriff and the city marshal here," Luke said. Before Razor could respond, Luke was asking that someone find the sheriff or city marshal.

"What about a doctor?" one asked.

"We don't need a doctor," Luke replied. "Just tell them Luke Shaw will wait for them in the train terminal."

The crowd grew larger as news of the shooting spread. In El Paso, shootings occurred every day, but the excitement never waned and always drew inquisitive crowds. Luke and Razor retreated to the sanctuary of the train terminal, where Luke was well-known. He told the clerk to clear everyone out of the terminal manager's office and let no one in except the sheriff or the city marshal.

"Luke, I'll fill you in on what just happened as soon as I explain this to the sheriff and the city marshal."

"Razor, I know them, let me handle it." Before Razor had time to protest, the sheriff walked in.

"Luke, what are you up to now? I thought we ran you out of Texas, and here you are again in trouble," the sheriff said with a big grin.

"Will Partlow! It's you and the marshal I'm worried about. A man can't walk down the street without being shot at. Do I have to come out of retirement and help clear out the riffraff?" Luke said, smiling.

"Well, seems as if you cleaned out some of it this morning. Did you know them?"

"No! They just started shooting at us as we walked out the door of the café," said Luke.

"We'll clean up the mess, Luke, and you come back anytime you like. We need all the help we can get. I would like to visit, but don't have the time. I'll fill the marshal in on what happened."

"Glad to see you, Will, be careful," said Luke.

Roberto and Enrique had not had time to pitch in to help. They would have if the shooting had lasted any longer. Razor had told them that they were vaqueros, not gunfighters, and they told him they would fight for the brand regardless of the circumstance.

Roberto and Enrique had gathered Razor's and Luke's horses. They were waiting for them outside the terminal. They saddled up and set out to catch up with the herd of heifers. It took them four hours.

It was then that Razor started explaining to Luke what the shooting was about. Luke cut him off. "Razor, that's none of my business. You owe me no explanation. It's over for me, and I hope for you also. They needed killing. Let's move on."

"Sounds good to me," said Razor.

It was inevitable that Marlow could not let it go. Now Razor could concentrate on going ahead and killing him then get back to the important thing, his lightning bolt. A smile came to his face. The scar on his neck had not hurt for months but his hand kept going there. It had been four hours since the shooting and he was conscious of his hand touching his scar.

Luke and Razor carried on a conversation during the entire drive. To stay out of the dust of the drive, they rode in front, leading the way. Luke never mentioned Amanda Gale but spoke of his boss frequently. He never talked of his boss's wealth but of his character. By the time the drive ended, Razor had great respect for Luke and his boss. Luke was even more impressed with Razor than before. Razor reminded him of himself and his boss. His boss had to meet Razor Sharp. Razor needed to hunt down Marlow but put it off to accommodate his new friend, Luke Shaw.

Chapter 28

The Killing of Ralph Marlow

Razor introduced Luke to Walks. Razor had told Luke of Walks' ability and the calming effect he had with the mustangs. After looking at several herds, Luke decided he would pick from the one-year-olds. Walks led the way into the herd with his horse at his heels. He slipped a rope around the neck of the horse selected by Luke and walked out of the herd with it. Razor made a halter with his rope and held her at bay. It took Walks only a little time to gather the other five horses. They returned to Mustang and used the telegraph in the bank to order a special boxcar to be delivered to El Paso for the horses' trip to Denver.

Razor insisted on helping Luke deliver the mustangs to El Paso. Enrique and Roberto went along to herd the horses. On the way to El Paso, Luke told Razor that he would like to bring his boss to Mustang to meet him. Razor had heard so much about his boss that he loved the idea. "Just wire me and let me know when."

After Luke departed with the horses, Enrique and Roberto headed back to Mustang. Razor would stay in El Paso or Juarez until he killed Ralph Marlow. He was not going to spend the rest of his life looking over his shoulder.

Razor started looking for Marlow as Luke's train pulled out of the terminal. He checked into the hotel near the terminal and put his horse in the public stable next door. A good night's sleep and an early breakfast revived his spirit. He put his belt and holster with one of the .45 Colts around his waist and slid his other Colt .45 under his belt in front. His ten-inch Bowie knife found a home on his left hip. With a plain bandanna around his neck, he was ready to stay on the hunt until Marlow was dead regardless of how long it took. During the daytime hours he looked in every room of every building in El Paso. At night, he looked in every saloon, whorehouse, café, and cantina.

After five days, he determined that Marlow was not in El Paso. He decided to go to the low river crossing that he was certain Marlow had used when running away from the shoot-out at the railroad terminal. He didn't want to be seen going into Juarez over the bridge.

Razor carried his saddlebags stuffed with jerky and hardtacks and two canteens of water. He walked across the Rio Grande into Mexico at the low river crossing east of the bridge. Razor decided to go to the southeast of the bridge and approach Juarez from there. He had bathed each day but hadn't shaved or changed clothes since he had left Mustang. Razor did wash his plain bandanna each day. He fit in with much of the population. His border Spanish came in handy, and on rare occasions, he used Castilian Spanish. After four days, he became impatient with his progress in locating Marlow and decided to use the custom all the Mexican police adhered to, and that was *donar*. In Spanish, it meant to donate, but in English, it was understood as a bribe.

He would feign desperation to find someone and have in his possession only the money to be used for bribes. Razor hid all his weapons and money in a cluster of chaparral except for one .45 Colt, which he would carry on his hip, and four silver dollars in his pocket. He crossed back into El Paso using the low river crossing and used the bridge to cross back into Juarez. He caught the eye of one of the policemen who was looking at him, and they walked toward each other. Razor was the first to speak.

Razor told him he was looking for a North American gringo by the name of Ralph Marlow. He described him and told of the rope scar on his neck. Razor knew immediately that the policeman had some knowledge of Marlow. He led Razor away from the bridge and on to a side street and asked why he was looking for Marlow. Razor told him he understood that Marlow was hiring some hands, and he was desperate for a job.

Razor took one of the silver dollars out of his pocket and slipped it into the policeman's hand. The policeman looked at the coins and said, "I understand that job is going to pay much more than this silver dollar indicates. Is this all the job is worth to you?"

"The job is worth a lot more to me. After I get paid, I could look you up and pay you much more. I only have a little more now."

"How much more do you have?" asked the policeman.

"Do you know where I can find him?"

"Yes! But not for one dollar."

Razor turned his pockets inside out and handed him the other three silver dollars. This was ten times more than the policeman made on his salary a day, and the *donar* he received a day was usually much less than this. But this was not nearly as much as Marlow had started paying him two days ago.

The policeman drew Razor a map as to where Marlow should be. When he was out of sight, Razor detoured to his hiding place to retrieve his saddlebags, weapons, money, and the two canteens. Razor was eager to locate Marlow. Walks and Finder had taught him patience, as all Apache practiced. He would be eager but patient in going to Marlow's hideout.

The policeman left and took a shortcut to Marlow's dwelling. Razor made a wide loop and neared the dwelling from the south and not from the expected north, where the front of the building was located. It had an eight-foot-high, two-foot-wide adobe fence around the house, with broken bottles and other glass lodged in cement across the top. There was a walkway on both sides and at the front of the house. The only exit off the property was through a split, tall iron gate with spikes on top that opened outward.

Razor needed a place where he could see the gate without being noticed. Two blocks to the north and across the street from the gate was an abandoned flat-roofed adobe building for rent. It had no front door, and he entered and looked around. A ladder was stored against the wall. Razor took the ladder outside and around to the back. If anyone saw him, he would tell them he was thinking about renting the building and wanted to check out the roof. Razor climbed the ladder and stepped over the three-foot skirt down onto the roof, pulling the ladder onto the roof behind him.

He moved to a position that gave him the best view of the gate. He was just in time to see the policeman who had taken his bribe rush out the gate. The officer went two blocks east, turned the corner, and started north.

Razor knew the policeman didn't want to run into him on his way from Marlow's house. Razor needed information on how many gunmen were in the house, but he also needed to stay clear of the police. He certainly didn't want to raise a red flag to the police that a killing was going to take place.

Razor sat on the roof of the adobe patiently, drinking from his canteen and chewing on hardtack while watching the gate. Five hours had passed when a skinny Mexican woman rushed away from the house. Razor could not tell where she went and continued to sit tight. An hour later she rushed back into the house. Four gunmen wearing bandoliers followed closed behind.

The sun was going down, and it would be dark within the next thirty minutes. The Mexican lady came to the gate and lit the coal oil lanterns on both sides of the gate and returned to the house.

Razor decided to get closer to the gate and climbed down from the back of the building. He left the ladder in place. By the time Razor got to the corner across the street from the gate, it was getting dark He stood against the back corner of the building, watching the gate.

In less than ten minutes, four men came out the gate and looked around. Seeing no one, they turned their backs to Razor and motioned for someone to come out. It was Marlow! Razor would have preferred to put the inevitable confrontation off until a more favorable battleground could be had, but he wanted to get this over with.

Razor had both .45s drawn and was walking fast toward the gate. Seeing Razor, Marlow reached for his gun and screamed to his men as he tried to go back inside. The four others turned, drawing their weapons. They were hit by the first four bullets fired by Razor, two from each gun. Marlow got off a wild shot that hit the ground three feet in front of the spot where Razor was standing.

Marlow had given up trying to get back through the gate when four others were trying to get out. He was trying to get off another shot when Razor squeezed off his fifth shot. Marlow wilted to the ground.

A bullet cut a path across Razor's left shoulder. His sixth shot finished off the shooter. Razor's left arm dropped to his side, but he held on to the gun in his left hand.

It was at that moment that the other four made their way out the gate. Those who were trying to make it past Marlow and the other four dead gunmen started firing at Razor. Having to step over the dead threw their aim off. They became less accurate when Razor started shooting into the crowd at the gate.

Razor knew Marlow was dead because he had taken time to shoot him between the eyes. He had backed up and fired three shots from his right gun at the men trying to exit the gate. He knew the gun was empty and slid it into his holster. He reached over with his right hand and took the gun from his blood-soaked left hand.

Razor grabbed the bandanna from around his neck and pressed down on the wound as he fired his last three shots and backed around the corner. He slid the gun in behind his belt. That's when he realized he had lost the bandanna in his haste to get off the last three shots. He heard a lot of screaming coming from around the gate, but he didn't know if anyone else had been killed but knew some had been wounded with his last six shots. He also didn't know how many there were behind the gate to start with. He could hear them shouting and running. There had been two shots fired at him, after he had been wounded, that were a little out of range, and when he rounded the building, a rifle shot hit the building close by.

Razor felt he had enough time to climb up the ladder and pull it up on the roof with him. He would then have plenty of time to reload. He would plan from there. When he had turned the corner of the back side of the building, he couldn't see the ladder against the wall. It was now pitch-black near the ground. He knew where he had left it, but he could only make out a bare wall. The ladder was gone. He had no option other than to keep running. He tripped on something and crashed to the ground. While he was getting up, he used his hand to push up from the ground and found the ladder under his hand. Apparently, it had fallen, or someone had pushed it down.

Razor leaned it against the wall, ran up the ladder, and jerked it up on the roof as three gunmen rounded the corner. They ran past the building, and he heard their footsteps fading away into the dark. He felt sure they would not be back. They would not want to explain what they were doing with the gringo bank robber or all the dead bodies. He ejected the spent cartridges and replaced them with live rounds.

Razor's adrenaline was pumping hard. He was thrilled he had killed Marlow without being killed himself. He hated that he had not killed him before now. It had taken time that he could have used looking for his pretty lady/lightning bolt.

He was still in danger and had to get back over the border. He checked his wound and determined it was a flesh wound that had greatly impaired the movement of his left arm, and it hurt like hell. He took his Bowie, cut his shirttail off, and bandaged the wound using his teeth and right hand. He pulled the shirttail as tight as he could and made a sling for his arm. Taking better care of it would have to wait until he got out of the tight spot he was now in. He knew he had to have left a blood trail. He hoped it could not be picked up in the dark.

He was startled when he heard all the commotion down below and saw a flicker of light. He eased over to the front of the building and peeked over the top of the small wall and saw torches being lit. A crowd was forming. The hollering and screaming were increasing. He saw mostly police in the crowd. Some branched out, with the help of people with torches. He heard an officer bark orders to a group of police to go to the border. Several raced north and two ran northeast toward the low river crossing.

Razor could see, by the light of a torch, a young boy at the corner had stopped where he had made his last shot. He was picking up the bandanna that Razor had lost. He saw him look around and slip the bandanna into his pocket.

Razor doubted the blood trail would be detected with the torches. They gave off enough light, but it was a flickering light that cast flickering shadows. He had to be gone by daylight.

After the last torch left the area around 10:00 p.m., Razor went to sleep and awoke at midnight. Several dogs barked at a distance, which was customary in Juarez. He opened his saddlebag and retrieved several strips of jerky and put them in his shirt pocket.

His left shoulder was sore, swollen, and stiff but the bleeding had stopped. He knew his shirt and trousers would be covered with blood. The blood and his arm in a sling would make him a prime suspect in the shooting. He would do his best to stay out of sight, but there was nothing else he could do about it now. He had to get across the border before daylight.

The searchers would expect him to go north to the bridge or northeast to the low water crossing. Instead, he would go southwest into the desert, loop back north, and cross the Rio Grande near the New Mexico Territory border and head back into El Paso.

The many miles he had walked and run with Walks would pay off. The adrenaline rush caused by the killing of Marlow was still with him and grew even stronger thinking about what it meant to him to be free from the danger of Marlow. Razor was accustomed to long treks and many in the dark. He felt mentally and physically strong, excited, and determined that nothing could stop him now. When leaving, he laid the ladder back down.

"Shhh, be quiet, Señor Sharp! We have some business to discuss."

Razor felt a gun poked in his back. It was pitch-black, but he knew exactly who held the pistol.

"We finished our business when you told me where Marlow was."

"You didn't tell me you were the rich gringo, Razor Sharp. Señor Marlow had to tell me. You need me now more than ever, and I am here now to help you."

"Why do I need you? Marlow is dead!"

"But so are many others, and you killed them, that's why you need me."

"They needed killing," said Razor.

"When you killed Señor Marlow, you cost me a lot of money. You are going to have to pay me."

Razor knew the shakedown would last forever and would end in a killing. He would put an end to it now.

Adrenaline does strange things to the human body. Razor turned, grabbed the gun with his right hand, and slid his thumb in front of the hammer and twisted it out of the hand that held it. He immediately backhanded the man to the ground with the gun. Razor put the ladder against the wall and dragged the crooked policeman up the ladder to the roof and threw him to the ground. Razor descended the ladder, found a large stone in the dark, smashed his head in, then threw the ladder on top of him. Razor checked to make sure he was dead then placed the stone under his head. He wiped the pistol clean of blood and placed it in its holster. Now he would never have to worry about this leech again.

Razor cautiously left the area. He quieted several barking dogs with his smooth, soft Spanish words that soothed them as he slowly moved away. He didn't use the jerky as a dog pacifier but was glad he had it in case he needed it.

By the time Razor neared the edge of the river, daylight was breaking. He found a drift log he could straddle and guide in the swift current to the north shore as well as a board in a drift that had washed up nearby. Razor placed the board on the log and held it tight with his foot. He trimmed the board so it could be held in one hand and used as a rudder.

Before entering the Rio Grande, he looked up and down both sides. Seeing nothing of concern, he put his two Colts in his saddlebag and left his canteens around his neck. He had no choice but to hold the saddlebags over his head with his left hand, knowing it would open the wound and again cause it to hurt like hell.

On his third attempt, he overcame his mental reluctance to raise his arm. As he pushed off, blood ran down his body, and the swift water pulled the log from the river's edge into the middle of the river instantly. Razor fought the current with his one arm, gaining two feet and losing one. He worked the log out of the current and eased the log onto a sandbar on the north side of the river. Easing off the log, he used the rudder to push the log back into the river current with hopes it would drift through Juarez unnoticed. It was another fifty feet before he would be hidden by the mesquite on the bank. Once he had cover, he lowered his left arm and dropped the saddlebags. He followed them to the ground. After several minutes, he rose, eased back to cover his exit trail from the river, and walked inland for about a mile.

He sought shelter under a thick grouping of mesquite and removed his shirt. The sun was up. He had arrived none too soon. He checked and cleaned his weapons then checked his wound. It was red and puffy and seeping blood. He built a small smokeless fire and heated water in one of his canteens. He took one of his bandannas out of the saddlebag and poured the hot water over it and carefully washed the wound.

He found the dried poultice powder in the saddlebag that Walks and Finder had ground to put on wounds to dehydrate them. He sprinkled on a liberal amount. He then washed the blood off the shirt the best he could. The blood that he could not wash off was sprinkled with sand dust. Then he tied a bandanna over his wound.

This time he didn't put a bandanna around his neck because he didn't want to be recognized. He let the shirt dry while he ate some jerky and a hardtack. He buried the small fire deep, put on his shirt, placed his arm back in the sling, and headed back into El Paso.

With a smile of contentment, Razor walked facing straight ahead but was looking for danger from all directions. Adrenaline made him strong. While he was in the desert, he ran most of the time. When he entered town, he removed the sling and bore the pain. He walked fast and directly to the hotel near the train terminal. The bloodstains on his shirt were indistinguishable. He had caught several stares along the way, but a smile in response by Razor diffused the stares. Back at the hotel, he ordered bathwater at the desk and went straight to his room.

After he bathed and put more of the poultice powder on his wound, he placed a clean cloth over it. He then put on clean clothes and didn't put his arm back in a sling. He went to the stable to retrieve his mustang and headed to Wells Fargo.

A strong, tall, dark, clean-cut man approached the border bridge that went into Juarez. In the middle of the bridge, he pinned on his US marshal's badge. When he reached the Mexico side he dismounted and asked to speak to the chief of police of Juarez in English, then in broken Spanish.

Razor waited in a small windowless office beside the bridge and in less than five minutes an official arrived and introduced himself as the chief of police for the City of Juarez, Hector Ramirez. In broken Spanish, but good enough for the chief to understand, Razor spoke. “Chief, I am US Marshal Sharp. I have a thousand dollars of gold coins to pay the reward money for the death of the North American bank robber Ralph Marlow. It is rumored you were instrumental in killing this bandit. If this is so, I’ll need for you to sign this affidavit of such, and the money is yours.”

“*Si*, I am the one,” said the smiling chief.

Razor emptied the saddlebag of gold coins on the table and had the chief count it. Razor had prearranged the three copies of the affidavit, one in Spanish, ready for the chief to sign. The chief didn’t count; he just stacked the coins as fast as he could and reached for the affidavit and signed the three copies without reading what was written.

“Chief, there is another reward of twenty-five thousand dollars for the return of what’s left of the one hundred thousand dollars that Ralph Marlow stole. If you find it, let me know.”

“I’ll be looking for it,” said the smiling chief.

Razor would not count on ever seeing the bank’s stolen money but thought it would be very interesting when everyone in Juarez and El Paso read in the newspapers of both cities that the chief signed an affidavit that he had killed the bank robber Ralph Marlow.

Razor left and returned to El Paso over the bridge. He had taken his marshal’s badge off and headed to the *El Paso Gazette’s* office. The *Gazette* printed the paper for El Paso and Juarez in both English and Spanish.

Razor was sleepy but so keyed up and excited he knew he would not be able to sleep, so he spent the last few hours of daylight searching El Paso for his lightning bolt. He reluctantly gave up at dark and returned to his hotel. Early the next morning, rested, happy, and eager, he bought several copies of the *Gazette* in both English and Spanish and headed to Mesilla. He looked for his lightning bolt on the way out of El Paso.

Chapter 29

Luke Shaw Takes His Boss to Mustang

When Luke arrived in Denver with the horses, Amanda Gale was there to meet him. "Did you find him?" were the first words out
of her mouth.

"I don't know, but I've found someone you should meet. Your man couldn't be better than the one I found."

"Luke, I don't want some man you just found. I want the one I asked you to find."

"But, Amanda Gale, you have not seen this one, and you should. You might change your mind."

"I'll never change my mind. I want you to find him."

"That might take a long time, Amanda Gale."

"Well, take the time. I'm not going to settle on anyone else! Oh, yes! I forgot to tell you! Dad wants you to come for dinner tonight."

That night at dinner with his boss, many things were discussed. Luke's boss knew Amanda Gale was having Luke look for a man she had seen twice and had fallen head over heels for. Finally, Luke mentioned he would like to take his boss and Amanda Gale to meet Razor Sharp at his ranch. Amanda Gale refused immediately. "I'm not going."

That must be the guy that Luke found for me, she thought. She was not going to waste her time on him when she could be looking for her guy in Santa Fe. She was certain that he lived there or close by.

Luke's boss responded, "Wire him and set up a time."

Two weeks later, Luke and his boss rode up to Razor's home. Razor had seen them coming from a mile away and was waiting on his front porch when they arrived.

"Get down and come on up," said Razor.

When they reached the top of the steps, Luke said, "Razor, meet Quick Tender."

Wow! thought Razor. He had read about Quick Tender. Some twenty years prior, Tender had been accused of murdering two deputies by a renegade sheriff who had placed a bounty of a thousand dollars on his head, dead or alive.

Quick Tender was the owner of the Great American Pacific Railroad and resided in the mountains around Denver, Colorado, with his large family. Luke had never mentioned his boss's name, and Razor had grown to like Luke's boss, but wow! Quick Tender!

Twenty years ago, the man single-handedly drove the Comanche out of Central Texas with a single shot between the eyes of sixteen of them! Razor didn't try to hide his enthusiasm about meeting Tender.

Tender was aware that Sharp was the man who was orphaned and had accumulated a massive herd of mustangs and salvaged a bank. He brought peace with the Mescalero Apache. He liked most Indians and spoke the Apache

Athabaskan language and Spanish. In less than an hour of conversation, Quick was amazed with Razor's depth of knowledge and understanding on any subject they discussed. He had never met anyone who was interested in so many of the same subjects that he himself was interested in.

Wow! If Amanda Gale met Razor Sharp, she would forget about that other guy, Quick thought.

The conversation went into the wee hours of the morning. None of them wanted to withdraw. Thoughts were shared about Indians, cattle and horses, as well as the future of the country. A lifetime bond was forming.

After both men had a few hours of sleep, the conversation continued. After a tour of Mustang topped off with a delicious lunch, the three returned to Tender's front porch where they enjoying seeing the first snowflake of the year. Coats were retrieved, and the conversation continued again.

Quick mentioned that he and his family had been invited to the reception that the governor of the New Mexico Territory was giving to celebrate peace with the Mescalero Apache. "Razor, as the guest of honor, I would like to furnish you and your entourage free transportation from El Paso to Santa Fe and back. Wire me and let me know how many there will be, and the private cars will be there. You see, I happen to know the man who owns the railroad," he said with a sly grin.

"I will, and I'm mighty appreciative of that, Mr. Tender."

After dark, the conversation moved inside, and dinner was served by Razor's cook.

Quick spoke, "Razor, do you have someone special you will be bringing with you?"

"Just a few of my friends. They are all employees but friends first," Razor said.

"There will be a lot of dancing and such and I thought you might need a dance partner," said Quick.

"Oh, I have a dear friend who lives in Santa Fe that I plan to ask."

"If that falls through, I have a seventeen-year-old daughter who would love to go with you," Quick said.

"I'll keep that in mind," Razor said.

That night Razor had a tough time going to sleep. The reason he wanted to take Bonnie Lou to the reception was that she would understand that he wanted to look for his lightning bolt after he explained it to her. If he were to be stuck with Mr. Tender's daughter, he would not know how to handle the situation if he did see his lightning bolt.

Quick was restless also. Razor Sharp was the one he wanted as his son-in-law. His thoughts wandered, *Amanda Gale could look forever and never find the guy she's trying to find. The one she has seen only twice in her life, or was it three times? Even if he could be found, he would never be as good a find for her as Razor Sharp. How could someone his age be so mature?* Quick paused and thought, *That's what some people said about me.*

Razor insisted on escorting them both back to El Paso. They would be spending two nights on the trail, and the trail would be dusted with snow. Razor enlisted Finder and Walks to accompany them with a packhorse carrying winter camping gear. It was a pleasant journey. Luke, Quick, and Razor enjoyed the crisp weather and continuous conversation.

Razor, Walks, and Finder spent the night in the hotel next to the train terminal. Quick and Luke spent the night in

Quick's private railcar. They had breakfast in the café together and were ready to depart.

"Razor, don't forget about my Amanda Gale. I think you would enjoy meeting her," said Quick.

"I won't forget, sir. I can assure you of that."

Razor was feeling guilty about his thoughts. *Was Tender trying to push his daughter on him, who was probably ugly! Uh, not good-looking?* His mind raced back to the fabulous time he had with Luke and Mr. Tender. He looked forward to seeing them at the celebration in Santa Fe.

Quick was thrilled that he had met Razor Sharp. He couldn't wait to tell Amanda Gale about him. He knew he could make this work. He would hog-tie her and drag her to the reception if he had to, but she was going to meet Razor Sharp.

Chapter 30

El Paso Gold Shoot-Out

The coal had been delivered, and Razor was ready to go to work. He had prepared the forge with the coal in place. He had transferred the gold nuggets to the shop in the wooden wheelbarrow his father had built. The insides of the molds had been painted with carbon black from his fireplace. Now it was dark enough to start the fire in the forge. The black smoke from the burning coal would disappear into the night.

It took two hours to get the forge hot enough to melt the gold nuggets. He poured the first melted gold into the one hundred coin-sized molds, by standing at a distance and lifting the melting pot with the overhead crane. He tilted the pot with a large extended wheel and filled the bar molds using the same procedure.

When it cooled, he tapped off the slag on top and dumped the coins and bars of gold out of the molds. The carbon black had given the gold the bright, slick finish he desired.

Razor cleaned the shop of all remnants left by the pouring of the gold and put things back in place. With a hammer, he marked every piece with the chisel that bore the Razor brand before putting the coins and bars back in the hidden chest.

The next day Razor left Mustang with one of his small gold bars. He headed for El Paso to get the bar assayed. He could have it done in Mesilla, but he picked El Paso in hopes of finding that beautiful young lady that he couldn't forget.

No luck on the girl, but the gold assayed at 999.5 pure gold.

Razor rode across the Rio Grande bridge into Juarez and had the metallurgist cut a stamp on the bottom of a high-carbon steel rod that would mark the gold bars with 999.5. He bought two different sizes.

Razor then sought several seamstresses and contracted with them to gather all their sewing machines and materials to make ten suits and several dresses. He would pick them up in a wagon and take them to Mesilla in three days.

Razor had lunch in Mexico then rode back to El Paso to look for his lightning bolt. He looked around the train terminal and in the hotel. She was not there, so he decided to go to the café across the street.

Whoa! Razor moved back from the open door of the hotel. Standing outside the café was the clerk from the assay office. He was pointing out Razor's horse to two hard-looking gunmen. They both had two guns tied down low on their hips. By the motion of the clerk's hands, he guessed that he was describing Razor to them.

Razor quickly checked his guns. He didn't want to have a shoot-out in the same place he and Luke had killed Marlow's six gunmen. He wouldn't have Luke here to explain the situation. Did they plan to rob him for the small gold bar? Or were they going to follow him to see where he got it and see if there were more?

Razor didn't know the answer but convinced himself that they had more on their minds than one small gold bar. He didn't want to be bushwhacked on a lonely trail or to have them follow him to Mustang. Razor decided to do what he wanted to do, and that was to put an end to it now. He checked his Colt on his right hip, sliding it in and out of the holster.

Razor left the hotel and was halfway to his horse before they saw him. His left hand went up high, waving at the clerk while his right hand rested on the Colt. "Why don't y'all join me for some lunch? I'm buying," said Razor.

The three were startled and tried to separate. By this time, Razor was in the middle of them. He figured the clerk would not participate in any gunplay, and Razor stayed in between the two gunmen with his hand still on the Colt.

The clerk said he had to get back to work and hurriedly left the scene.

"Gentlemen, let's get down to business," said Razor. "This is as good a place as any. This happens to be my lucky corner. Two weeks ago, on this corner, six men tried to kill me. All six of them are now dead. I know what your intentions are, and I don't plan to be bushwhacked, nor do I plan to have to look over my shoulder for you to keep you from jumping my claim. I may get killed, but I assure you, one of you will die today—if not both of you."

Razor was creating doubt in them both. There was no money in killing him. They wanted to kill him after they found his claim.

They wanted nothing to do with a shoot-out. They were bushwhackers and wanted a sure thing. They were hesitant as to what they should do. Razor was pushing the issue and not giving them an inch. This was new territory for them, and they didn't like it one bit. They each knew one of them would die but saw no way out.

They both had been trying to move to get Razor from between them. When they thought they had, he moved back between the two men. They both went for their guns and fired as Razor dove to the ground, firing at one then rolled over and fired at the other. Both were hit by bullets meant for Razor, and Razor's two shots would finish them off.

The two were struggling to regain control of their bodies. Razor didn't know where the all the bullets went but knew his shots went into their hearts. While they were bleeding out, one was trying to find his other weapon. He had been shot by his partner. He was now struggling to draw his other gun with his left hand. Razor would have to pay close attention to him.

The other was bleeding out of his throat. Both of his hands were around his neck, trying to stop the flow of blood, then one of his hands moved down to his heart to stop the flow of blood from there. Razor didn't have to worry about him.

The one trying to grab his other gun was successful but didn't have enough strength to raise it up or to pull the trigger.

Spectators rushed out to see the remains of the dead. This was a dangerous situation for Razor. He kept his two guns drawn and observed the crowd to see if there were any others who might want to become involved.

Razor asked that someone locate the sheriff and tell him that Luke Shaw's friend would be waiting for him in the train terminal.

Razor rushed to the terminal and was recognized by the terminal manager as a friend of Luke Shaw and Quick Tender. He was welcomed into his office to wait for the sheriff.

Razor had been confident he could take the two gunfighters. These were tough times in this part of the country, and measures had to be taken that were usually not needed in civilized cultures. El Paso was not a civilized culture. Razor knew he had done the right thing for his future safety but longed for the day when he could live in a peaceful society.

These two gunmen had nothing to do with Ralph Marlow or Raiman Callaway. Even though Marlow and Callaway were dead, he knew that danger lurked around every corner in places like El Paso. This knowledge probably saved his life.

When the sheriff arrived, he was led into the manager's office, and the manager left, closing the door behind him.

Razor stood and said, "Sheriff Partlow, I'm Razor Sharp. I was with Luke Shaw several weeks ago. I hate to bother you again, but I need your help."

"That's what you get for hanging around someone like Luke Shaw. Any friend of Luke Shaw has to call me Will," the sheriff said, laughing. "Razor, Luke never mentioned your name before, and I figured it was for a good reason, and I understand that. I've heard a lot about you, and it's all been good. I've already figured out what happened outside, but what put you on to them?"

"Will, you need to talk to the clerk at the assay office. He fingered me to the two men outside. I had been at the assay office earlier to get a small bar of gold assayed. I came out of the hotel and saw him pointing out my horse and describing me. I couldn't hear him but figured it out by the hand signals he was using."

"That's good news, Razor. We've had several prospectors robbed and some killed after they had assays done. Razor, I'll take care of everything outside, and your name will not be mentioned. I've had my eye on those two for a long time but could not catch them in the act. If I can ever help you again, don't hesitate to ask."

"Thanks, Will. I don't want to get the reputation as a gunman."

"I understand that, Razor."

Razor stayed in the terminal until everything was cleaned up outside. He had seen his lightning bolt here before, so why couldn't he see her here again? It didn't happen, and he reluctantly left for Mesilla to spend the night.

On the way to Mesilla, he thought of El Paso's terrible reputation and what had happened to him that day. He never liked to dwell on bad things, but he determined that El Paso was a lot worse than the terrible reputation it had. He put it to bed with the thought *They needed killing*, and he would move on.

Razor liked sleeping in the barn at the freight yard, especially in cold weather they were experiencing now. Warm and comfortable, under two horse blankets, he dreamed about his lightning bolt. He had to find her. These were the most pleasant thoughts he had ever had and was asleep in minutes. Maybe he would see her again in Santa Fe.

The next morning, Razor washed himself with water from the horse trough. He had to break a thin layer of ice to get to the water. It was a refreshing experience. Most of the crew was now working out of Mustang. Several of the bank guards and guards at Bonnie Lou's former house still used the bunkhouse and chow hall. The meals were cooked as requested. A small remuda was kept and cared for by the stable boy who was also cleaning the bunkhouse for more guests.

Razor ate breakfast and told the cook to prepare for fifteen more people who would arrive in a couple of days. Razor went to the telegraph office and telegraphed Miss Scott. Razor wanted her to round up Finder, Walks, Enrique, Roberto, Mr. Stew, Calhoun, and Jacob. She was to bring them to Mesilla.

Razor then found US Marshal Lester Block and insisted he go to Santa Fe with them for the celebration. He told of wanting to buy everyone new shoes and would have shirts, suits, and traveling clothes made by seamstresses. This was his appreciation for everything they had done for him. Lester was thrilled to be a part of the celebration.

Two days later, the crew arrived. The next morning, they all went to Juarez, including Marshal Block. Calhoun drove the wagon with Miss Scott as the only passenger. It was shoe-buying time. Razor bought everyone a new pair of shoes. He insisted Miss Scott buy three pairs. They picked up the seamstresses and their materials and machines and took them back to the freight yard. Five days later, all were ready to travel.

Razor had been communicating with Bonnie Lou over the telegraph for several days. She was excited that Razor wanted to escort her to the governor's celebration party. With Razor being the guest of honor, it would put her in the spotlight of the whole territory.

Quick Tender had been insisting that Amanda Gale go to the party and at least meet Razor Sharp. "I don't want to meet Razor Sharp. I don't want to meet anyone who you or Luke try to fix me up with. I'll find my man on my own terms," Amanda Gale said.

"Amanda Gale, people from all over the Territory of New Mexico, Colorado, Arizona, and the State of Texas will be there. Why don't you come anyway? You might the man you have been looking for!"

"Okay, I'll go if you promise you or Luke will not try to introduce me and try to fix me up with Razor Sharp. He would be in my way if I did see the one I want."

"I'll order Luke not to introduce him to you. Paul has already said he was going to look at the girls. He can keep you company."

Chapter 31

Amanda Gale

Miss Scott and Jacob married two weeks before they were to leave on the Santa Fe trip. They were going to make that their honeymoon trip. Razor was Jacob's best man, and they were married by the new preacher, at the new church, in Mustang, New Mexico Territory.

All the new white-face heifers were now over thirteen months old and had started breeding. If everything went according to plan, there would be two thousand head of cattle on the range next year. The Army was buying horses as needed and would be buying steers from Razor, their preferred vendor, by the end of next year. The bloodline of the horses was improving back toward the original thoroughbred line they came from.

Razor had enough gold bars to ship to the Denver Mint to cast his Razor-brand coins. He still was using the ones he cast in Mustang. None had ever been turned down. He was still getting enough gold nuggets from the X, without mining, to continue his gold bar production.

Razor had not forgotten his lightning bolt. He was going to turn everything over to Miss Scott—now Mrs. Walters. That is, everything but the X. Not that he didn't trust her, but his father told him to never tell anyone. He was sure that she and Jacob had wondered about the gold but would never ask.

Afterward, he was going to spend 100 percent of his time looking for the girl he'd seen at the courthouse until he found her. He knew he would not be truly happy until he did.

Finder and Walks were doing a wonderful job at the sawmill. Walks had learned to speak both English and Spanish. They had an eager crew with the Apaches. They were teaching them Spanish and English while on breaks and lunch. Most of the home construction was completed. Many of the employees had built homes in Mustang. The sawmill always had orders. Lumber was needed for bigger barns, adding bedrooms, chicken houses, etc.

The vaqueros were happy with the steady employment and having family members living in Mustang. They were proud of the Razor brand. They rode with pride. When seen by outsiders, the Razor brand brought them respect.

Food crops were planted. Apricot and pecan trees were favored. Grapes and dewberries were plentiful, and it was common for people to barter among themselves for food items.

Razor did some deep thinking. He was not happy because he could not find his lightning bolt. Could he find someone else who would make him happy? He might be forced to try.

He was happy when he spent time with Luke Shaw and Quick Tender. Tender had invited him to Colorado to spend some time with him there. He could give up his pursuit of Miss Lightning Bolt temporarily and ask if he could join him around Christmas. He had never been around anyone at Christmas but his mother and father. Gathering with friends during the holiday season was an enticing idea. He would wire Tender and see if that would be okay. He didn't want to impose on him or his family, and if it did, he could make it some other time.

He sent the wire, and within minutes, Quick Tender had wired him back. "Kathy Gale and I would love to have you here to celebrate Christmas with our family. Plan on leaving with us from Santa Fe, after your celebration party with the governor."

This pleased Razor. He didn't think he could stand the heartbreak of not finding the love of his life much longer. He had to move on. But in what direction. He would decide that after his visit with Quick Tender. He would also enjoy his visit with Bonnie Lou.

Razor decided to go back to Juarez and buy some winter clothes. He found a sheep-lined winter coat with sheep-lined gloves of high quality. Sheep-lined chaps would help when riding in deep snow.

The rope burn around his neck didn't look as bad to others as it did to him, but he wanted to continue to keep it covered anyway. He bought every different color bandanna they had.

He went to a cantina frequented by the elite Spaniards in the area. They brought their families for dinner and to enjoy the music and flamenco dancing.

Razor loved the food and the music, but he had gone for a different reason. He looked back and smiled at the girls who smiled at him. All of them were well dressed, and most were very good-looking. The Spaniards seemed to always be happy. He was seeking happiness from them. His heart didn't race. He felt nothing.

"Amanda Gale! Razor Sharp is going to spend Christmas with us," said Quick.

"Dad, I'm leaving. I'm unhappy enough about not being able to find this man. I'm not about to spend Christmas with someone I don't know and don't want to know. He would probably try to get after me, and I couldn't stand it," Amanda Gale said as she stormed out the door.

Razor had a meeting with Mr. Stew, Mr. Walters, Calhoun, Roberto, Enrique, Walks, Finder, and the surveyors shortly after he arrived in Mesilla. They decided to fence the whole two-hundred-thousand-plus-acre ranch with barbed wire. It was critical that they start on the east property line so they could keep the Longhorns and the new heifers separate. The Goodnight-Loving cattle trail that came from east Texas and went to Denver had cattle drives of Texas Longhorns that numbered into the thousands. The herds came from the south, skirting the Comanche strongholds, then into New Mexico following the Pecos River all the way to Fort Sumner and beyond. It would be too tempting for a lovesick Texas longhorn to ignore the bellow of young heifers. The new road entering the ranch and the road leaving the ranch would have a cattle guard. The fence would start west of the Goodnight–Loving cattle trail. There were cedars on the property to furnish all the posts that would be needed, including the large corner posts.

Once the property line fences were built, cross fencing would be added as needed. Roberto and Enrique assured Razor that they could get enough labor to finish the job in less than a year. Calhoun and his teamsters would haul the wire they would pick up in El Paso that would be shipped in by rail. They would haul the posts along the property line as the surveyors marked the line and holes were dug. The wire haulers would follow along the line with the barbed wire. The crews were trying to mimic the rhythm of the railroad construction crews. The rhythm improved with the passing of a very short time. At the rate the work was going, the fence would be completed in eight months.

Razor returned to Mustang and met with Jacob and Mary Ann. He told them of his decision to spend Christmas with Quick Tender and his family. He didn't know when he would return and wanted Mrs. Walters to be in control of all operations. "If there is a problem, I can be reached by telegraph anytime. I've always told Mr. Stew, Finder, Walks, Enrique, Roberto, and you, Jacob, if I were not around to always come to you, Mrs. Walters. There won't be anything different."

"Jacob, tighten security before we leave for Santa Fe. I know that the way you handled the horse thieves added to our reputation that no one should mess with Mustang, but we should always be cautious. Let everyone know that they are to tell no one that we will be gone for a few days or when we will be back."

"Have Calhoun arrange for a wagon to carry our luggage to leave a day ahead of our departure. We will leave the next day and regroup past the Sacramentos."

"Mrs. Walters, have Joe Brine come here to run the bank while we're gone. Have his assistant handle deposits and cashing checks while Joe is gone. Any loans or other business can wait until he returns. I'll tell the rest of the crew everything on the train. Any questions?"

"One other thing, Jacob, don't do anything to get fired while I'm gone," Razor said with a big grin.

Razor went to Mesilla three days before he was scheduled to leave for Santa Fe. He got there at dark and went to the freight yard. He turned his horse into the corral with the remuda. He went to the barn without eating and climbed to his bed in the loft. He pulled the horse and saddle blankets tight over him to keep out the frigid night air. Then he knew why he wanted to go there. It was to forget about the lightning bolt that struck him that was bringing so much unhappiness and to think about his first and best friend, Bonnie Lou.

On the day of departure, Razor telegraphed Bonnie Lou and gave her his estimated time of arrival in Santa Fe and asked that she meet him at the terminal. Calhoun had arranged to have the wagon and horses taken to the freight yard in Mesilla and kept there until their return. Quick Tender had arraigned for a Pullman sleeping car, dining car with a kitchen, chef, and servers. A private passenger car was attached.

Razor then told everyone of his conversation with Jacob and Mrs. Walters. He pointed out that nothing was changed. Mrs. Walters was in charge.

"If you need something, ask her. If they have a problem, ask her. That's the way it has been since she started running the bank. The reason I'm bringing this up now is that I am going to be out of pocket for a while. You all know what to do. She can contact me anytime. I'll be looking for new ventures we may go into, and I need all your help in keeping everything running and under control. Remember, always defend yourself and the brand, and the brand will always defend you and yours."

Everyone was excited about the trip. Razor was looking forward to it, too, and was excited about spending time with Bonnie Lou, Luke, and Quick Tender.

They all knew Bonnie Lou and liked her. The ones who had not seen her lately were amazed when they saw the beauty of the young lady meeting the train. She was poised and comfortable with herself and was glad to see them all, especially Razor Sharp.

The private car was put on a siding. Razor, Bonnie Lou, and his entourage were carried by carriage to a large hotel near the capitol building and the town square. The reception was to be held in the ballroom of the hotel. Bonnie Lou waited in the lobby, while the others were escorted to their rooms to freshen up.

Razor was to meet with the governor, Quick Tender, and Luke the next morning. Razor had informed Jacob and Mrs. Walters that he wanted to spend some time with Bonnie Lou alone and was taking her to the square for lunch.

After selecting a café on the square, they sat at a table outside the front entrance. They were sitting close together, and Razor was holding her hand. She was telling him how much she liked it there in Santa Fe. "There are a lot of good-looking guys here, but I haven't found the right one for me yet. You should think about moving here," she said. "There are a lot of beautiful girls here, too, and most are well-educated. We could have a great time together, exploring the city and looking for our mates," she said.

"Bonnie Lou, when you find the right one, you will know it. Don't waste any time in telling him he is the one. Don't lose him." He decided to tell her about his lightning bolt after all.

Amanda Gale and Paul were walking along in front of the many cafés on the square.

"Oh! Oh! It's him, Paul! Oh no! He's holding her hand! He must be in love, or that may be his wife!"

She turned away with tears forming in her eyes. "Why have I been such a fool? He must be a cheating husband, or he would not have looked at me the way he did. What am I going to do? I want to die, Paul!"

"There's always Razor Sharp, Amanda Gale."

"Oh, be serious, Paul!"

Through sobs, she admitted, "I still love him, Paul." She looked back over her shoulder, and Razor was even closer to Bonnie Lou and holding her hand tighter.

"I'll tell you one thing, Amanda Gale, he has a very beautiful girlfriend or wife," Paul said.

"Paul, go back and see if she has on a ring, would you? If she is only a girlfriend, I can take care of that. I'll stay here. Please hurry!"

"Amanda Gale, if she is not already married, from what I've seen, I want her. Wait here, I'll be back shortly."

Paul hurriedly rushed back to the café where they had seen them. They were not there. *Maybe it was the next café,* he thought. They were not there either.

"Amanda Gale, they're gone. I looked everywhere. Listen, I'm coming back in the morning. I'm going to find her. Married or not, if her husband was looking at you the way you said, he must not be interested in her, and I plan to take her away from him. Then you can have the love of your life."

"I won't act too proud not to do that, Paul. "I know I love him, and I'll make him love me."

Early the next morning, Amanda Gale and Paul were at the square, moving from one café to the next. The hours passed, and they didn't see either Razor or Bonnie Lou. "Amanda Gale, we must go to the governor's reception. If we do nothing but stick our heads in, smile, and be seen by Dad, then we can come back here and continue our search."

"Let's make another round, Paul. Then we can run the whole way, make our showing, and get back here."

"Sounds good to me," Paul said.

Bonnie Lou stood by Mrs. Walters and Jacob at the reception. She had on a lovely red gown with a small bouquet of white roses pinned on it. She was so proud of Razor and cherished their friendship. Her smile reflected such.

Accolades were poured on Razor by the governor, Quick Tender, Luke Shaw, Bankers, Marshal Lester Block, and the Lipan Apache, Water Finder. Finder told of Razor's undying faith that the Mescalero Apache wanted peace as much as the white man did. He talked about Razor's hardships and his learning the Athabaskan dialect and teaching Spanish and English to those who desired to be taught. Finder astonished the audience with his ability to speak perfect English.

Razor thanked the governor for the celebration and everyone who spoke and those who attended. The governor then asked everyone to stay and visit and introduce themselves to Razor Sharp.

The clapping and cheering were still going on when Amanda Gale and Paul rushed in.

They didn't want to leave until their father had seen them there. Suddenly, Paul saw Bonnie Lou and pointed her out to Amanda Gale.

"I wonder what she's doing here?" Amanda Gale asked.

"I don't know, but she is going to see me," said Paul as he rushed off.

"I'm Paul Tender," he said as he looked in her eyes then at her ringless hand.

"I'm Bonnie Lou Callaway, Paul," she said while looking in his eyes and with her knees weakening.

"Who are you with, Bonnie Lou?"

"I'm here with Razor Sharp," she said while looking into Paul's eyes.

"I would love to meet him. Would you introduce me?"

"Of course! Will you stay with me until he is free?"

"Definitely, Bonnie Lou. Were you with him on the square yesterday afternoon?" Paul asked while still holding her arm.

"Yes, I was, Paul. He had just arrived in town, and I hadn't seen him for a long while. We are good friends."

"Bonnie Lou, would you walk over here with me? I would like for you to meet my twin sister."

"I would love to meet her, Paul."

Without releasing her arm, Paul led her away toward Amanda Gale.

"Amanda Gale, I want you to meet Bonnie Lou Callaway," said Paul just as Quick Tender appeared. "Here you two are! I've been looking for you both! Stay here! Don't move! I'll bring Razor Sharp over to meet you!"

"But you promised," said Amanda Gale.

"I promised I would not let Luke introduce him," Quick said as he rushed to get Razor.

"Bonnie Lou, who were you having lunch with on the square yesterday?" asked Amanda Gale.

"Just a friend," she said as she again looked into Paul's eyes.

Quick reached into the crowd of people around Razor and grabbed Razor by his arm. "Come with me. I want you to meet my daughter, Amanda Gale."

Razor really didn't want to go. A large crowd was increasing every minute he had stood there, and he was looking for his lightning bolt. There was just two much he needed to do. As he was reluctantly being dragged away, he spotted her. In fact, they were headed straight toward her. His thought was, how could he get away from Mr. Tender now that he had his lightning bolt in sight?

Amanda Gale was thinking that she didn't want to waste time meeting Razor Sharp. She needed to get back to the square and look for that elusive man who had so impressed her. At that moment, she saw her father leading a strong, tall man toward her. She fainted before he got there.

Sharp reached down and picked her up in his arms. Quick led them to one of his rooms and Razor laid her down on the bed. Bonnie Lou retrieved a wet hand towel from the bathroom and rushed to place it on Amanda Gale's head. Razor was kneeling on the floor with one of his arms under her head when she woke up.

She put her arms around him, looked into his eyes, and whispered, "Are you the one, Razor Sharp?"

"Yes, I am the one, Amanda Gale."

Made in the USA
Monee, IL
27 February 2023

28521588R00148